APRIL'S GLOW

JULIET MADISON

Print ISBN: 978-1-916978-77-5

To my cat, Pepper, who passed away the day after I finished writing this book. The story just so happens to have two cats as characters, and I hope you will live on in them.

R.I.P. and thanks for being part of the family.

CHAPTER ONE

I
f there was anything worse for April Vedora than being
stood up, it was being stood up on April Fool's Day. A week
before her birthday at that. And two days after having really bad
sushi and spending half the night getting intimate with the toilet
bowl. The only thing that could make life worse was if it rained
while she sat at the picnic table by the wishing fountain in
Miracle Park, waiting for her first ever internet date to turn up;
which, by the way, had taken at least eight months to pluck up
the courage to agree to. So much for courage. Courage could go
and get flushed, like the bad sushi.

'Stupid creep,' she huffed, as she stood and smoothed down
her long, paisley skirt, having given the guy exactly one hour
and ten minutes to turn up. She'd sent a text twenty minutes
prior, which had met with no reply.

April gazed into the distance at the blue-skied horizon
between the trees framing the park, blurring her peripheral
vision and the evidence of perfect lives, lovers, and happy
families that littered the park like colourful confetti. Her zone-
out was broken by a soccer ball hitting her left leg, which had it
not been for a sudden loss of balance due to the impact, she

1

wouldn't have noticed. She leant on the picnic table to steady herself. The moment was like life, really. A bump here and there, sometimes you'd fall, sometimes you wouldn't, and even though sometimes you got sick of the repeated bumps and falls and didn't care whether you got back up this time, the human instinct was to put that hand out and regain balance. The innate desire to keep going, get back up again, and move forward. Lately, it seemed like all April was focused on was moving forward, but when would she have a chance to get somewhere, *be* somewhere: not always in a state of needing to aspire to something greater? The ever-rolling wheel of life. Did it ever stop?

'Sorry, lady,' said a blond-haired boy as he came to retrieve his ball.

'No worries, kid,' she replied.

No worries? Little did he know.

She didn't know if she wanted kids. Maybe a few years ago, when her life had been completely different, but not now. Things had changed big time, and priorities had shifted. Besides, having set up a new business, she'd need at least three to five years of building it up to make enough of a profit, and a family lifestyle would make it difficult. Anyway, even if she did want children, it would take two, and she was missing that vital component. And after the no-show of today, her love-life was looking like a no-go.

The breeze ruffled her wavy chocolate-coloured hair as she walked across the main street. She distracted herself with inane thoughts as though she was simply out for a Sunday afternoon stroll and hadn't just been humiliated...

I really must book my next appointment with the hairdresser. Need more garnet highlights before the last ones grow out too much.

And when was the last time I went to the dentist? Should do that too.

But maybe I'll book a massage first. Yes, massage first, then dentist. Or maybe the other way around.

Okay: hair, then dentist, then massage. Done.

She nodded discreetly to affirm her mundane decision, then eyed the appealing window display in Mrs May's Bookstore. An explosion of colourful children's books mixed with an array of Easter eggs sat on the display shelf. April was sure there had been more Easter eggs last week when she'd walked past. Some little darlings had probably nicked a few when their parents weren't looking. Then again, she wouldn't be surprised if they'd been eaten by someone else...

'Been eating the display items again, Olivia?' April asked as she walked through the open door into the store.

Olivia, granddaughter of Mrs May herself, glanced up from her computer at the counter. 'Me? Never.' She winked. 'Want one?'

April shook her head, then eyed the display. 'Actually, yeah, I could do with one.'

Olivia moved from behind the counter and grabbed a couple of eggs. 'Bad day? Oh! I almost forgot, your date! What happened?'

'Absolutely nothing. Looks like Mr Maybe-He's-Perfect-For-Me is more like Mr I-Like-Standing-Women-Up-Just-For-Fun.' April sighed.

'Oh no!' Olivia popped the small chocolate egg into her mouth, then mumbled, 'Idiot.'

April savoured the temporary sensation of smooth chocolate melting in her mouth. Temporary. Like everything good in life.

'Here.' Olivia handed April a book. 'Might make you feel better.'

She chuckled at the cover showing a rugged Australian

landscape decorated by a bare-chested man in jeans, boots, and an Akubra hat. 'Really?'

'I've read it. It's a heart-warming and… stimulating read, in more ways than one.' Olivia tilted her head and cast a suggestive glance out the corner of her eye. 'And it has a happy ending.'

'Happy schmappy. Why can't our lives be like books?' She got her purse out to pay for the book and Olivia pushed it away.

'On the house, my gift to you, Hun.'

'Aw, you're too kind. Let me buy you coffee sometime.'

'Just give me the biggest slice of your birthday cake next weekend and we'll call it even.'

'Deal.' She smiled at her new friend. They'd only known each other since April opened her candle store six months ago and had introduced herself to some of the local business owners. Olivia and April had clicked and bonded over chocolate.

'Hey, forget about that guy. Block him and try someone else.'

April waved her hand. 'Nah, I think that's it for online dating.'

'What, one bad experience and you're calling it quits?'

'You can talk, Miss I-Don't-Need-A-Man.'

'I'm perfectly happy being a single mum, thank you.' She tucked her tousled hair behind her ears.

'Then I will be too. The single part, that is, not the mum bit.' She smiled.

'So no more men for now? Oh, I was looking forward to living vicariously through you.' She pouted.

'For now, I'll live vicariously through this book.' April held up the paperback. 'With Mr I'm-Too-Hot-To-Wear-A-Shirt Cowboy.' She held it to her cheek, put her hand on the man's abs, and moaned.

'Careful, you might scare the customers.'

'Or they might think it's a really good book and buy a copy.'

'True.' Olivia's expression turned all motherly; a tilt of the head, concerned creases around the eyes. 'Seriously though, don't give up. You deserve someone great after all you've been through. You never know, this time next year you might get your own happy ending.' Olivia patted April's cheeks and went off to help a customer.

Happy ending? Right now she'd settle for a happy beginning.

CHAPTER TWO

'Enjoy the rest of your day, sweetheart.' Clarissa Vedora kissed her daughter's forehead and handed her the bag of presents. 'Don't eat them all at once.' She winked.

April peered into the gift bag containing a variety of body products, a scarf, and chocolates.

'As nice as the body lotions and shower gels smell, I'll try to resist eating them.' April patted her mother's arm and she laughed. 'Thanks for lunch, Mum. And thanks for coming too, Susie.' She leaned over and kissed her aunt's cheek, then glanced briefly at the empty chair where her father should have been.

'My pleasure. You have a good time tonight,' Susie said.

'Tonight?' April's mind went blank for a moment. 'Oh yeah, my dinner party. After the wild shenanigans with you lot, I almost forgot.'

'You might need a rest when you get home before your friends arrive,' Susie advised. Her cure for everything—a cold, a bad day, a good day, a negative horoscope—was a rest. *Take a nap,* she'd say, *grab forty winks, have some shut-eye!*

April faked a yawn. 'Good idea.' Though she'd probably

stop by her store to see how her employee, Belinda, was doing, then she'd make sure the house was relatively tidy, then she'd scroll through her Facebook birthday messages.

They walked out of Café Lagoon and Jonah waved them goodbye from behind the counter. If he was a little older, she would have been happy to go on a date with him, he was such a cutie. But he sometimes talked about this girl he knew who moved away and travelled a lot for her career, and by the look in his eyes whenever he spoke about her, he still had a thing for her. Poor guy. Stuck in a small town looking after his parents' business when he probably wanted to see the world. Or maybe he was happy here and wanted the small-town life. He had a permanent smile plastered on his face.

April turned to the left and her mother and aunt turned in the other direction, then her mum turned back and leaned in close. 'Don't worry about your father, he would have made it if he could have.'

She waved her hand in dismissal, despite the deep-seated hurt that twinged in her chest. 'Doesn't matter. More fun with you two anyway.'

April checked her phone. No message or call from her dad to wish her happy birthday either.

'You're probably right.' Clarissa gave April's hand a squeeze. 'He cares, you know that, but...'

'He also cares about the booze.' She exchanged a knowing glance with her mother. 'Anyway, better go. Thanks again, chicky babes.' April blew a kiss to them.

'Oh, April, you make me feel like your friend, not your mother.' She smiled.

'That's coz you are.' She winked, waved, then turned. She didn't know what she would have done without her mother after the most traumatic day of her life two and a half years ago, when her life took a one hundred and eighty degree turn.

April approached the pedestrian crossing, then as always, checked the road carefully before crossing to make sure there were no hoons ignoring road rules. Sundays in Tarrin's Bay were always busy, tourists visiting the Tarrin rock formation, the beaches, boutiques, and—hopefully—her store. Lucky it wasn't market day or she may not have been able to take her birthday off work, as market days always brought in more customers since her store was so close to the park and harbour.

She turned the corner and walked past the first few historic terrace shops, their intricate framework, decorative signs, and old-fashioned charm comforting her. She'd been lucky to score one of them to lease, and if it hadn't been for the high competition urging her to make a quick decision, she may have missed out. But life was short, she knew that, and opportunities needed to be seized.

A customer walked out of April's Glow as she arrived. April tried to peer discreetly into her shopping bag to see if she could tell which candles she'd bought, but Belinda had wrapped them all neatly in the store's trademark rose-pink tissue paper. However, the unmistakable scent of her bestselling vanilla frosting candle wafted around the air. It was the closest thing to eating a fluffy vanilla cake with mouth-watering frosting without actually eating it. She really should tout it as a weight loss aid. Calorie free, simply smell and enjoy.

She walked into the store, and a symphony of sweet, spicy, and refreshing aromas enveloped her. The dark wood panelling on the walls framed shelves piled high with colour-coordinated candles of varying sizes, along with candle holders, lanterns, oil burners, and the odd decorative item.

'Ahh, home sweet home.'

'I think you've walked into the wrong building, boss.' Belinda stepped out from behind the counter and rearranged the vanilla frosting candles where the customer had been on a candle-buying rampage.

'Okay, *second* home sweet home.'

'I'd be happy to live here, better than sharing with my noisy housemates.' Belinda tucked a strand of black hair behind her multiple-pierced ear, her purple nail polish glossy in the light of a nearby lantern on the shelf. 'Anyway, what are you doing here on your birthday?' She waved her hand at April. 'Shoo! Get lost, enjoy your day.'

April smiled. 'You know, I could fire you for being all rude and stuff.'

'But you won't, you *need* me.' Belinda grasped April's arms and squeezed them with excessive enthusiasm, her eyes bulging.

This was why she came by the store, not only to check how the day's sales had gone so far, but because she needed a touch of fun from her quirky, eccentric, young employee, and a hint of the aromas and colours that covered her heart in a warm, soft, fluffy blanket and took away disappointment. She really shouldn't be disappointed; she knew her dad may not show up and had learned to brush his absences under the carpet. And her mother and aunt had given her a beautiful birthday lunch. At thirty-three, she had a lot to be thankful for in life.

'Okay, but first, how are the sales?'

'Good, and that's all I'm saying. I forbid you to think about business stuff till tomorrow.' Belinda ushered April towards the door. 'Go get drunk.'

Ain't gonna happen. April never had more than one or two drinks at a time, and only a few times a month, if that. She kept silent. She hadn't discussed her father's alcoholism with her employee; there was no reason to. They'd become like friends since she hired her four months ago, as they weren't exactly shy, making it easy to get to know each other. But some things were best kept private.

April stepped out onto the sun-speckled sidewalk, the aromas whooshing away like they'd been sucked into a vacuum. She walked up the road, around a few corners, and onto her street. As she neared her house, she noticed a white Ute parked outside the house next door, and several boxes piled up on the front porch.

So the new neighbour is finally here.

She slowed down, seeing if she could get a glimpse of the person. But the door was shut and the curtains drawn. She hesitated before walking towards her front steps, wondering if she should knock on the door and welcome them to the street.

Why not?

Impulsivity was her strong point. She blamed it on being an Aries. Not that she really believed in all that horoscope stuff.

Oh, hang on. I should bring a gift or something.

She should have brought a candle from her store. Maybe she could go grab one from her house. April lifted the bag she was carrying.

Or...

She withdrew the fruit-and-nut chocolate her aunt had given her, and always gave her, for some reason. Bless her little mistaken soul. April didn't have the heart to let her know the truth after all these years. Somehow, she thought that April liked it. But really, if one was going to have chocolate why would one spoil it with such healthy things as fruit and nuts? Yep, she could give it to the neighbour. Maybe they liked healthy chocolate.

April wandered up the pebbled pathway and onto the porch, vaguely aware of the scent of paint; the weatherboard panels had recently been painted an eggshell colour by the previous owners before selling the property. Her sense of smell had heightened since starting up the candle business; assessing various aromas was now part of her job.

She knocked on the door and waited, the chocolate in her hand. Hopefully they didn't think she was going to give them the gift bag with her own presents. She really liked the Belgian chocolates and swirly patterned scarf her mother had given her. And hopefully they wouldn't be able to tell that the fruit-and-nut chocolate was a reject gift.

Who would answer the door? Probably a lonely old man, a widower, and maybe he would hook up with Nancy Dillinger on the other side of April's house and have a love affair. It would give Nancy something to do apart from peering through her curtains. Or perhaps the neighbour was another medical professional like Sylvia Greene who lived two houses up, and they would walk to work together and discuss difficult cases. But it was probably an old man, the Ute looked like it had seen its fair share of use, and more and more elderly people were moving to the town these days.

She thought she heard footsteps, but then only silence.

Should she knock again? Maybe the old man was hard of hearing.

Nah. She left the chocolates on the doorstep and scribbled a note on a scrap of paper from her bag—*Welcome to the neighbourhood. From Number 3.* She added a smiley face.

When she went inside her house, she patted Romeo, her grey tabby cat, refilled his food bowl in the laundry, then peered out the kitchen window. The neighbour's kitchen window was directly opposite, but the venetian blinds were closed. On the back deck was a reclining timber chair that hadn't been there before. One chair, not two. Most likely a single occupant, as she'd thought. Wind chimes hung from the deck ceiling, thin, cylindrical metal rods surrounding a yin-yang symbol made from wood.

What person moves into a new house and hangs up wind chimes before unpacking the important things?

Then again, if April moved house again, she'd probably unpack the candles right away and base her furniture arrangements on where she wanted each particular candle.

She gave up her surveillance and flopped on the couch to check her birthday messages on her phone.

Hope all your wishes come true! many of the messages said.

Wishes. What would she wish for if wishes came true?

She stared at the ceiling for a moment, as though tiny stars would magically appear and one would shine bright, urging her to wish upon it.

Apart from the obvious wishes people would choose—peace, more money, perfect health—she couldn't make up her mind about what she wanted. After last week's non-existent date, she knew what she didn't want, and that was a start. Yes, she would make *anti-wishes* instead.

Anti-wish #1: No more money worries.

Anti-wish #2: No more accepting free samples from the bakery near April's Glow—in other words; no more unnecessary weight gain and sugar comas.

Anti-wish #3: No more unreliable men. Actually, no more men. At least for the rest of the year.

There.

'May my anti-wishes come true...' she whispered to herself. Romeo sashayed over and pounced onto her lap, meowing and looking at her with his big glossy eyes.

'Okay, Romeo, I'll make an exception just for you. You're my number one man.'

He curled into a ball and purred in satisfaction, then flinched as a door slammed shut next door.

'Damn. Where's my doorstopper?' Zac Masterson asked himself, as the loud sound put his reflexes on high alert. He rummaged through boxes and sighed, then kicked off his boots, reopened the front door, and propped them against it. Cool afternoon air rushed into the dim house. His new home. Now that the nosy neighbour had gone inside, he could get back to setting things up in peace. No interruptions, no distractions. He wasn't ready for being sociable, not yet.

He stepped out on the porch and almost trod on something. Glancing down, his eyebrows rose at the sight of a block of chocolate with a note attached. He picked it up and read it, a tiny smile tugging at his lips.

He glanced next door to Number Three; a red brick house most likely built in the sixties, with a weathered timber fence separating the property from his. He'd hid in the bathroom when he'd heard the knock. Hopefully the person thought he was out, picking up supplies. Or maybe they even thought he was deaf. He'd been tempted to peer out the window to catch a glimpse of his new neighbour, but resisted. No doubt he'd see the mystery person soon. Maybe it was a woman with a husband and kids, though he hadn't noticed any play equipment in the backyard. Or maybe an elderly person like the woman he'd seen in the next house up, looking out her front window. Although he hadn't seen her close up, her grey hair had contrasted with the bright yellow curtains she held aside.

Anyway, it didn't matter. He was here to keep to himself, get through what he had to get through, and figure out his next steps. People would only complicate things.

He opened the fruit-and-nut chocolate and popped a couple of squares in his mouth. *Not bad.* He hadn't had chocolate for ages.

Effortlessly carrying the boxes inside, Zac mentally planned where things needed to go. The house was bigger than he was used to. He could live in a tent and have all he needed, but he had more space now, more luxuries, and he planned to make the most of it.

As he carried the last box in, he caught sight of a kid riding a bike past his house. Automatically, he checked the road to make sure no cars were about to swerve around the corner; then, satisfied the kid was safe, he went inside and closed the door, locking it.

He stood in the centre of the living room, staring at the empty fireplace that he planned to fill with firewood over the coming months as autumn merged into winter. A memory of sitting around a campfire with friends invaded his mind. Friends. Most were long gone now. Here he was, in a new town, starting all over again like a kid in a new school. But he wasn't ready to make friends. In time, perhaps. He knew he couldn't continue this way forever, but for now, solitude was his best mate.

Zac glanced at his laptop charging in the corner on the floor. As it often did, inspiration hit him unexpectedly, so he sat on the floor and opened his computer. He clicked the web browser and opened his anonymous blog: *Winning The War Within*.

Words formed in his mind and he typed quickly:

BIRD IN A CAGE
> *I know I should be living out there*
> *Interacting and doing my share*
> *But it's easier somehow to go it alone*
> *No one around, no ringing phone.*

> *Sometimes I get a glimpse of an alternate life*
> *I'd have a job and friends, maybe even a wife*
> *But as fast as the glimpse appears it dissolves*
> *And I return to the words around which my*

life now revolves.

> *The words they are comfort, companion, and friend*
> *They make sense of the chaos, the grief they mend*
> *But I know these words must come to life; be born*
> *To give flight to the bird, its cage must be torn.*

He read through it a couple of times then clicked 'publish'. The last line lingered in his mind...

One day he would fly again, metaphorically speaking. He didn't know when, he didn't know how. But he hoped—*wished*—that somehow, he would find the strength to tear down the bars of his cage and set himself free.

CHAPTER THREE

'D on't forget to make a wish! Ready?' Olivia placed the cake on April's outdoor table, her hand creating a curved barrier between the flaming candles and the night air.

'Ha! I've actually made *anti*-wishes,' April replied.

'Anti-wishes? What kind of weirdo are you?' said Zoe, one of her oldest friends—she'd known her since primary school.

'Takes one to know one.' April winked, and Zoe blew her an air kiss. The happiness of their friendship was directly proportional to the severity of their fake insults.

'Well, whatever you want to wish for or not wish for, get ready, time to sing happy birthday!' Olivia was used to running birthday parties, having had eight years of experience with her daughter, Mia. April wouldn't be surprised if she whipped out a game of pass the parcel or pin the tail on the donkey. Or maybe she'd broken with tradition and hired a surprise stripper. That would be one hell of a way to welcome the new neighbour to the street, trying to sleep to the sounds of tipsy women laughing and talking loudly over hyped-up music and watching the shadow of a gyrating muscular male through the living room window.

Nancy next door would probably like it though. She might even join the party.

But no, she was sure Olivia hadn't planned such a surprise. And her cousin, Lisa, who sat demurely opposite her, holding her wine glass with her careful, dainty fingers, was more of a quiet, reserved type.

Zoe snapped a photo as the candles warmed April's face and the scent of wax drifted up to her nose. April smiled, then for the second photo, stuck out her tongue and squished her cheeks together. It was her birthday tradition, to have a funny-face photo for every birthday, ever since she'd done one in high school with Zoe, who had suggested repeating it each year.

When she returned her focus to the cake, she caught a flash of movement to her right. One of the sheer curtains framing the neighbour's kitchen window billowed. The venetian blinds were slightly open. Maybe he'd seen her wacky birthday pose and wondered what he'd gotten himself into, becoming this crazy person's neighbour. She also wondered if he'd seen her earlier, setting up the outdoor table with her candles. She'd rearranged them about five times before she was happy with the layout. Then she'd remembered she was at home and not at work and didn't have to be such a perfectionist about her display abilities to impress the customers.

April swayed as her friends sang 'Happy Birthday'.

'Hip-hip-hooray! Hip-hip-hooray!'

April reviewed her anti-wishes in her mind, then blew out the candles. Bar one.

'You must be too old. Can't blow all of the candles out in one hit.' Zoe chuckled.

'Hey, you're six months older than me,' April replied.

'I get the feeling you're going to keep holding that over me, right up to when we share a room in a nursing home one day.'

'Who says I'm going to share with you? I might share a room with the resident hottie.'

'I might be *married* to the resident hottie.'

'Ladies! Your candle, April.' Olivia pointed sharply to the cake. She wouldn't put it past her to blow it out on her behalf and say, 'There, all done. Happy birthday! Now let's play a game'.

April thought about what she actually would like for the year ahead... *oh why not?*

I wish for a year of business success, and happy, memorable moments.

There. Not too specific. A general wish. She blew out the remaining candle and her eyes flicked up to the sound of the neighbour's window closing.

'Somebody doesn't appreciate our singing,' said Zoe.

'Hey, speak for yourself!' Olivia placed her hands on her hips.

Guess the guy's not deaf after all.

Lisa smiled and observed. Small talk wasn't her thing. She only spoke when there was something to say. But when she did speak, it was either a hilarious one-liner, or something profound and helpful. April would never forget how her cousin had comforted and supported her, back when her life had taken an unexpected detour. And the pink candle-in-a-jar that sat on her bedside table, given as a gift by Lisa to lift April's spirits, was what had sparked the idea for opening a candle store and starting her life over. She owed a lot to Lisa.

'Have you met your neighbours yet?' Zoe cocked her head towards the house.

April shook hers. 'I think there's only one person. See—one chair on the deck. And there's a Ute out front. Probably an old guy.' She picked up her one-and-only glass of wine and lifted it to her lips; the crisp, grapey scent taking over the aroma of the citronella candles.

'Could be a couple, and they might *share* the deck chair in a loving embrace.' Zoe spoke with a flourish.

'Half their luck,' Olivia mumbled.

Lisa cleared her throat. It was like a proverbial drumroll… Lisa's going to speak! 'Or, maybe they *had* two chairs but one broke because they had more than just a loving embrace on it.'

Wine spurted from April's mouth and narrowly missed the cake. Zoe guffawed and Olivia giggled. 'Oh God, Lisa, you're a hoot!' April laughed.

Lisa shrugged as if her suggestion was a completely plausible explanation for the solitary chair.

'Here you go, Ape,' said Zoe, handing her the kitchen knife. 'Slice it up and make another anti-wish?'

'Seriously, I'm thirty-three, I think you can stop calling me Ape now.' She took the knife and positioned the tip at the centre of the chocolate mud cake, then slid a glance back at Zoe. 'Zooey.'

'Hey, I know we had that whole discussion back in school about you being an ape and me belonging in a zoo, and seriously, Ape suits you. But Zooey? It's just not funny anymore.'

'As long as you call me Ape, I'll call you Zooey.' She slid the knife through the cake in one smooth motion. She forgot to make another wish, or anti-wish, but the knife touched the bottom anyway, which meant her anti-wish would be void. Not that she believed in superstitions.

She cut four slices and, as promised earlier, handed Olivia the biggest slice.

As they dug into the rich, dense cake, April dug deep inside her heart to unearth some much-needed hope. She'd be okay. She *was* okay. She had built her strength back up in the last two years, both emotionally and physically. And she had two close friends, a great employee, a cousin who was more like a sister, her mother, and Lisa's mum, Aunt Susie. And of course there was Dad. Though he wasn't there for her much, he was still around. She still had a father. She had a lot more than many other people. But she had also lost a lot more than other people.

Before April allowed herself to remember the past, Zoe lifted a glass of wine. 'A toast!' April lifted hers, as did Olivia and Lisa. 'To April, and a year of amazing business success, laughter and happiness, and... what else?'

'Um...' Olivia tilted her head towards the starlit sky.

Zoe raised her glass even higher. 'And a hot, passionate fling with a gorgeous man who has a body to die for!'

Olivia and Lisa clinked their glasses to Zoe's but April hesitated. 'Um, yeah maybe not that last one, Zooey.'

'Why not, Ape?'

'Too complicated.' She flicked her free hand in a dismissive wave. 'I'm not ready for complicated.'

'Who says it has to be complicated?' Zoe replied.

Complicated. Why *did* it have to be? It hadn't been before. At least in the beginning. Meet a guy, fall in love, get engaged, and then... well, that's when things *had* gotten complicated. If things had turned out differently that unforgettable day, she'd now be married to Kyle living the life she had planned. But life could change in an instant, and the thought of giving love a chance again after all she'd been through was exhausting. The non-existent date last weekend had been the sign, even though she didn't believe in signs. Though two and a half years had passed, it was still too soon.

But she clinked her glass against Zoe's and the others' anyway. 'To uncomplicated,' she said.

'To uncomplicated!' they chorused.

The next morning, April let Romeo outside and left his water and food bowl on the back deck. He scooted off with enthusiasm and dashed into the nearest bush, then dashed back out of it and leapt onto the bird bath, balancing precariously on the thin edge, dipping his paw in tentatively and trying to scoop some of the water up. No matter how many water bowls she left around for him, he always preferred to find his own source whenever possible—in the garden, the kitchen sink, and the shower or bathtub.

'Bye, Romeo!' she called out. She locked the back door, grabbed her handbag, and opened the front door. April stopped when something caught her eye on the doormat. A lone flower sat in a glass jar half filled with water, a note attached with an elastic band. *Huh.* She picked up the beautiful flower; long, slim petals radiating out from the centre petals, the bright red colour reminding her of her store's 'passion' candle. The note said:

Happy birthday, April.

That was it. No name, and she didn't recognise the handwriting.

She smiled, glanced around the street to see if anyone was around. They must have left it early, or maybe one of her friends had left it last night when she wasn't looking, when they had all shuffled outside in a cluster of chatter.

It couldn't be the new neighbour, he or they didn't know her name.

She looked towards Number Five. It was probably Nancy Dillinger who'd left the flower, the dear thing. She was nosy, in a polite way, but the few times she'd spoken with the woman she could tell she was a nice person with a good heart. But she didn't recall seeing any unique flowers like that in her garden. Though she wouldn't put it past the woman to pinch flowers from someone else's.

'How sweet,' April said out loud, taking the flower inside

and placing it on the dining table next to her citrus candle centrepiece. She took a photo of it with her phone, then noticed Romeo's confused look through the glass pane of the back door at seeing her back inside. 'Sorry, Romes,' she said with a pout. 'Still going to work.' She went out the front and walked down the street.

How nice, to get an anonymous gift. She walked briskly, and couldn't shake the feeling that someone was watching her.

CHAPTER FOUR

O n arriving home that afternoon, April expected Romeo to be waiting at the back door, meowing loudly and waiting to come inside for dinner. But he wasn't there. She opened the door to the back deck and stepped outside.

'Romeo!' She leaned on the deck railing and scanned the garden. 'Romeo!'

Where was the little rascal? She eyed the trees. Maybe he was up too high and didn't want to come down or was stuck. 'Come on, Romeo. Get your furry butt over here!'

'You're saying it wrong.'

April flinched. She turned left to face the source of the male voice at the house next door.

Holy moly. She almost toppled over the railing. The sight of him paralysed her voice box.

'You're supposed to say, "Wherefore art thou, Romeo?"' he said, as a small smile lifted one corner of his lips.

'Oh, I'm ah...' She watched him standing there, in a tight-fitting white singlet of all things on this cool afternoon, watching her with his chocolatey eyes, a dark shadow of a beard across his jaw. He was definitely no old guy, couldn't be more than thirty... thirty-five at the most. 'Just looking for my cat,' she explained.

His tattooed arm muscles bulged as he folded them across his chest. 'Your cat's name is Romeo?' The tone of his voice went upwards at the mention of her pet's name.

She stiffened. 'Yes. Why? Do you have a problem with that?' April didn't know why she felt defensive. Maybe it was his amused smirk, or the way he stood still with such a strong presence and confidence, like he was the king of his backyard.

The man held up his hands. 'No, not at all. What one names one's cat is one's own business.'

What was with all the 'ones'? Did he time-travel here from Shakespearean times or something?

April glanced around, if only to tear her eyes away from his commanding physique that had her captivated like a teenager with hormone overload. 'Romeo, Romeo!' She looked back at the man who now wore a full-on smile, his hand waving in circles encouraging her to say more. She rolled her eyes and released a small smile of her own. 'Romeo,' she said in a floaty, girly voice. 'Wherefore art thou, Romeo?'

Cringe-worthy.

The man chuckled, then cocked his head towards the back corner of his garden. April squinted, peering into the bushes. Two glassy eyes shone in the dark corner behind the orange tree. 'Oh, Romeo! What are you doing over there?' April huffed, stepping down the deck steps and approaching the weathered wooden fence that separated her house from Number One. 'Sorry,' April said. She leaned her hands on the top of the fence that came up to her shoulders and got a closer look at her hidden cat. He was having a stare-off with another cat, a tortoiseshell tabby. 'Is the other cat yours or have all the neighbourhood cats flocked to visit the new resident in the street?' she asked.

'Not all the cats, just yours,' he corrected. 'She's mine

actually, picked her up from the shelter yesterday. Supposed to leave her inside for a week or so to get used to the place, but she had other ideas. First time she goes out and she's already found herself a boyfriend.'

'Don't worry, Romeo is de-sexed.'

'Good to know. Though I think making out is the last thing on their minds at the moment.' He glanced at the cats, now sharing occasional hisses at each other.

How was it that within minutes of meeting her new neighbour she'd already quoted Shakespeare, mentioned the word de-sexed, and now they were chatting over the fence about cats making out?

'Romeo,' April called out. 'Come on, back home now.' Her cat ignored her, his unblinking eyes fixed fiercely on the other cat. She glanced down the length of the fence, thinking she'd have to go around the property and through his house to get Romeo. The man didn't seem the slightest bit interested in helping her out. 'Um, would you mind, ah...' She gestured to the animals.

The man raised his eyebrows like he didn't know what she wanted.

'Can you, um... can you please pick up my cat for me?'

He shrugged again. 'They'll finish when they're ready. You can't force a cat to do anything.'

'But I need to bring him inside for his dinner, and I have... things to do.'

The man placed his hands in the pockets of his jeans as he watched the cats. April furrowed her brow. Clearly, *he* didn't have things to do.

The wind chimes on his back deck jingled as the breeze picked up. Maybe he was a wind-chime maker, or some kind of artistic person who didn't rush anything. 'Well, if we're going to stand here and wait for nature to take its course...' April took her hands off the fence and crossed her arms, catching his glance as he turned to face her. 'So, what do you do?'

'I don't do,' he replied.

'Huh?'

'I'm a human being, not a human doing.'

And a slightly weird, albeit incredibly attractive human at that.

'Obviously, but you must do something. I mean, everybody *does* something, right?'

Romeo hissed loudly and the man's cat reciprocated. Then she pounced into the bushes, and Romeo followed. Leaves rustled chaotically, and hisses and growls emerged. April nibbled her bottom lip. If she could, she would climb over the fence and retrieve her cat, but it wasn't the most practical solution. 'We really should—'

'Shh,' he said, 'give them a minute.'

Shh? He was telling her to 'Shh'? Maybe he was one of those nature documentary people, observing animals in their natural habitat and commenting on their behaviour.

April's stomach grumbled. She needed to get inside and make a start on dinner. Going for the direct approach wasn't working with this guy, so apart from the idea of launching herself into his garden, maybe she should get him talking a bit more and then he might be kind and pick up her damn cat and give him the hell back. 'What's her name?' she asked.

The man shrugged. 'Dunno.'

'You have a pet cat and haven't named her yet?'

'I'll wait till the right name comes to mind.'

'You like waiting, don't you.' Oops, that was supposed to be a thought, not speech. That happened to April a lot, words just seemed to come to life on their own.

'Patience is a virtue,' he replied.

'Patience is a pain in the arse.' Oops, another thought

turned speech. The man looked her in the eye again, his gaze narrow and his head tilted a little, as though she was an animal in his nature documentary, and he was trying to understand her behaviour and impulsive speech. April shoved a chunk of her wavy hair behind her shoulder. 'Anyway, if she has no name, how do you expect her to come to you when you need her to?'

'She'll come to me when she wants to. Cats are very independent.'

April drummed her fingers on her folded arms, while he seemed more relaxed by the minute.

'See? Look.' He pointed to Romeo who was edging slowly away from the bushes and the other cat.

'That's it boy, over here,' she said. She made little clicky sounds with her tongue, then wished she hadn't, as the man released a slight chuckle at her Skippy the kangaroo-sounding clicky noises.

'Treat them a little more like humans and they'll be more receptive, you know,' he said.

'Are you a vet?'

'No.'

'A nature documentary maker?'

'No.'

'A...' She'd run out of ideas, and he was also getting more amused with her by the minute, judging by the grin on his face. Geez, the guy had nice lips. He probably used lip balm. They would be soft to kiss. *April! No men, remember? And definitely no strange, unhelpful men who lived next door.*

'Hey there, buddy. Thanks for the warm welcome to the neighbourhood.' The man effortlessly leaned down and picked up Romeo, who although tense, didn't try to scratch him or leap from his grasp. He handed him over the fence to April and she held onto her pet tightly for fear of him escaping.

'I think I'll call you The Cat Whisperer,' she said to the man.

'And I'll call you The Cat Matchmaker.' He turned to his Cat-Without-A-Name who was hiding under the small gap beneath the polished timber deck. He picked her up and patted the top of her head. 'Come on, Juliet, how about some dinner?' He stepped onto his deck and opened the back door, but not before he turned his head back briefly and flashed April a satisfied smile.

The door clapped closed and April stood by the fence, her mouth slightly agape. Had he just named his cat *Juliet* in response to her cat being called *Romeo*? She didn't know whether to laugh or tell him not to be so silly, but he had gone back inside without so much as a 'nice to meet you' or 'my name is so-and-so'.

April shook her head and turned towards her house. But when she stepped up onto her own deck and glanced back at the scene where the weirdest first meeting of all time had unfolded, something beside the reclining timber armchair on the deck caught her eye, and surprise fluttered in her chest. A terracotta pot sat there, and a unique flowering plant bulged from the potted soil; long, slim, red petals radiating out from the centre.

CHAPTER FIVE

'But how did he know my name? Do you think he checked my mail in the letterbox or something? The snoop!' April discussed what had happened with Belinda the next day at work.

'Hang on,' Belinda replied. 'Didn't you say he closed the window during your birthday celebrations?' She leaned on the counter with her bony elbows. One had a tattoo of a feather on it.

'Yeah, so?'

'Well he must have heard your friends singing 'Happy Birthday' to you. They did use your name, right?'

'Oh yeah. But I could have been one of the friends, he didn't know it was *my* house. Unless...' He must have seen her setting up outside when she'd gone all OCD with the candle table decorations.

'He's seen you; he heard your name; he left a flower on your doorstep. What's with all this over-analytical crap? Enjoy the gift, girl! I mean, boss.'

April smiled. 'You're right. He's just unnerved me for some reason. He's a bit weird. Didn't even introduce himself.'

'Did you introduce *yourself*?'

'No, but...' Damn. 'Okay I get it. Anyway, back to work, my insightful young employee.' April shooed her away from the counter and opened the stock list on the computer. Monday was usually slow, and being the start of the week, she liked to do the ordering of stock at the start of each week. That way they'd have plenty of the popular items ready for the weekend surge in sales.

'God, I love this smell.' Belinda sniffed a lime green candle like it was oxygen. 'I wish there was some kind of permanent aromatic nose attachment so I could smell it all day without having to pick up the candle.'

'Like a scented nose ring?' April suggested with a chuckle.

Belinda pointed at her and raised her eyebrows. 'Yes! You could be onto something there, woman. What a cool invention. We should invent it.'

'I'll leave that business venture for you, I think.' April had a belly button ring, and her ears were pierced, but that was it. She didn't think she had the kind of nose that suited a nose ring. Didn't want one anyway. Belinda had enough piercings for the both of them. And tattoos.

April resisted the slight shudder in her nerves that sometimes threatened her sense of stability.

She hadn't thought of her tattoo for a while. She'd loved the result of her impulsive decision to get one, after the redness had died down. It had made her feel unique and powerful, like she was expressing her own identity and projecting her confidence into the world. But now, that confidence, along with the tattoo, was gone.

'I think you should order more of these,' said Belinda, and April returned her focus to her job. 'With my enthusiasm and strange smell addiction for whatever is in this baby, I reckon I can sell a truckload for you.' She held the lime green candle up and stroked it like it was a cuddly pet.

'Your wish is my command.' April opened the website of one of her suppliers and added the candle to the shopping cart.

If only enticing scented candles were all that a person could get addicted to.

When she had finished her order and was about to change the window display, her phone beeped with a text message.

> Sorry I missed your birthday. Would have been there if I could've. This bad back of mine is making it hard to get around. How's about my baby girl pays me a visit sometime? Miss you.

April's heart softened as it always did when she heard from him, then hardened. She was tempted to go see her dad on her lunchbreak, or after work, make sure he was eating properly and looking after himself as best as someone like him could. But she'd had enough of the ups and downs, the hot and cold, the abandonment followed by re-entry into her life. The inconsistency of his parental role. If she was to move forward with her life, she needed to put herself first. And that meant avoiding the inevitable hurt that came with continually bending to her father's needs. Not that she'd let him fend for himself completely, but he'd had plenty of opportunities and support to get help for his addiction, but hadn't committed to the process. They'd done all they could, for so long, but what more could they do?

She typed back:

> I'm pretty busy with the new business, will see how I go for time over the next few weeks. Look after yourself.

What she really wanted to type was: *Stop drinking. Please, Dad. No more.*

But he wouldn't stop. And there would be more. And more of everything else that came along with that; the drunken accidents, the fights and needing to be called in to the police station, the hospitalisation from dehydration and malnourishment, the guilt trips he'd give her because *'no one looks after me.'* She'd tried. Her mum had tried. But after the divorce Clarissa had said enough was enough. She'd check up on him occasionally, but there were boundaries she intended to maintain. At least her dad's neighbours knew his situation and often checked on him, which gave her some peace of mind. But she couldn't be his carer. She had her own life to lead, to rebuild after all that had happened.

She wouldn't waste her life by watching him waste his.

April slowed as she walked past her new neighbour's house after work, noticing the bundle of mail sticking out of the letterbox, and a parcel sitting on the doorstep. It was almost six. Maybe he was out?

'Probably waiting for the mail to come to him when it's ready,' she joked to herself.

Heavy clouds hung overhead in the darkening sky. April yanked the mail from the letterbox and marched up to his porch. She glanced down at the parcel, the sender's label said 'Fast and Fresh' and had a logo of a basket of fruit. If it was fruit, she didn't know how fresh it would be sitting out here all day. And why would someone get fruit home delivered anyway, when the shops were a quick walk up the road?

Holding the mail in one hand, she knocked on the door with the other, then adjusted her handbag strap over her shoulder.

Her gaze flickered to a window at the side as the curtain moved. Then the door opened slightly and the man stood there as though trying to hide something behind him. Either that, or he could be worried she might barge in and start making herself at home or something.

She waited for him to say hi, but he kept silent, looked at her with eyes that seemed older than his years.

'Just bringing in your mail,' she said. 'Not that I'll be doing that on a regular basis, but it looks like it might rain, and it was sticking out of the letterbox.'

'Thanks.' He snatched the mail from her and went to close the door but April held out her hand and stopped it.

'And there's a parcel here.' She glanced down at the box. When he didn't bend down, she added with a hint of sarcasm, 'Would you like me to pick it up for you?'

He didn't reply, simply bent down and lifted the box as though it was as light as a feather. He was wearing that singlet again, and now that she was closer, she could make out one of the tattoos on his outer arm: a Chinese-looking symbol.

'Nice tatt,' she said.

'One of many,' he finally spoke.

'I figured that.' Her eyes scanned his skin, but now the box in front of his chest obscured her view.

'I'm April.' She held out her hand, even though his hands were firmly holding the box.

He turned around to go into his house.

Oh great, he's ignoring my attempt at being neighbourly. What a jerk.

She shook her head and was about to turn away herself when he placed the box down in his kitchen and came back to the door. He held out his hand. 'I'm Zac.'

Oh.

She grasped it, and even though she'd been taught to shake

hands with a firm sense of confidence, she held his like a limp fish as both the touch of his warm skin and the sight of his intense eyes looking directly into hers overwhelmed her ability to focus.

'I already know your name,' he added. 'Overheard it the other night.'

Oh yes. The flower. 'So it was you who left the gift on my doorstep.'

He shrugged. 'Maybe.'

'Clearly it was since you didn't say "what gift?"' She smirked, but he remained silent. 'Well, thanks. It was nice.'

He gave a single, small nod.

'Anyway, I've done my neighbourly duty, I'll leave you to it.' She turned.

'So what do *you* do?' he asked.

April turned back to face him. 'Huh?'

'For work. What do you do?'

'I thought you weren't interested in doing, only being.'

'That's correct. But you are obviously interested in doing. So what is it? Real estate, journalism, school teacher?'

'Keep guessing.'

'Just tell me.'

'Okay then. What I do is own and run a candle shop in town. April's Glow.'

A tiny smile flickered on his lips. 'Nice name.'

'Thanks. Yeah, it was named after, well obviously *me*, but there's a story to it as well. Because when I was young ...'

Zac chuckled.

'What?' April adjusted her bag strap again.

He shrugged.

'Why are you laughing?'

'You're amusing to watch.'

'Amusing?' April's cheeks went warm and she diverted her

gaze to the porch railing. She was just talking, what was so amusing about that? Well, now she wouldn't tell him the story of how the shop got its name. He could suffer in suspense.

'Candles, huh?' he said. 'I like candles, actually. I'm not a fan of artificial light.'

She tilted her head. 'Well maybe you'd like to visit my shop and help your neighbour out by making a sizeable purchase.' She grinned, opening her bag to retrieve a business card. If she could find one. 'I'll give you my card. Hang on.' She pulled out her purse where she kept a few spares in the zippered compartment. She unzipped it and withdrew a card, but a couple more came with it and fell on the ground, along with ...

Oh my God.

April's eyes widened in horror at the flat, square-shaped item, its shiny foil packaging glinting in the porch light as though saying 'look at me!'

'You have promotional condoms for your business? Cool,' Zac said.

Oh God, oh God, oh God.

April bent down and picked up the item, dropped it again, then picked it up again, along with the fallen cards. Shame she couldn't pick up her dignity.

'No, it's not promotional, it's just... it's... I don't usually have ...' She shoved the items and her purse in her bag and tensely held the strap on her shoulder. She only had *one* in her purse at Olivia's insistence when she'd agreed to the internet date. *'Just in case,'* she'd been advised. Not that she'd planned to go that far with someone she'd just met. 'Anyway, I should go.'

'Aren't you going to give me your card?'

She eyed his unperturbed expression, which looked like he was used to people dropping condoms around him all the time, just another day at the office. Maybe he *was* used to it. Maybe he was some kind of male prostitute and that's why he kept to himself and stayed home and maybe April was the tenth, eleventh, or even twelfth woman to arrive on his doorstep that day.

She carefully reopened her bag and took out a card, and handed it to him.

He studied it and nodded, then slid it into his pocket.

'Anyway, bye.' April's voice was high-pitched. She turned away again and stepped off the porch, desperate to get away. But something made her glance back, as Zac walked back inside his house but left the door wide open. 'Aren't you going to close the door?' she said. *Why can't I stop talking and leave?* 'Oh wait, let me guess. It'll close when it's ready, right?'

He shrugged, his hands in his pockets.

'You never know who could barge right in.' April gestured to the door. 'A thief, or a serial killer, or ...' *or a woman with your mail.*

'I can protect myself,' he replied. 'And... I have a feeling you can too.' He grinned and closed the door, leaving April standing in his front yard, wishing she could sink into it and disappear forever. Then the rain came pouring down.

CHAPTER SIX

S he was struggling. Struggling to stay afloat, to breathe, to find her footing. April shot up in bed, sweat sticking to her pyjama top. The dream was a regular occurrence, but instead of drowning in a dark pit of thick nothingness, she had been surrounded by, almost engulfed by ...

What the hell?

She laughed. Shook her head. Dreams were crazy. Like the hundreds or thousands of colourful plastic balls in children's play centres, she'd been submersed among thousands of colourful condoms, as she flailed about and panicked like she was in quicksand. And Zac was there. He tried to rescue her, but fell into the pit and got engulfed too.

April was alone in her dark bedroom and yet her cheeks flushed with embarrassment.

She considered taking one of the sleeping tablets she still had in her medicine box, but hadn't taken one for over a year and didn't want to start that again. She'd almost become addicted. Besides, they'd make her drowsy and she wouldn't be able to focus at work.

She glanced at the clock. Almost three am. She rolled

around in bed for a while trying to get comfortable, but within ten minutes made her way to the kitchen, rubbing fatigue from her head. She flicked the switch and noticed she'd forgotten to close the venetian blinds before bed. She froze. Zac's light was on next door, and he stood in the middle of his kitchen, just like her. Only he wasn't wearing flannelette pyjamas and nor did he have crazy bed hair. He had normal, neat, cropped hair, and his chest was bare, apart from tattoos. His kitchen window was high and blocking his lower body, so who knew what he was wearing, if anything, down below.

He waved. Not a 'Hi! It's me! Fancy seeing you here!' wave. A 'Hey neighbour' wave. She waved back, then ran her hand discreetly through her hair but it got caught in a knot. She looked away to fill her glass of water, and when she looked back he was holding something large and square. He held it up. A whiteboard. On it he'd written: *What's your number?*

Oh, nice one. Loser. Trying to hit on her by standing in his kitchen half naked and doing the old *Love, Actually* trick.

April eyed her own whiteboard that hung on the wall beside the fridge. It had the quote 'each day is a new beginning' handwritten on it. Lisa had suggested a while back that she have motivational quotes around the house to help with lifting her mood, after it had fallen deep into that dark, hopeless pit she sometimes dreamed about. She was supposed to change the quote each week, but this one had been on there a month. She lifted the whiteboard off the wall and rubbed out the quote, replacing it with: *Why?* She held it up to the window.

Zac rubbed out his own and started writing something, then he held it up:

You're up, I'm up. Might as well talk.

April wrote:

Why not just talk over the fence?

Zac replied:

Because I'm naked.

April gulped and quickly rubbed out her last message, replacing it with her number.

Seconds later her phone rang from its charger in the living room. She picked it up and returned to the kitchen. 'You're not really naked, are you? I bet you're wearing something, at least,' she said.

'Only a smile,' he replied, and she glanced at him through the window, his smile sending a warm flush to her cheeks.

'Aren't you cold?'

'Nope.'

'Do you always walk naked around your house in the middle of the night?'

'Yep.'

Why am I asking such questions? 'If Nancy Dillinger was your neighbour you'd probably give her a coronary.'

'Is she that lady next to you?'

'Yep.'

He took a swig of water. 'Nice hair, by the way.'

Oh man. The problem with having naturally wavy hair was that it had a mind of its own. You never knew what kind of strange arrangement you'd end up with in the morning; on a good day it could look like rolling hills of the countryside and on the bad days like the Sydney Opera House.

April defensively patted her hair and frowned. 'I'm sorry I didn't do my hair before coming to the kitchen in the middle of the night to get a glass of water. I'll do better next time.'

'Or shave it like mine. Number three. Then you don't have to worry.'

'I'm sure your choice of style would look just wonderful on me.' April glanced down, tapping her right fluffy-polka-dot-socked foot on the floor. 'Why are we on the phone anyway?'

'Because I called you.'

'Clearly. But what do you want to talk about? Need insomnia cures?'

'If I needed them, I'd be Googling and not asking advice from someone suffering the same problem.'

'What makes you think I'm an insomnia sufferer? I could be having a one-off waking episode. Which is actually what's happened.' No need to tell him about the bizarre dream. 'I should get back to sleep. Have to be up for work in four hours.'

'Do you love your job?'

'Huh? Yes.'

'What's your passion?'

'My passion? Candles, of course. Why?'

'But what is it about them? Why candles?'

She frowned again. 'Because, um... I *like* them?'

'I like them too. But that doesn't mean I want to run a candle store. So why do you?'

'Well, some of us actually have to *do* things to make a living, so candles are what I chose to, you know, allow me to have electricity, buy food and clothing—which, clearly—you've forgotten to do.'

'It's because they give you hope, isn't it.'

Bam. It was like he had pried open her heart and soul and read her like a book. *How did he know that?* 'It's because, well, they smell nice, and look nice, and people like them and buy them and I get income from it. That's why.' She ran her hand across her bed hair and had the vague sense she'd messed it up worse than before.

'Bring one back for me,' he said. 'Any candle. You choose. And I'll pay you for it.'

She stood closer to the window and leaned one hand on the sink. 'Why don't you come into the store and choose your own?'

'Because I want to see which one you pick for me.'

'Is this some kind of personality quiz or something? Are you a psychologist who analyses people based on their purchasing tendencies?' *How did you know why I love candles? What is that tattoo on your shoulder? Why are your pecs so damn beautiful?*

'I'm just a man. I need a candle for my house. I want you to choose.' He shrugged. 'I'll see you and the candle at the end of the day.' He ended the call and put his phone down, switched off the light, and walked his naked self out of the kitchen. April's phone was still attached to her ear, her hand unable to move. This Zac guy was the weirdest person she'd ever met. But somehow, his weirdness drew her to him. She wanted to discover more. She wanted to stay on the phone and talk at three am. She even wanted to peer over and... *No, April. No men. No thinking about men, no flirting with men. No men.*

She flicked off the light and returned to bed. Lying on her back, she became aware of a cool film of sweat that had pooled at her lower back. She rubbed it away. It was also on her chest. She rubbed it dry against her pyjamas, but her hand lingered between her breasts, and she thought of Zac's hand. She quickly removed it and rolled over. Maybe it was time to see what the real estate market was like in town. She didn't know how she could handle living here, next to him. And it had only been a few days. And he didn't look like he was planning on going anywhere else anytime soon.

If he hadn't ended the call when he did it would have been dangerous. Things, feelings, were welling up inside, things he hadn't allowed to well up for a long time. It was crazy, he hardly knew the woman. But it felt like he'd met her before. Anyway, *she* was dangerous... to the stability he'd worked so hard for, to his focus. But danger drew him close like a magnet. Always had, always would. As long as he didn't get too close, he'd be okay.

He could be friendly, a good neighbour, flirt a little, but that was all.

As he returned to his room and shut the window, a bird squawked far in the distance; a reminder that in a couple of hours the sun would start to rise. As it always did. Knowing that no matter what, the sun would shine with each new day, had kept him going over the last several months.

One day at a time, he reminded himself.

And there were only one hundred and forty-four of them to go.

CHAPTER SEVEN

April checked her income and expenses spreadsheet on the computer at work and winced. There were so many expenses in the early stages of running a business, but as long as she had enough to cover her living expenses, it'd be worth it in the long run.

'It's all for a good cause,' Belinda said. 'What's with the worried face?'

April flicked her hand. 'It's nothing. Should have budgeted a bit better, I guess. But yeah, I wanted to do this.'

Providing a heap of complimentary candles for the upcoming Anzac Day service in a couple of weeks would put a dent in her income, but it would be worth it. Sure, her business name would get exposure, but that wasn't the reason. Knowing that candles from her store would bring light and hope to those remembering a traumatic past made her feel good. Like she was making some sort of difference, however small. Just as one small candle had given *her* hope.

She recalled how Zac had picked up on this. Or maybe he had guessed. Either way, it had nudged a part of her inside that didn't want to be nudged. That part that if she allowed herself to become too aware of, might release a whole lot of stuff she wasn't ready to face. She had to stay focused, happy, and keep moving forward. If she kept going, kept getting further away from her own past, maybe it would gradually disappear.

April grabbed her handbag.

'Let me guess, Café Lagoon?' asked Belinda. 'Why not try some place different for lunch?'

'Well, last week I went to the café around the corner, remember?'

She nodded. 'Or you could get some takeaway and sit in the park today. Fresh air, sunshine, maybe perv on random cute men.' She raised her eyebrows twice.

'Actually, I *will* go someplace different.'

Belinda held out a hand to high-five, but April didn't take it.

'I have some leftover soup at home. Need to save money. I'll eat there and be back in an hour.'

'Bor-ing.' Belinda dropped her hand and slumped, then straightened up. 'Oh! Unless... perving on not-so-random cute men who live next door perhaps?'

April shook her head and was about to exit the store when she remembered. A candle for Zac. She peered at her shelves and displays.

Just a man.

Needs a candle for his home.

You choose.

She couldn't get him anything too girly, or too sweet smelling, or too... what sort of candle could he possible want?

Men like food, right? Food, and... spicy stuff. Right?

Cinnamon. She grabbed the burnt orange-brown triple-wick candle from behind the display of cinnamon sticks wrapped in twine.

'Shoplifting?' Belinda asked.

'Living dangerously.' April winked and walked out.

She wouldn't give it to him yet, like she'd rushed back on her lunchbreak to obey his strange demands. She quickly walked past his house and into hers. Romeo meowed profusely at the back door and she let him in. 'Shh, Romeo, the neighbour might be having an afternoon nap.' She hoped he was, at least. Then she could eat her lunch in peace and not get lost in some weird discussion about cats or Shakespeare or condoms.

A combination of carrots, celery, and broccoli in her spicy vegetable soup warmed her stomach as Romeo weaved under and around the dining table chair, his tail held high like a flag. She scrolled through Facebook but nothing caught her interest. Just the usual 'look what I had for lunch' and 'so-and-so is feeling sad because such-and-such has discontinued her favourite lipstick shade', and... *Argh!* Why did people think it was appropriate to post pictures of spiders they'd found around their house? Actually, that would be a good Facebook status. She typed it in and hoped the culprit who she didn't actually know in real life but was a friend of a friend of a friend of someone she'd known fifteen years ago, would see it and get the hint.

Her phone rang with an unknown number. If it were a telemarketer, she would sing an annoying children's song really loud. Then she'd post on Facebook that she'd done that and people would comment with 'LOL' and 'good one!' and 'thanks now I have that song stuck in my head'.

'Hello?' she answered.

'Chosen a candle yet?'

April's spoon clattered into the bowl.

'Well, have you?'

'Patience is a virtue,' she replied.

'I thought patience was a pain in the arse.'

Why did their conversations never go the way normal conversations should go?

'I'm on my lunchbreak. I have to go back to work soon.'

'I know. I heard you come home. That Romeo of yours has a loud meow. I think he's sexually frustrated. Anyway, you haven't answered my question.'

April's mouth dropped open a little. 'If you must know, yes, I do have your candle. And you can wait until I feel like giving it to you. I'm enjoying a well-deserved break right now.'

'Let me guess, mindlessly scrolling through Facebook or YouTube videos?'

Was the guy a psychic?

'I'm... um, that's none of your business.'

'You should try meditation. Calms the mind, refreshes the body, that sort of thing.'

'You should try not calling people you hardly know with your impatient demands and advice.'

Silence.

'Do *you* meditate?' she asked. 'I bet you do. You seem like the type.'

'I do. But there is no type. I am who I am.'

'You're Zac, a guy who doesn't feel the cold, has tattoos, a cat called Juliet, and who likes to *be*. That's all I know.'

'Do you want to know more?'

Silence.

'I should get back to work.' She cleared her throat. But bubbles of curiosity popped madly away inside. She *so* wanted to know more. But she couldn't give in. Men were complicated, and this one was, without a doubt. No complications allowed.

'Can I have my candle first? Please? Also, I have one for you.'

'You have a candle for me?'

'Sort of.'

'You either do or you don't.'

'Come and see for yourself. I'm out back.' He hung up before she could object.

He probably had one of those cheap, petroleum-based tea light candles he'd half used and would give it to her as a joke. And he'd better pay her for the cinnamon candle, she couldn't afford to give any more freebies.

She went out to the back deck. Zac was laying on the grass in his backyard, hands behind his head, gazing up at the sky. At least he was wearing a t-shirt. And jeans. His feet were bare. Romeo scooted off to the bushes and April made her way to the fence. She held up the candle. 'That'll be thirty-seven bucks, thanks. And add three dollars for home delivery, so let's round it up to forty.' She gave a nod, though he wasn't looking her way.

'Bring it over,' he said. 'Come join me. You have to look at this cloud.'

'Huh? You want your candle, come here and get it. I don't have time to laze away the day looking at clouds.'

'You should make time. You're missing out.'

April sighed. 'You can leave the money in my letterbox and I'll drop the candle over after work when you've finished your important cloud-gazing work.' She walked back up to her deck.

'Hey, hang on.'

She turned.

Zac got up and walked to the fence, extracted his wallet from his back pocket. 'Here you go.' He held out a fifty-dollar note.

She met him at the fence and took it. 'I'll have to go inside and get change for you.'

'Keep it,' he said, his eyes allowing no objection.

'Well, um, thanks. Here's your candle.'

He accepted it and lifted it to his nose. 'Cinnamon. How did you know?'

'Know what?'

'That it's one of my favourite spices.'

'I didn't. But I mean, who doesn't like cinnamon?'

He shrugged. 'And three wicks, much better than one. Now I feel special.' He offered a small smile.

'It's just how they make those ones.' April flicked her hand. 'So where's mine, huh?'

He raised his eyebrows.

'My candle? You said you had one for me.'

'Oh yeah. You have to come over to get it.'

Yeah... no. He was clearly only interested in one thing, trying to hit on her and invite her over for a midday rendezvous. 'Nice try. My job is calling.'

'But if you don't come and least look at the candle, it'll be gone soon.'

'How so? Planning to give it to another neighbour?'

'You'll know what I'm talking about when you get here.' He grinned. 'C'mon, this fence isn't too high. Jump on over, I'll give you a hand.'

It was a shame that someone so damn attractive was such a ladies' man. If he spoke to people normally and showed respect and didn't demand they do things, he'd be a decent catch. Not that she was looking for one.

April smiled to herself. *Time to scare him off with the reality of my situation.* Then he'd probably leave her alone to live her life in peace and he could continue cloud gazing and meditating and whatever the heck he liked to do. Or be.

'Yeah, I can't just jump on over,' she said. 'Even if I wanted to.' She bent down and rolled up the fabric of her left trouser leg, exposing her prosthetic limb.

Zac peered over and looked for a moment.

'Still want me to "jump on over"?' She made quotation marks with her fingers. When she'd signed up to internet dating, she'd clearly stated in her profile that she was an amputee, so that if anyone wanted to meet her, they knew in advance and she wouldn't have to do the big reveal. That was why when someone had wanted to meet her and then stood her up as a stupid April Fools' joke, it had made her angry. Just once she'd wanted something to go right in her life.

'Sure,' Zac said.

Huh?

'Come around the side gate.' He started walking down the side of his house. 'You coming or what?' He looked at her like he didn't have all day. Which he clearly did.

No one had ever reacted like that before. Or *non-reacted*. 'Aren't you going to ask me what happened to my leg?'

He shrugged. 'Right now, I just want to show you this candle.'

April edged slowly along the fence, towards her own side gate that mirrored his, her eyes not leaving his gaze. He wasn't pretending that the prosthesis hadn't surprised him, he appeared genuinely uninterested, unaffected.

Without speaking, she unlatched her gate, walked around the front towards his house, then through into his backyard.

What on earth am I doing?

Zac returned to his spot on the grass, lying on his back. 'See?' He pointed to the sky.

April peered up, shading her face.

'You have to get down here to see it properly.' He gestured to the ground.

'I'm supposed to lie down next to you, get grass stains on my work clothes, and look at the sky?'

'Yep. Hurry up.'

April laughed, shook her head, crouched down, and manoeuvred herself onto her back.

'See?' Zac said. 'That one over there. The bit at the top looks like a wick, and that cloud puff is like a flame. Cool, eh?'

It took a moment until her brain formed the image from the cotton wool clouds. 'Huh. There you go.' If she'd had her phone she would have taken a photo, but Zac must have read her mind because he got his from his pocket and snapped a picture.

'Just sent it to you.'

She turned to glance at him, only realising then how close his face was to hers. The sun gave his stubble a light sparkle. There were slight creases at the corners of his eyes, and his irises were dusty green with flecks of orangey-brown, like... cinnamon. 'Thanks.' She quickly looked back to the sky. 'But you lied. You can't *give* me that candle, only show me.'

He chuckled. 'Oh, but I did. In here.' He tapped his temple. 'Material things are never really ours, only our memories. Like the clouds that move and change shape, life and *things* are fleeting.' Zac got up and released a masculine-sounding exhalation. 'Back in a sec. Have to write that down!' He scurried into his house.

April sat up and leaned back on her hands. She shook her head, which she seemed to be doing a lot around him. He's a writer. That must be it. 'Are you some famous novelist living a secret life in Tarrin's Bay, and that's why you won't tell me what you do?' she asked when he returned.

'Nope. I just write poetry. On my blog. That's it.'

'And you make money from that?'

He shook his head.

'So it's a hobby?'

He shook his head again. 'It's way more than that.'

Okay, maybe he was a billionaire who wanted to see how the other half lived for a while. Or he could have won the lottery and didn't want people to know he never had to work another day in his life.

April stood. 'I'll stop being nosy. Thanks for the, ah, cloud candle, and I hope you enjoy yours. Even though it's not really *yours*. I hope you enjoy it... in *here*.' She tapped her temple and smiled.

'I already am.' He smiled back.

April walked to the side gate. She turned. 'One more question, though. What did you mean, your poetry is way more than a hobby? I mean, if you don't make money from it?'

Zac held the cinnamon candle in both hands, close to his chest. 'Without it, you would not be standing here, in this yard, talking to me right now.'

In a daze, April left, gathered her things and walked back to work. With every answer he gave, more questions swirled up inside, desperate to be asked, answered, and understood. Suddenly all the candles in her store seemed insignificant and uninteresting compared to the variety of colours, shades, and flavours of this intriguing human being who lived next door.

CHAPTER EIGHT

What was abnormal to her was normal to him. He'd thought he'd noticed something a little different in the way she walked, the way she held herself. The way she favoured her right leg. Seeing her prosthesis was actually a welcome relief. Finally, someone who knew. Someone who'd experienced something major. Someone whose blessed life had been marred by the reality of something that 'only happens to other people'. Not that he'd wish trauma on anyone, and not that he didn't wish April hadn't been through whatever she'd been through, but as morbid as it was, it was reassuring to find someone who in some way might understand the life he'd lived.

Zac went back inside and looked around his sparse house. Still more to do, but no rush. But there was something missing. Something he needed to do soon, to make the place feel right.

He went to the corner of the living room and opened a box marked 'personal'. He retrieved a tattered shoebox and opened the lid, memories gushing out and hitting him like a blow to the head. Although it hurt to look at the photos, ignoring them would be worse. He would not do that to his best friend, the person who'd been the closest thing to a brother he'd ever had.

Zac placed the framed photo of himself with Johnny, when they were about eleven years old, on the mantle above the fireplace. All goofy grins, skinny limbs, and tanned faces from many Australian summers spent in tropical Far North Queensland. Next to it he placed the photo of Johnny in his army uniform, taken before his first rotation in Afghanistan, and another of himself with Johnny, before their second rotation, and only months before ...

The visual memory formed with painful clarity then shattered into thousands of tiny shards. How had Johnny gone from alive to dead so quickly? At what point had he ceased to exist? What was his last thought, his last sight, his last feeling? It had all happened so fast. It was so incomprehensible, so unfair, so ...

Zac's thoughts and memories never finished themselves, never rounded out, always broke off and hung about in uncertainty and disbelief, without the closure he needed. That's one of the reasons the poems helped. He could finish a poem; he could try to make sense of things and give it an ending. That elusive little dot at the end of a sentence. September first, in just under five months, would be that little dot. It would mark the end of one thing, and the beginning of another. Getting there in one piece was another matter, but if there was one thing that growing up without a proper family had taught him, it was to rely on himself. Get himself through. He could do it. He had to. If not for himself, for Johnny.

Zac straightened up and that familiar pull of the muse beckoned him. Or was it resolve? Resolve to not just *get through*, but try to make the most of his existence. He'd been the lucky one, though the guilt had paralysed him for too long. Maybe now it was time to not only survive, but thrive. He owed it to the ones who didn't come home. Somehow, he would find a way to live for all of them.

Zac opened his laptop and typed into his blog. The subscriber list had grown by around a hundred in the last week alone. He didn't know how. He didn't do much promotion. But word had gotten out. *Who is the mystery poet?* some would comment on his posts. Who *was* he, really? That, he was still figuring out.

THE ILLUSION OF TIME
Life is fleeting though we realise too late
Before we know it we've sealed our fate
We think that forever will take much longer
But time grows weaker and our regrets, stronger

An affinity for infinity has always ruled my mind
But here in this body, time is my bind
I believe in the eternal, for the soul not the flesh
And so while I am here, body and soul I must mesh

Live bravely with passion, don't let pain make you numb
And don't rely on forever, it will not come
Life is in the now, that's where we have to live
Don't wait, don't hold back, give all you've got to give.

He seriously got you to lay on his lawn and look at clouds?!

Zoe's text reply to April's detailed summary of her lunch break spent with Zac was followed by several emojis showing varying states of surprise and shock. She'd also sent the same summary to Olivia, who'd replied:

> Reading bedtime story to Mia, will reply
> properly later!

April lay in bed, her bedside candle glowing a light pink, though not as bright as her phone. She replied to Zoe:

> Yep. What's he doing to me!

> Seducing you with his charm and quirkiness by
> the looks of it. Can you send a photo?

> No! How am I supposed to take a discreet
> photo?

> Who said it has to be discreet? Waltz on over
> there and take charge like he does, tell him to
> smile, and bingo!

> I don't waltz. And that'll only spur him on.

> Exactly. A good fling will set you free.

> 'Uncomplicated', remember?

> Ape, complicated is living next door to a guy
> who is as hot as you say he is and not making
> the most of it. You'll send yourself mad.

> Zooey, there is more to life than hot guys and
> flings.

> I know, like hot neighbours and flings.
> Seriously, he sounds intriguing. Go with it. Get
> to know him. If he flirts, flirt back. See where it
> goes. Enjoy your life, girl.

He *was* intriguing. And the whole cloud thing was kind of

cute. Not to mention him being the only person to treat her like a normal person after seeing her leg. Who was he, really? Some philosophical blogger poet dude with plenty of time on his hands. But what else? Finding out could be more interesting than television, or Facebook. She would give it till the end of April to suss him out further. If he seemed to be just a perpetual bachelor looking to charm his way into her life only to weave his way back out and leave her emotions in a mess, she'd forget the whole thing. But if they had the potential to be friends, then that would be worthwhile. Anything more than that she couldn't comprehend right now with someone she barely knew, but... images formed in her mind, and she shook them away. Just a normal human response, imagining someone naked. Not that she had to imagine *too* much, after the three am naked-in-the-kitchen *Love, Actually* incident. She had barely thought of anyone of the opposite sex since Kyle, but the accident was over two years ago. Maybe things were shifting, and like Zoe said, it was time to enjoy her life... get her *glow* back, like her mother had said when she suggested April take up a new hobby, or do art therapy, or group therapy for amputees, or something to help her deal with what had happened and get that natural spark back in her daughter.

Her phone beeped and she jumped. It was Olivia:

Your life is so interesting, why can't mine be like that?

You have a beautiful daughter, you're a lucky woman.

I know. And here's a pic of her sleeping, isn't she adorable?

Olivia often sent photos of Mia, or posted them on Facebook. Mia, and the bookstore, was her whole life.

Takes after her mum.

Aww. Hugs. Sooo… read any of that book yet? Might help take your mind of Mr Neighbour. Or make you think of him, one or the other!

April withdrew the rural romance book from her bedside drawer, laughing that it was on top of the unused condom box she'd bought at her friend's insistence.

She eyed the cover model's bare chest. *Not as nice as Zac's,* she thought, then replied to Olivia: *I'll start reading it tonight.*

And though she tried to deny it, she knew that deep down she also meant that from tonight, she'd start enjoying her life more. And if that enjoyment included a certain man with a name starting with Z, then so be it.

As Zac allowed the water in the bathtub to surrender his tired muscles to the welcome feeling of weightlessness, words floated through his mind. Random at first, then related. Phrases, joining and merging together like one drop of water connecting with another. He'd thought it was another poem about Johnny, or about his tumultuous journey, but no. This time, the words were different. Unfamiliar. Dangerous. But they came anyway. He got out of the tub, not bothering to dry himself off as he walked to his laptop and allowed the words to spill onto the screen:

UNTOUCHED
We've smiled, we've spoken
Though you don't know that I'm broken

I'm already caught in your net
But we haven't even touched yet

The feel of your skin
My yang to your yin
I want it. But I'm scared
I'm open. I'm bared.

He stood suddenly, naked and vulnerable. Then he closed the laptop down hard and went to his room. The calendar next to his bed reminded him to stay focused. No complications, no risks, and that meant no women. He had to keep the status quo until September first. But how could he strike a balance between making the most of his life and making sure he didn't risk going back to his old ways?

It was time to call someone he hadn't felt the need to call in a while.

CHAPTER NINE

'I don't know, but it's like, as soon as I decided to give the man a chance, get to know his crazy self a bit better, he suddenly became "busy" and distracted. Like, "Oh, sorry, I have so much unpacking to do," and, "I'm painting my spare room," and, "I need to clean out Juliet's cat litter".' April sighed into the phone to Zoe, as she walked to Lookout Point to meet with one of the organisers of tomorrow's Anzac Day service.

'Better go back to playing hard to get,' Zoe replied.

'I was never playing hard to get, I was never playing anything. Just being me.' April shooed away a fly that had followed her up the hill, probably attracted to her new hairspray she'd bought to tame her wavy, freshly garnet-highlighted hair. 'Anyway, I'm a busy businesswoman, no time for games. If he wants to talk to me, he knows where I am, I'm not going to make much of an effort to get to know him anymore.' Her breath panted a little as the uphill walk made her heartbeat faster.

'Fair enough, but can you at least get that damn photo? Otherwise I'm coming over this weekend to check him out. Which I should anyway, I haven't seen you since your birthday.'

'If you're coming on the weekend, prepare to help out in the shop,' said April. 'Mondays and Tuesdays are more like weekends to me these days, Belinda's now closing up on those days so I can go home early. Might even get another day off soon.'

'Monday night it is then. The twenty-minute drive will give me a good chance to practice my singing. If you're lucky, I might treat you to an encore performance at your place.'

'Ha-ha, lucky me!' April's tone held sarcasm. 'Loser.'

'Takes one to know one.'

'Losers Are Us. See ya.'

'Bye.'

She put her phone in her bag and wobbled slightly as she trod on a pebble. Though she slowed a little, she didn't stop, and a smile lifted her lips as she realised how far she'd come. She'd been taught to look carefully where she was walking, as without the sensory input from the sole of her foot to inform her brain of changes in texture or slope on the ground, she had to rely on her sight. But now, sometimes, she forgot about the foot and it was only when she lost her balance that she remembered.

A man in an Akubra hat met her at the rocky lookout, along with a few other people who were setting up some of the displays and seating for the service. She was instructed on where to bring the candles and he gave her a rundown of the proceedings. The sun was low and glary, and the strong breeze pushed around them like an annoyingly overconfident sales person. As he spoke about a friend of a friend's grandfather's time in the war, the contrast to where they now stood was so strong she felt unworthy of being there. In this beautiful place, this safe town, this beautiful natural landscape.

'We're lucky, eh?' he said, glancing around the horizon where the deep blue of the ocean merged with the sky.

'Sure are.'

He eyed her leg, the ankle of her prosthesis visible under the hem of her long skirt. 'How long's it been?' He gestured downwards.

'Two and a half years.'

'Not an ex-soldier, are you?' He raised his eyebrows.

She chuckled. 'Me? I wouldn't cut it as a soldier. No, it was a car accident.'

'Sorry to hear, love. Guess you've got to count your blessings.'

She'd heard that and its variations many times after that awful day, when the reality of being an amputee, among other trauma, had driven her deep into depression.

'At least you survived.'

'At least it was only below the knee.'

'At least it wasn't your right arm.'

And she knew they were thinking: *'At least you weren't paralysed from the neck down like Kyle.'*

Kyle. He was the unlucky one. What if she had been sitting in his seat in the car? She shuddered to think of the possibility. He would have been her husband by now. But a drunk driver had changed that for them. And if she hadn't been adjusting the volume on the car radio and singing along, maybe she would have been able to react faster to the car coming towards their side who'd run a red light. Maybe less damage would have occurred had she been able to brake sooner, or swerve more sharply. Maybe then the impact would have been one inch further away from Kyle's spinal cord.

Maybe, maybe, maybe.

She would have stayed with him. She'd committed to being his fiancée and future wife. But his family said no, and once he was able to communicate clearly, he'd said no too. He'd wanted her as his wife, not his full-time carer. Maybe if he'd been a paraplegic, but quadriplegic? She'd known it would be incredibly difficult, especially with her own injury to recover from, but the accident hadn't killed her love for him. Though he survived, she hadn't only lost her leg that day, but her man. Her future. Life had dealt her a new one, and she was still figuring it out.

'I have a lot to be thankful for,' April said to the man, and before he could ask any more questions, she thanked him for his time and confirmed she'd arrive early to set up the candles.

The atmosphere the following morning was far removed from what it had been the day before. The sun had not yet splashed the sky with its glow, and the moon over the ocean created an eerie presence. Her candles, most held by the many attendees, and others framing the staged memorial area around the microphone and podium, glimmered in the sporadic breeze, the flames protected by their tall heatproof casing. A universal symbol of hope. Remembrance.

As names of soldiers were called out, and prayers and poems recited, she thought of Zac and wondered what sort of poetry he wrote. She'd never been into poetry, but hearing special words spoken into the dim expanse of Lookout Point, the sound of waves crashing and rolling beneath as their background music, she realised its power, its potential. It was a way to make sense of what had been, give structure to the chaos that had occurred, and immortalise the heroes who had perhaps stood here many years gone by, dreaming of a future they never got to experience.

Yes, she was lucky. She may not have got the future she'd planned, but she had a future.

When the service had ended and the early sun warmed the air and started waking up the town, April glanced down towards the harbour on her left, and saw him. Zac. In the distance, standing alone on one of the piers. Why had he not come up to take part in the service? She walked down the hill. Maybe they'd cross paths on her way back home. But by the time she got to the bottom he was already walking further ahead, going the long way around, towards the beach instead of the town.

Probably best. She would go home and make use of her rare day off while the shop was closed for Anzac Day. He'd go to his place and do his own thing, and they need never be more than courteous but distant neighbours. Later she'd join some of the locals at the pub for dinner. Her mum wouldn't be there though, she boycotted pubs. She would catch up with her for lunch tomorrow instead.

After chatting to some locals in Miracle Park on the way home, April arrived back in her street and found Zac planting a small tree in his front garden.

'Poet *and* a gardener, huh?' she said, stopping in front of his house. So much for leaving him to his own devices, her mouth didn't like to cooperate with her brain. 'I'll leave you to it,' she added, about to walk off.

'Wait,' he said.

She looked at his face, his eyes tight and squinting in the morning glare.

'I've got something for you.'

'Another cloud candle?' April glanced upwards.

'No. Something you can actually take with you. Into your house, I mean, not when you die.'

She tilted her head. She didn't know how to respond to that.

'Sorry. I'm sure you'll live a long healthy life. I'm just saying. You know, after our conversation a couple of weeks ago.'

'That we can't take material possessions with us when we die, yes. I remember.'

'It's inside.' He brushed soil from his bare hands and walked towards the front door. April followed, but hung about on the porch. A subtle glow caught her eye and she peered into his house, noticing the fireplace. But it wasn't lit, the candle on the mantle above was. The cinnamon candle.

'I'm glad the candle is getting put to good use,' she said. 'But they look nicer when lit at night.'

Zac wandered to the mantle. 'I know. But I thought today would be good.'

'Because of Anzac Day?'

He nodded, and before she knew what she was doing she had stepped into his house without asking permission. 'Is that you?' She pointed to a photo of two kids. She recognised the shape of his jaw, even in the youthful roundness of the child's face. She looked back to the door she'd stepped through. 'Sorry, I shouldn't barge in. My legs and my mouth have a mind of their own.'

He chuckled. 'It's okay. Yes, that's me and my friend.'

April's gaze wandered to the photo next to it. 'And all grown up. Same friend?'

He nodded. 'Yep.'

'You're a soldier?' It made sense. His commanding presence and posture. His tattoos, the intensity and seriousness he sometimes had. When he wasn't chuckling or commenting on how she was 'amusing to watch'.

'*Was.*'

'How long have you been off duty?'

Zac glanced up to the roof. 'Almost three years now.'

'Wow. You must have seen a lot. I mean, I don't need to know, but... is that why my prosthesis didn't shock you?'

'I've seen much worse.'

'I can imagine. Although I can't. Not really. I won't begin to even... I should stop talking. I'll stop talking.' She turned away from his gaze and brushed her hair from her face.

'It's okay, April.'

She narrowed her eyes a little. 'I saw you, at the harbour. You weren't at the dawn service?'

He shook his head and slid his hands into his pockets. 'Prefer to honour those who've served in my own way. And also, it's ...' He ran his hand across his short hair. 'Doesn't matter. Oh, your gift.' He went to the kitchen.

April furrowed her brow. 'What is this gift you speak of?'

He held out his hand, a small seashell resting on his palm. 'Found it when I was walking over the sand dunes. Made me think of you for some reason. I think because it has these little speckles on it, like cinnamon.'

April took the shell and studied it with a smile. Golden brown specks were scattered across it like freckles. And one edge of the shell was broken off. There was also a larger patch of golden brown near the centre, like a birthmark. 'It's unique,' she said. 'I like it. Thanks.'

'Don't thank me, thank Mother Nature.'

'Okay then. Thanks Mother Nature,' she spoke loudly in case Mother Nature couldn't hear her from within the confines of this man-made enclosure.

Maybe the reason why Zac had been distant the past two weeks was because of what today represented, and it triggered memories for him. Painful memories, just like the month of September did for her. 'Sorry if I've been a nosy neighbour, pestering you about what you do and how you pay your bills. I'll mind my own business now and try to be normal. So, if you need to borrow a cup of sugar anytime, let me know.' She laughed.

'I don't use sugar,' Zac replied.

'Oh. Then if you need to borrow a cup of... Sugar substitute? Chia seeds? Or... coffee?'

'I'll be sure to remember your offer.' He grinned, then walked April to the door.

Before stepping off the porch she turned to face him, his eyes grey and tired-looking, like he hadn't had enough sleep. Which if he'd been up since before dawn like she'd been, he hadn't. 'Hey, a few of us will be at the pub tonight for dinner, if you'd like to come?'

Zac took a step back. 'Um. Thanks. But I'll pass.'

'Okay, but if you change your mind, let me know.'

He scratched his head, and his mouth opened like he wanted to say something, but no sound came out.

'Well, I'll be off.'

'April.' He lightly touched her arm and she glanced down at his hand. He had nice hands.

'Yeah?'

'Thanks for the offer. It's nice of you. But the reason I can't is, well ...' He nibbled one corner of his lip. 'It's a bit embarrassing, really.' He rubbed the back of his neck.

'What is?' she asked. 'That you don't want to be seen in such a state of obvious self-neglect with your unimpressive physique and unshaven face? And those tattoos, I mean, you look like a badass. People might get scared.' She nudged him with a wink.

Zac smiled. 'Yeah, I've let myself go. Too many meat pies.' He patted his belly that clearly received no less than a hundred or more crunches per day. 'Nah, the thing is, and I haven't told anyone this, except for... anyway, the thing is, I have a mild case of agoraphobia.' A slight hint of pink coloured his cheeks. 'Crowds. I just can't do them. It's hard to explain. I need quiet. Not too many people around. A pub, or any similar place, it's... I'm not quite there yet.' He lowered his gaze and lifted the edge of his doormat with his foot.

April felt a surge of pity for the guy. Well, not pity so much as sadness. A man like him, in his prime, clearly traumatised by things in his past... of course it was understandable that the war would have affected him in some way. He didn't appear to have any physical injuries, but he probably had post-traumatic stress, or maybe the crowds and open spaces just triggered anxiety for some reason.

April touched his arm as he had hers. Somehow, it felt both rough and smooth at the same time. 'I understand. No problem.' She offered a small smile. 'Thanks for telling me.'

She gave a small wave and stepped off the porch, but as per usual, she thought of another thing to say and had to turn around again. 'You know what? I feel like eating in tonight.' April put her hands on her hips and surveyed Zac's front garden. 'Care to join me?'

Zac's eyebrows shot up. 'You're inviting me over for dinner?'

'Looks that way. I can pick something up, or find something to whip up.'

He rubbed his chin. 'The thing is, I've already defrosted some chicken for tonight. How about you join me here instead?'

Now April's eyebrows rose. 'You're going to cook for me?'

'No, you can cook. I'll just provide the ingredients and kitchen facilities.'

She eyed his unchanged facial expression.

'I'm kidding,' he chuckled. 'You can clean up instead.'

April laughed and warmth spread throughout her cheeks.

'Seriously, I've got it covered.' He held up his hands. 'Just come over when the sun goes down.'

'You've got yourself a deal.' She gave a nod. 'Would Juliet like Romeo to join her for some gourmet cat pellets?'

Zac laughed, and his Adam's apple bobbed. 'I think the cats can sort themselves out for tonight. See you later on.' He smiled and closed the door.

So much for not bothering to get to know him anymore. The pages of his book of life were starting to open, and she was sure tonight would provide many more answers to the questions that had been forming in her mind. It was time to get to know Zac, for real. Not just chatting over the fence, not the odd, random conversations at his door, but real, proper, dignified conversation over the dinner table. A sense of anticipation fluttered inside. She had been looking forward to dinner at the pub, but this... this she was looking forward to *way* more than that.

CHAPTER TEN

April tried to take a nap, but despite fatigue from the early morning, her mind wouldn't switch off. Housework helped. She vacuumed floors, scrubbed the shower, cleaned the kitchen, then collapsed on the couch and watched the last half of an old movie on TV before her eyes drooped closed.

She shot up when she awoke and turned her wrist to look at her watch. 'Crap!' It was late afternoon. April went to the bathroom and turned on the shower. When she was ready, she stepped in and moved the shower stool aside. She stood one-legged on the slip-proof mat, under the warm stream, aware of how good her balance was these days. If she'd tried to shower this way before the accident her leg would have become fatigued by now, but her right calf muscle was hard and strong. She swivelled bit by bit on her toes to turn around and wash her back, and when she'd finished, sat for a few brief moments on the stool to rest her muscles. Putting her prosthesis back on was a welcome relief. When it had first been made for her, it had, strangely, felt like a burden. Something needed, and gratefully accepted, but also a reminder of her limitations. Learning to use it had been like trying to switch to using her left hand instead of right. Except worse. There had been the constant fear of falling, which still affected her sometimes, but hardly ever anymore. At first, as a new recipient of helpful modern technology, she'd spent hours staring at it like it was some stranger intruding on her personal space. And that had made her feel silly. She wasn't sure how long it had taken before she'd felt like it had become part of her; her friend, her guide, her helper. But eventually it had.

April changed into a long slinky black skirt, and a slim-fitting V-neck top with three-quarter sleeves: purple with a black trim. When her hair was dry and make-up applied, she fed Romeo and locked her house, making her way to Zac's with a small bag, and a bottle of wine that, luckily, she'd had in the fridge. Or maybe she should have asked if he wanted her to bring dessert. Anyway, she could always pop back home if they needed anything else, though if he hardly ever left the house, he was probably well stocked with everything they would need.

His front door was wide open. Soft, earthy, instrumental music greeted her. 'C'mon in,' he called out from the kitchen.

She stepped inside and instinctively glanced at the candle and photos on his mantle. The candle flame flickered and emitted the warm, cinnamon fragrance.

The scent of garlic and herbs also filled the house, as Zac opened the oven door and turned over the chicken pieces.

'What's cookin'?' she asked.

'Don't you mean what's cookin', good lookin'?'

'Nice try. So does it have a name?'

'Nope. But let's call it Wednesday Chicken.'

'Sounds irresistible.' She chuckled.

'Would you like to name it then?'

'I'll need to eat it first before knowing what to call it.'

'Then I'll eagerly await your input.'

They continued their conversation like a tennis match until

Zac washed his hands and finally met her gaze, then it dropped to the bottle in her hand.

'Oh, here. I didn't want to come empty-handed so this was all I had at home. Unless you have something else?' She held up the bottle of red.

'Um, I have homemade lemon, lime, and bitters, I'll just have that. But feel free to have the wine yourself.' He slid his hands into his pockets then removed them and twisted to face the high cupboards. 'Oh, I'll get you a glass.'

'That's okay, I'll have what you're having.'

'You sure? It's up to you.'

'Yep. I'll just put this over here.' She moved the wine to the corner of the kitchen counter near the knife block. 'Creative in the kitchen, huh?' she asked.

He shrugged. 'If there's something I want, I'll make it. You cook?'

'Yeah, but I'm not that great. So it's probably good you didn't come over.'

'It's not that hard. Find instructions online—easy.'

'Somebody's confident.'

He shrugged again. 'I like to look after my health, it's easier to do that if you're self-sufficient.'

'So tonight's meal could be called Healthy Wednesday Chicken.'

He smiled. 'It could. It's an improvement. But I'll be expecting something more creative from you after dinner.'

'Good thing I'm not drinking the wine then, otherwise I might call it something ridiculous like Healthy What Day Is It Chicken.'

'Ha!' Zac's laugh was natural, but he scratched his head awkwardly. *Was he just being polite and pretending my humour was humorous?* 'Oh.' He walked to the mantle and picked up the candle. 'Should put this over here.' He placed it in the middle of the round, rustic wooden dining table.

'You've unpacked a bit more, I see,' April said, eyeing the combined living and dining room. There were now books on the bookshelves that had been empty when she'd been here earlier. She scanned the titles but didn't recognise any of them.

'It's becoming more like a home, bit by bit.'

April peered closer at the books. 'Novels or nonfiction?'

'Nonfiction, mostly. They've helped me a lot. You read?'

April scratched her arm. 'Ahh, my reading is on par with my cooking. I mean, I can read of course, I just forget. Or my mind keeps me occupied with other things. Or I read Facebook. But, oh! A friend gave me a book recently, so I've been reading some of that.' She was three-quarters of the way through the book that was as much about the rugged masculinity of the hero as it was about the rugged country landscape. Fine with her.

'Oh yeah? What's it about?'

April diverted her gaze as she recalled the shirtless man on the cover. 'Something about a guy who moves back to the country, to the place he grew up, and reunites with old friends and enemies.'

'And?'

'And... there's like, arguments and stuff, and he has to help his adoptive dad run the farm, because he's sick, but he's keeping a secret from him, and there's also this girl, I mean woman, who he meets and she has this food business, like she makes jams and stuff from local produce, but she has a secret too, and ...' And in chapter nineteen they finally get it on in her kitchen when she's showing him how to make blueberry jam and he gets some on his face and she licks it off and ...

'Hang on, so is it the sick adoptive dad who has a secret or the guy who moved back home?'

'The dad.'

'What's the secret?'

'I don't know yet.'

'Well, tell me when you find out.'

'I will.'

'Cool.'

April grinned. 'Or you could just read it after me.'

'But I like how you tell the story.' He grinned too. 'And let me guess, the guy and the girl hook up?'

'Several times.'

He laughed. 'Maybe I will read it then.' Zac put two plates on the kitchen counter then some cutlery. 'And you'll have to read one of mine.'

Umm... She didn't feel that inclined to read some New-Age self-help book, but what could she say? 'I'm not a fan of self-help,' she said. Of course, the truth. No filter needed.

'Have you ever read any?'

'No, but—'

'Then how do you know you're not a fan? And anyway, they're not just self-help, there are books about spirituality, philosophy, poetry, and the science of the universe.'

'Sounds riveting.' Well, she would probably like the poetry, after today's enlightening experience.

Zac went to the bookcase and extracted a book. 'Here, start with this, it's not too lengthy and you can read small amounts at a time.'

April took hold of the small book, *The Prophet*, by Kahlil Gibran. 'Is this really you and you're hiding behind a pseudonym?'

He laughed again; this time more high-pitched as if she was being ridiculous. 'Yes, and I time-travelled back to the early twentieth century just to write it.' He opened the cover and pointed to the original publication date.

'Ah. Okay, I can't refuse a challenge. I will read it. On one condition.' She lifted a pointed finger.

His eyebrows rose.

'You visit my store one day.' She held up her palm facing him as his posture shifted and his confident stance slackened. 'I know, I remember what you told me today, and I know I don't know anything about the agoraphobia or what you've been through, but I do know that you didn't always have it, and that anyone can get through anything if they really want to, so I want you to promise that one day, even if it's in a million years, that you'll walk through the door of my store.'

'Do I have to buy anything?' he joked.

'That's optional.' She shrugged.

'Good. Because I'm not a fan of pushy sales people.'

'So will you?' April held the book near the bookcase. 'Or should I put this book back and never become enlightened to its magical secrets that have helped you immensely?' She raised her eyebrows at him the way she'd seen Olivia do to Mia when she wanted her daughter to obey.

He shook his head, not to say no, but as a show of his amusement. 'How could I imagine going through life knowing that you never got to read that book? You've put me in an incredibly difficult situation here.' He half-smiled. 'So yes, one day, I promise, I will walk through the door to your store—well, not literally walk through the door, that would hurt—but I'll visit your store, yes.'

April held out her right hand and he shook it. His large hand enveloped hers with a gentle firmness. 'Deal.' She placed the book next to her handbag on a lone bar stool that stood at the kitchen counter. 'So can I do anything to help, with my awesome kitchen skills?'

Zac ushered her to the table and pulled out the wooden

chair for her. 'Hmm, how about you take a seat and I'll get everything sorted.'

'Works for me!' She tapped her fingers on the table. 'But seriously, if I can help with anything, I'm not *really* that bad.'

'I'm sure you're not, but there's nothing else much to do, so sit back and relax.' He took a bottle from the fridge and poured some of the liquid into two glasses. 'There you go, one hundred percent natural ingredients, hope you like it.'

April sipped the lemon, lime and bitters as the ice cubes crackled and clanked together. 'I like it. It could make a good candle flavour. I mean, fragrance. If lemon, lime and bitters could be a fragrance.'

'I don't see why not. Do you have many food or drink related candles?' He leaned on the kitchen counter and sipped his drink, then swirled the glass around in small circles.

'Sure do. Cinnamon, obviously,' she eyed the candle centrepiece, 'and chocolate, vanilla frosting, watermelon, even coffee.'

Zac nodded slowly. 'Have you ever taken a bite out of one when you were hungry? Just to try it?'

She chuckled. 'I've been tempted. Some of them smell so delicious it's hard not to.'

'I bet you don't have a Healthy Wednesday Chicken candle though.'

'Umm, I don't think that would be a great seller. And I definitely need to improve on that name. Leave it with me.' She tapped her temple.

'Speaking of Healthy Wednesday Chicken ...' He placed his glass on the counter and grabbed an oven mitt, opened the oven door and pulled out a large baking dish, steam rising in curvy streams.

'Actually, that smells really good. I think I would totally buy a candle that smelled like that,' April remarked.

'As long as I get commissions. Fifty percent.'

'Of course.'

He placed the dish on top of the stove, and April took another sip of her drink. *So far so good.* The night had just begun, things were flowing well, and he didn't irritate her the way he had before. The photos on the mantle caught her eye again, and she wondered about other people in his life. Did he have any?

'Anzac Chicken?' she blurted.

Zac half-smiled. 'Are you going to randomly blurt out name ideas throughout the evening?'

'Probably.'

He grinned. 'Not bad, but I don't think it would do the Anzacs justice. Unless we remove the An and make it *Zac's Chicken?*'

'Ha! Might as well call it Ego Chicken. Or, I'm Such A Damn Good Cook Chicken.'

'Now you're talking.' He nodded and gave her a thumbs up.

He plated up the meals and carried them over, placing one in front of her. 'Ooh, thank you. Looks yum.'

'Dig in, neighbour.'

She sliced off a morsel of chicken breast and skewered it with zucchini, eggplant, and tomato. The tender chicken warmed her mouth, and a rich, enticing, slightly sweet flavour blended with the vegetables. 'Very nice, Zac,' she said. 'I do give you permission to call it Zac's Chicken.'

He swallowed a mouthful and shook his head, then said, 'Nah, you can do better than that. Keep 'em coming.'

'I will. So what gives it this beautiful, rich flavour?'

'I marinate it in caramelised balsamic vinegar with fresh herbs, garlic, and a few other secret ingredients.' He smiled. 'Do you want to bribe me for the recipe?'

She was about to take another mouthful but replied, 'No, I'll just invite myself over here whenever you make it.'

'How about, for every book of mine you read, I'll cook you dinner.'

April tilted her head. 'How about every *chapter* I read?'

He tipped his head back in a chuckle. 'Not gonna happen. Gotta make you work for it.' He eyed her silently for a moment, and she thought he was going to say something like, 'on second thoughts, sure, come over for dinner after every chapter you read!' Which, if she read one every night, would mean she'd have dinner with him every night and never have to cook another day in her life. Now there was a good plan.

What was that look in his eye? It had only been there a brief moment then disappeared. Maybe she imagined it. Maybe the candlelight had just reflected off his irises and made them look... different.

'So where were you before—'

'You didn't get to—'

They spoke at the same time.

'You go,' she said, flicking her hand towards him.

'I was going to say, you didn't finish telling me the story of how your store got its name, that day when you ...'

Dropped the you-know-what in front of you.

'Oh yes,' she interjected, before he could embarrass her. 'Well, since you're being so hospitable, I guess I can tell you now.' She took a sip of drink then cleared her throat. 'Okay, so obviously, candles glow, right?'

He nodded.

'And my name is April. So, April's Glow! Ta-da!'

Zac blurted a one-shot laugh. 'Yeah, I'm not buying it, neighbour. Tell me the *real* story.'

April put down her glass. 'Am I that bad a liar?'

'I'm just really good at reading people.' He swirled his drink in front of his lips then took a sip.

A random thought flashed through her mind as she wondered what sort of people he'd had to read in his previous vocation. What kinds of people had he met, fought, and seen hurt or killed? The idea of war seemed so far removed from him, sitting here in his modest dining room, eating good food, and talking about such luxuries as candles and books. Her gaze dropped to the tattoo on his inner right wrist as he put down his glass.

'What does that mean?' She pointed to the Chinese symbol that looked like a fancy letter N or H.

'Hey, don't change the subject,' he replied.

'But it'll only take you a second to tell me.'

'If I tell you now, then you'll ask me about my other tatts and explaining them all could take quite a long time.' He crossed his arms in front of his plate. 'So, April's Glow. Spill.'

'Okay, okay.' As she began talking, he uncrossed his arms and resumed eating. 'Well, there *is* the reference to glowing candles, and my name, but the thing is, when I was a child, I had a skin condition called rosacea. It gave me these inflamed red patches on my face, around my cheeks, and I hated looking different to other kids.' She took a quick mouthful of food then continued. 'Anyway, to make me feel better, my mum used to tell me that I had red cheeks because there was so much love inside me that it was bursting to get out and be shared with everyone. She didn't tell me it was called rosacea until I was older. Up until I found out she had always called it *April's Glow*. She made it sound like a special thing.' April smiled. 'So once she told me that, I wore my red cheeks with pride. If anyone asked why they were so red I'd say: "It's April's Glow". Some people would laugh and others would say "why don't *my* cheeks glow?".'

Zac gazed at her with interest as she patted her cheeks.

'It eventually went away, as you can see my cheeks are perfectly normal now, except when—'

'When you drop embarrassing items on my front doorstep.'

April paused with her fork in mid-air. 'Um, yep.' She lowered her gaze. 'And they're probably glowing a bit right now.'

Zac laughed. 'Sorry, couldn't resist.'

April shrugged. 'Anyway, when I got the idea for the candle store, I thought how candles make people feel good, or, like you said, give people hope, and I was reminded of how my mother made me feel better about my condition. So the name seemed like the perfect fit.' She rested her elbows on the table and clasped her hands together above her plate.

Zac nodded slowly. 'Nice. I like it. Much better background story than me calling my dinner Wednesday Chicken simply because I made it on a Wednesday.'

'Yeah, it's always better for things to have a greater meaning. Speaking of which, what does your tattoo mean, huh?' She leaned forward, pinning him with her determined stare.

He glanced at his wrist. 'It's the symbol for strength.'

'Oh. See? Only took you a second to tell me.'

He stayed silent.

'Unless, is there more to it? And why the wrist?' Something told her that he wouldn't be the type to get a tattoo just because it looked good or seemed like a cool idea; with his deep mind surely each would have significant meaning.

'I told you what it means, now I get to ask you a question,' he said.

April leaned back a little. 'Okay, fair enough.'

'Do you have a tattoo?'

April took a big breath. 'I did. But sadly, my tattoo is no more.'

Zac looked confused for a moment; then, as she glanced

down at her prosthesis he opened his mouth in realisation. 'No way. Really?'

'Yes way. Of all the places to get a tattoo and it just so happens to be on the part of me that I end up losing. Loved that tattoo too.' Her smile disappeared.

'Have you thought about getting it redone on your other leg?'

April's eyes widened. 'No. I can't.'

'Why not?'

She pushed back a clump of wavy hair from her face. 'Because it wouldn't feel right.' She could feel her face warming up, even though she wasn't embarrassed. 'What if... It could ...'

She stopped trying to form sentences when Zac's hand covered hers. 'It's okay. You don't have to tell me.'

She looked at his hand on top of hers, and his forearm with its manly skin and light shading of hair, corded veins, and the shadows formed by his sculpted muscles. It was as beautiful and unique as the grainy wooden table that lay beneath their connected hands.

She looked back into his cinnamon-speckled green eyes. He knew. Somehow, he knew that she had the invalid fear that if she got another tattoo, the same fate might manifest for her remaining leg. But she didn't want to talk about fears. Wouldn't. He may be comfortable with getting in touch with his inner self and reading all those books and pouring his heart out into poetry, but *she* wasn't. She was comfortable with living her day-to-day life, being out in the world, talking to people. But interestingly, *he* wasn't. They were like opposites. Magnetically attracted to balance each other out. One thing they did have in common was the ability to ask direct and honest questions and think them perfectly valid and not at all confronting or inappropriate. But being on the receiving end of those questions... she wasn't used to that. Zac challenged her. He was a mirror, and she wasn't sure she was ready to look closely at the reflection.

Her hand flinched a little and he removed his. 'I might get another tattoo one day, but not on the leg. And not the same one,' she said.

'Can I ask what it was?'

'Seems silly, but it was a tattoo of my budgie that I had as a kid. My first and favourite pet. I took a photo in and the artist made a design from it, and did the tattoo in full colour. Budge, his name was.'

'The bird or the tattoo artist?'

April laughed. 'What do you think?'

Zac laughed too, lightening the mood.

'So you still haven't asked what happened to my leg,' she mused.

'Do you want me to?'

'I don't know. It's usually the first thing most people ask me.'

'I'm not most people.'

'I've discovered that.'

They both took another mouthful of food, then a sip of drink, like they really were in a mirror.

'Okay, so tell me, if you like, what happened?' Zac asked.

'Car accident.' She filled him in on the details of the crash and how her fiancé had ended up paralysed. She didn't fill him in on the details of her recovery, which was as much emotional as it was physical.

'You're a strong woman, April.' He stood and refilled their drinks.

She lowered her gaze. 'Maybe I should get a tattoo like yours.' Why couldn't she accept a compliment with a simple thanks? She *was* strong, had earned the compliment.

'Something tells me you'd suit something a bit more "out there",' he said. 'Maybe a butterfly, or hey, if you like some of the insight in the book, you could have one of the phrases tattooed.'

'Skin poetry huh?' She nodded. 'Not a bad idea. Do you have any?' Her eyes cast a subtle scan down the length of his body.

Was her subconscious using her interest in his tattoos to try to get him half naked?

He turned around and she thought he was going to take his shirt off, but he simply lifted the back of it up a little, exposing a sentence in cursive font tattooed on his lower back:

As my heart beats, so too does yours

'Not really poetry, but close enough,' he said.

'It's nice.' The tattoo, and his skin. 'And the reason for it?' She resisted the urge to reach out and touch it. Touch him. His skin was like a warm fireplace, enticing her towards it.

'To remind people that we're all the same. We're all in life together, no matter our differences.'

'Huh.' April kept her gaze on the tat, until his shirt dropped down over it and he returned to his chair. 'I like that. So, you walk around shirtless quite a lot?'

He chuckled. 'Used to, in summer anyway. But now I don't do so much walking around, except in quiet places. Nature, secluded beaches, for example.'

April nodded. 'Well, I feel privileged to have seen the tattoo that others are being deprived of.'

'It's nice to show it off for the first time in a long while.' He smiled, then his hand moved to his wrist tattoo and he rubbed it a little. 'Anyway, enough about tattoos, would you like second helpings of the Chicken With No Name?'

April took the last mouthful, then replied, 'No thanks. It was delicious, but I'm full.'

Zac stood and picked up their plates. 'Satisfying Chicken?' he suggested, a curious crease in his brow.

'Pathetic,' she said, crossing her arms and leaning back in her chair. 'You can do better than that. I mean, with the name. The chicken was far from pathetic!'

'Nice save,' he said. 'I was about to throw you out.' He chuckled as he walked to the kitchen, rinsed the plates then placed them in the dishwasher.

She stood too and stretched her arms above her head. 'I'm glad we're finally talking like proper human beings. Most of the time,' she said. 'I was trying to get to know you these past couple of weeks, but it didn't seem like you wanted to all of a sudden. But this is nice. So thanks.'

Zac turned to face her. 'My pleasure. And sorry if I was a bit distant, was just dealing with some stuff.'

She held up her hands. 'Hey, no worries. And I'm a bit of a nosy person, so I wouldn't have been offended if you simply didn't want to tell me your life story.'

'Well, we've started making up for the past two weeks tonight,' Zac said.

'We have. But in my mind are at least another three hundred and fifty-seven nosy questions, so watch out.' She pointed his way.

A curious expression crinkled his face. 'How about thirty-six?'

'Huh?'

'Have you heard of the thirty-six questions that went viral on the internet?'

'No, and that worries me, because I spend a lot of time on Facebook. How could I have missed something that went viral?' She feigned shock and brought her hands to her cheeks.

'There was a lot of hype about this list of questions that had the potential to help people fall in love, but the research and story behind it was interesting. It's about deepening connection between two people, whether they be friends, lovers, or strangers, by facilitating mutual vulnerability and self-disclosure. It's like a fast track to emotional intimacy.'

'Sounds scary.'

Zac leaned his elbows on the kitchen counter. 'Not really, you just answer questions about who you'd invite over for dinner, what you'd most regret not doing or saying in life, what you'd take from your house if it was on fire, that sort of stuff.'

Curiosity swirled up inside, but a slight hint of tension crept through her muscles. Vulnerability was something she didn't care to feel. She could chat and gossip like a pro, but how open and honest she was depended entirely on the nature of the topic.

'So what do you say, wanna do them?' His unblinking eyes awaited her agreement.

'Are you saying you want me to fall in love with you, Zac?' A flirty tone sweetened her voice and she put one hand on her hip.

'No, I'm saying do you want to do the thirty-six questions and see if we can make up for the past two weeks of me being a distant, boring neighbour, while you were being your normal, nosy self?'

April's amused laughter filled the house, and from somewhere Zac's cat meowed.

She could just say *no*. Say thanks for dinner and be on her merry way, but Zac had opened some kind of invisible door inside that she hadn't known was there. She didn't exactly want to answer thirty-six questions about herself, though the three he'd mentioned sounded okay. But she desperately wanted to hear *his* answers, and it was that reason that made her say 'yes'.

'Awesome! I'll get us some dessert and snacks and we can move over to the couch and get started.'

What am I getting myself into?

'Ah, Zac?' she said.

'Yeah?' He looked up from the fridge where he had bent down to get something from the freezer.

'I have a name for your meal,' she replied. 'Since I have no idea how you got me to agree to this... this... experiment thingy, and we've revealed a few significant things about our lives already, I've deduced that there must be some kind of truth-extracting ingredient in your chicken.' She planted her hands on the kitchen counter. 'I officially name your meal: Truth Chicken.'

Zac straightened up. He held a tub of something up in the air. 'And we have a winner!'

And she had officially decided that she was crazy, knowing full well she couldn't back out of this now, and hadn't even thought to ask to see the actual questions first. They were most likely, most definitely, about to become more than just neighbours, in the weirdest, most unconventional, yet irresistibly intriguing way.

CHAPTER ELEVEN

———————

Excitement surged through Zac's bloodstream. He had been longing to find someone to do the questions with. But with his solitary existence, there hadn't been many options. He knew deep down it was probably a bad idea, and he'd been advised to distance himself from April for the past two weeks, but today, on this day that marked remembrance, he wanted to remember other things too. What it felt like to look into someone's eyes for longer than a simple glance. To talk openly for hours. To be heard, noticed, understood. What it felt like to tell someone else about your life, your journey, your dreams. And to listen to theirs and see that spark in their eyes, that light that reminded him he wasn't the only one trying to move forward in life and find meaning with his existence.

And dammit, he wanted to know her. *Really* know her. Maybe he had moved next door to her for a reason. The universe could have planted him there on purpose and he had to discover why. Or maybe it was a test, a challenge, to see how strong he really was. To see if he could resist knowing her, discovering her, wanting her.

Either way, tonight he was going to do what he damn well

wanted. And the fact that the questions were structured and systematic gave him some kind of control. Unlike random conversation that went in multiple directions and could be more dangerous, this conversation would have a beginning, a middle, and an end. He just had to follow the process, and then it'd be done. He'd know April a little more, she'd know him, and he could finally feel those things he'd wanted to feel again. If only for a little while. Then he could get back to his plan.

'Here you go.' He handed April a bowl, then grabbed a plate of cheese and crackers from the kitchen and placed them on the small coffee table.

'Looks nice. Do I have to name this too?'

'No. It's organic coconut ice-cream, and those bright coloured things on top are raspberries and blueberries.'

'Oh really? I was wondering what on earth they could be,' she said with a sarcastic tone.

She dug her spoon in and Zac couldn't help but watch her lips envelop the spoon to devour the dessert. They were pink and plump, and when she smiled, they reminded him of a bow, like one you'd find on a gift.

He sat on the couch, next to her, but not too close, at right angles with one knee casually bent.

'So where are these questions?' she asked.

Zac got out his phone. 'I'll look them up.' He found the article mentioning the research of Dr Arthur Aron and others who had developed the experiment. 'So we take turns to read out and answer each question, until we've done all thirty-six.'

'Sounds easy enough.' April cleared her throat. Zac wasn't buying it. She was apprehensive. 'Do we have to be one hundred percent honest?'

'That's the idea,' he said. 'And I'll know if you're lying, remember?' He smiled. 'But that doesn't mean you have to give absolutely everything away. You can be honest but still keep secrets.' He was telling himself as much as her. Though there were things he wanted to share, to take the burden off his mind, there were things, well, *one* thing in particular, that he wasn't sure should come out into the open just yet. If ever.

'Okay, let's get this show on the road. Question one?' She clasped her hands together across her right knee.

Zac cleared his throat. 'Given the choice of anyone in the world, whom would you want as a dinner guest?'

'Will you be offended if I don't say you?' She laughed.

'Nope, because I'm not saying you either.'

'Great, glad we've got that sorted!'

'Right. So who would you choose?' Zac asked.

'Um ...' April looked up at the ceiling. Then her gaze dropped, as though the answer had fallen in front of her, but she dismissed it with a wave of her hand. 'Oh, this is too hard.'

'We're only at question one and you're giving up?'

'No, I'm just saying it's too hard.'

'Watch what you say, your thoughts and words become your reality, you know.'

'They do? Okay, I'd love a million bucks and a holiday to Europe.'

Zac shook his head with a chuckle. 'I can see we're going to be here all night.' Question one and they were already getting off topic. He was going to have to pull the reigns. 'Did you know we're only supposed to spend a short amount of time on each question?'

'Oh. Okay. Sorry. Right, my answer is ...' She drummed her fingers on her knee.

'I'm waiting.'

'Geez, impatient pain in the arse you are.'

'I do my best.' Zac shrugged. Then he leaned a little closer. 'You already thought of someone, didn't you? But you didn't want to say.'

April's eyes widened. 'Mind reader. They must teach you well in the army.'

'Nah, it's all in the body language. I read lots of books remember?'

She sighed. 'Alright then, I did think of someone, but it's a silly answer.'

'No judgement here, just say it.' He relaxed his posture deliberately to help her feel comfortable.

'I instinctively thought of my ex-fiancé, Kyle. There.'

'Oh?' Zac had been expecting her to say some B-grade celebrity. But this surprised him.

'Not that I'd be able to have dinner with him, and not that he'd be in a position to be a dinner guest, because of the... anyway, it's more that I never really got to say the things I wanted to say to him. When I said goodbye. I just basically cried and was a blubbering mess. Wasn't pretty.' She scratched the back of her neck and looked away.

His heart ached for her and what she must have gone through—losing her leg and then her fiancé, though intrigue surfaced at what her other answers would reveal. He had the feeling there was a whole lot more beneath her assertive, honest, outgoing personality. 'What would you say to him? If you could.'

She looked up, her chest rising tightly, as though she'd thought her answer was over and done with and they could move on. 'That's a bit personal.'

'Yeah, but maybe it'll help if you get it out in the open.'

She scoffed. 'But he won't hear any of it.'

'I'll hear it. And you'll get it out of your head. It'll feel better.'

She eyed him with caution, and Zac knew she was trying to determine how much she could trust him with her personal thoughts and feelings. 'Look, all I'd say is that even though he ended up a quadriplegic, I still would have followed through with my promise to be his wife. I would have supported him. Somehow. I would have stuck with him.'

Zac nodded slowly. 'I'm sure he knows that, even without you telling him.'

'But it's like I didn't get to express it properly, and I didn't get to talk to him about the things we'd been through together, the times we'd shared, thank him for the memories. It was like our life was in some alternate reality or was just a dream, and the accident woke us up.'

Zac processed her words, his gaze running over her face with its rounded cheekbones, and the furrows between her eyebrows that deepened when she spoke of things that upset her.

'Anyway, your turn,' she said, exhaling a whoosh of air.

'Write him a letter.'

'Huh?'

'Kyle. Write him a letter. Get it all out, once and for all. So you can move on.'

'After all this time? It seems silly. And I don't want to bring up the past for him when he's probably just getting used to his new way of life.'

'Then don't send it.'

'What? What's the point then?'

He shifted his position on the couch, draping his arm over the back of it. 'The point is it'll help *you*. Free up your mind and heart for other things.' Like... him? Was he unknowingly trying to help her move on so she would consider him an option? It was crazy, and he should stop it right now. He was in no way ready for anything with anyone, and would in no way surrender to the possibility. Thirty-six questions, deepen their friendship, enjoy some interesting adult conversation for once, and that was it.

Her eyes went distant for a moment. 'I'll think about it.'

'Good. Okay, my turn.' He rubbed his hands together. 'Who would I have for a dinner guest, hmmm.'

'The Dalai Lama?'

He smiled. 'Don't give me ideas, let me think for myself.'

She made a show of zipping her mouth shut.

'Megan Fox.'

April looked at him with eyebrows raised in disbelief. 'Seriously?'

'Why not?' He chuckled. 'Okay, I'll choose again. My mother. My real mother. I've never met her.'

'For real? So you're adopted?'

Oh, how he'd longed to be, in the past. But no one ever made that commitment to him. He shook his head. 'Grew up in foster care, had a few different families. My mate Johnny,' he cocked his head towards the mantle, 'he got lucky, found two awesome parents after we both stayed in the same foster family for a while.'

But his friend's luck hadn't lasted.

'So that's how you met him?'

'Yep. His new parents made sure we kept in contact and hung out over the years, which was great. I used to wish they'd take me in too, but they only wanted one apparently.' Or they simply hadn't wanted *him*. 'So I guess I'd ask my mother lots of questions and just kind of hang out, to see what it would be like.'

Would she be like him? Had he inherited some of her traits? Had she somehow impacted on the person he was now?

April nodded. 'Maybe you'll get to do that one day.'

'Maybe. But it's probably best to leave things be.'

'Or you could write her a letter. With all your questions.'

Zac picked up a cracker and topped it with cheese. 'Good advice. How'd you come up with that?'

'Heard it somewhere.' She waved her hand around.

After they'd answered questions about whether they'd like

to be famous, if they rehearsed telephone calls, and what would constitute a perfect day, Zac asked April question number five: 'When did you last sing to yourself? To someone else?'

April swallowed stiffly. 'I don't sing.'

'Surely you've sung at some point. In the shower, while doing housework, at work?' Zac sang to himself all the time. Lyrics floated of their own accord out of his mouth, like the poetry floated from his fingertips onto the computer screen.

'Well yeah, but I don't anymore.'

Zac moved his hand around in circles to encourage her. 'So... when was the last time?'

She grasped her fingers and massaged them like they were sore, avoiding his eye contact.

'It's a simple question.'

'Yeah, well, it's not a simple answer.' She stood. 'Could I please have some water?'

Zac stood. 'Sure, I'll get some.' He filled a glass and handed it to her. 'Hey, we're both in this together. No need to be worried.'

They sat again and she took a deep breath. 'The last time I sang was in the car. To Kyle. Right before the drunk driver slammed into us.'

Crap. 'Oh. I see.'

'The thing is, I can't even remember what song it was. Like the trauma erased it from my memory. But I had the volume up loud, probably a good thing since I was singing and I can't sing very well, and I was really getting into it.' She shook her head and he sensed her regret. 'I keep thinking if I hadn't been singing along, I could have reacted faster when I saw the car out the corner of my eye. Maybe things would have been different, even if it were only a slightly better outcome.'

Zac exhaled loudly, recalling his own wonderings about that day that changed everything for him. What if they hadn't stopped the vehicle? What if he hadn't gotten out? 'Regret is an uncomfortable thing. I've had a few of those in my life. But you can't let it eat away at you. We do what we can in the moment and that's all we can do. We can't know what's about to happen, only in hindsight.'

'I know,' she replied. 'But even now, I can't listen to music. At least, not music with lyrics. I have atmospheric instrumental music playing in my store, but... songs with words, I don't know why, I just can't take it. I guess they're like crowds are to you. My friends know to leave the radio off if they drive me somewhere.'

Wow. The woman must have been repressing her emotions for quite a long time. 'So you haven't listened to actual songs since the accident?'

'Nope. Not intentionally anyway. It just reminds me of that day. And also, songs and lyrics, they trigger emotions, memories. Makes me vulnerable and uncomfortable. So I avoid it. A bit wimpy, I know.'

He shook her concerns away with a flick of his hand. 'These questions are a bit uncomfortable and vulnerable, but you're doing them. That's pretty brave.'

'Yeah, but it's different. Anyway, so that's the last time I sang to myself and to someone else. You?' She gulped the rest of her water.

'Today. I sing around the house all the time. But to someone else? I think it was when I was in Afghanistan, unless I sang after I got back when ...' His mind rewound to another time in his life he'd rather forget. 'No, must have been Afghanistan. I was trying to make a new recruit feel more at ease, so I sang a song, and the others joined in. The fun didn't last long, but at least it brought a smile to the young guy's face for a little while.'

She smiled. 'That's nice. Are you a good singer?'

'You'll probably find out at some point and you can decide for yourself.'

'I'll prepare my ear plugs.'

They continued the questioning, and bit by bit he learned more about April and her life and her upbringing, while sharing some more about his, though he was careful not to let too much slip. They reached the last question of the first of three sets. After this, the questions would get more serious. More revealing.

He handed the phone to April, and she read it out: 'If you could wake up tomorrow having gained any one quality or ability what would it be?'

This was one of those moments where he'd be honest, but still keep a secret. 'Flying would be pretty cool, but,' he scratched his head, 'I think I'd just like to be able to walk around a crowd and not feel a sense of panic.'

April's brow did that furrowing thing again. 'I feel for you. I really do. I wish I knew the magic solution.'

'You and me both. But in time, I'm sure I'll find a way to overcome it. Anyway, don't want to dwell on that now, what about you, what ability would you choose?'

April's face lit up like one of her candles and she shuffled on the couch, an excited smile on her face. 'I'd totally want to be able to do magic. Like a witch. Click my fingers or say a spell and make stuff happen. Oh, the things I could do.' She rubbed her hands together and faked a witch's cackle.

She had nice teeth. White and straight. He'd broken one of his own when he was overseas and wasn't able to get it restored until he'd returned home. But hers, hers were perfect.

'I said, your turn. Earth to Zac?'

'Huh? Oh.' He grasped his phone as she handed it to him. What was wrong with him, getting entranced by her teeth?

They exchanged more questions, talking about good and

bad memories, dreams and accomplishments. Then question number nineteen came around. April read it out: 'If you knew that in one year you would die suddenly, would you change anything about the way you are now living? Why?'

Hell yes. So why wasn't he? Why wasn't he trying harder? Maybe he was putting too much pressure on himself to move forward all at once. 'I would work harder to connect with the world again. With people. I'd want to experience more. Feel more. Take risks. Be spontaneous.' The idea of being able to do all of that sent ripples of excitement through his body, but those ripples got snagged on fragments of fear along the way. If only he could yank those fragments out and toss them aside, he could start living this way now.

His mind probed deeper... what sorts of experiences would he want? What would he want to feel? What risks would he take? In what way would he be spontaneous? The answers came in the shape of her face, the subtle complexity of her eyes, and the cute bow of her lips. He'd done a lot in his life already, taken a lot of risks, experienced things not everyone got to experience. But he'd never experienced... love. Real love. Though he wasn't ready, something inside made him crave it. Maybe it was because he'd never felt like he belonged as a child, when no one wanted him. He'd been too boisterous and challenging. But now, now he was older, different, and in need of companionship. But that alone would not be enough one day. He wanted, *needed*, more.

'So you'd basically live life to the full,' she said.

'Yep.' An image of himself dying flashed through his mind, in despair at having missed out on the things he was currently missing out on. 'And I would also have lots of sex.'

A laugh shot from April's mouth. 'With the same person or multiple partners?'

'That depends.'

'On what?'

'On whether the person I wanted, wanted me.' He couldn't believe where this conversation was heading.

'And if they didn't?'

'Then I guess I'd go for the multiple partners option.' But somehow, he knew that wouldn't result in the type of satisfaction he craved.

'And if they *did*?'

'Then... I'd seriously hope I didn't only have one year to live.'

His gaze connected with hers as his answer met with silence. They both knew how precious life was. How it could be gone, or irrevocably changed, in the blink of an eye. And she knew what it was like to have found the love of her life but be unable to be with him.

Whether these questions could make people fall in love, who knew? But he was definitely feeling a stronger connection with her.

April ate a cracker, then said, 'If you could choose anyone, who would it be? And don't say Megan Fox.'

'To have lots of sex with?' He raised his eyebrows. 'I don't think that's on the question list, neighbour.'

'I know. I'm just asking, while we're on the topic. Neighbour.' She eyed him with a curious and cheeky gaze. 'Be honest.'

His heart rate intensified as images flashed in his mind that he didn't know if he should be thinking. 'If I found out right now, in this moment, that I only had a year to live... I think I would want to have it with you, actually.'

A cracker crumb fell from her lips and she froze.

'You wanted me to be honest.' He held up his palms.

Her cheeks became pink. 'Out of every possible woman in

the world, you're telling me you would want *me*?' She tapped her fingers against her chest.

He looked away from her stare. 'Well, I'm guessing if I only had a year, maybe I wouldn't be well enough to travel far, so the fact that you're my next-door neighbour is quite convenient. And you already know a lot about me, so we wouldn't have to waste extra time getting to know each other. Makes perfect sense.' *Any excuse.*

She laughed again, but with a high-pitched hint of discomfort. 'What makes you think I would even want to... to... do that... with you?'

Her embarrassment was adorable. 'I'm sure you'd take pity on a dying man, yeah?' He exaggerated a wink.

'Umm...' She grabbed two crackers. 'I have no idea how to respond to that.'

'April... what's your surname?'

'Vedora.'

'April Vedora, have I made you speechless?'

'No, I'm just hungry.' She gobbled up her crackers, took another, and pointed to her mouth. 'See? It's rude to eat and talk.'

'But you're doing it.'

A smile attempted to escape from her lips. 'Guess I'm rude then.'

'Guess you are.'

She chuckled and another crumb fell from her mouth. 'I'm also messy. Sorry.' She brushed her lap with her hands.

April told him how she'd spend her life if she only had a year to live, trying to fit in as much as possible, and every now and again adding 'Oh! And I'd do blah-blah...' and 'Oh! How could I forget blah-blah ...' He found it rather cute.

When question twenty-eight came around, it was easy.

'What do I like about you? Hmm, that's a tough one,' he

said, rubbing his jaw between his fingers and pretending to experience great difficulty.

She whacked him on the arm.

'Okay, okay. I like that you're honest and not afraid of speaking your mind. You just say stuff. Regardless of how the other person might respond.'

'Huh.' She nodded with a small smile. 'Thank you. Some might say that's a negative trait.'

'Then they would be the ones who would want to hear what they want to hear rather than the truth. The truth is always better.'

'I'm glad I can continue to be my honest, direct self with you then,' she said, then glanced around. 'You need some colour in this place, Zac. Are you trying to depress me or something?'

He sat up straighter. 'Hey, I happen to like neutral, earthy colours, thank you very much.'

'And I'm saying it needs some colour. A bit of earthy red, a splash of purple even. Maybe I'll get you some more candles.'

'You do that.'

She grinned. 'Okay, guess I better rack my brain for something I like about you. Umm ...' She mimicked his jaw rubbing.

'It doesn't have to be one thing. You can say multiple things, if you're having trouble narrowing them all down.'

She whacked his arm again and he laughed. He was starting to enjoy being attacked by her.

She eyed him like he was a specimen she was examining under a microscope. 'I'll give you three.' She bent one of her fingers with another, beginning her countdown. 'Firstly, I like your conversation skills. At first, I thought you were weird, but now I think you're interesting.' She bent another finger. 'Secondly, I like how you go with the flow. Like, you're relaxed and don't seem to let things bother you. Then again, maybe that's because you don't have a business to run and have the freedom to be a lazy bum all day.'

He whacked her arm this time.

'And thirdly, I like ...' She eyed him up and down. 'Oh what the hell, I'll just say it. Your bod is pretty impressive, dude. Okay, all done, is your ego nicely stroked?'

Warmth spread through his body. *Oh yes, it sure was ...*

'Oh, only three questions to go,' April said around half an hour later. 'Your house, containing everything you own, catches fire. After saving your loved ones and pets, you have time to safely make a final dash to save any one item. What would it be? Why?'

'Easy. My photo up there.' He pointed above the fireplace to the picture of him and Johnny in their uniforms. 'It means a lot to me. Other stuff doesn't matter, only memories.'

She nodded. 'The first thing I thought of, seems a bit silly, but I feel like I'd want my hope candle.'

'Hope candle?'

'It sits beside my bed. Never seems to run out, it's like the never-ending candle. It was given to me after my accident to remind me to stay hopeful and strong, and always makes me feel better. Though if it was a fire that destroyed everything, I'd probably be too afraid to light it after that!'

The remaining two questions were answered without too much difficulty, and Zac leaned back against the couch.

'Is that it, are we finished?' she asked.

He leaned forward, remembering something. 'Oh, hang on. There's also an optional exercise.'

But did *he* want to do it?

April peered at the phone screen. 'We have to stare into each other's eyes for four minutes? *Four* minutes?'

He noticed her jaw clench a little, and his own mirrored

hers. Maybe they shouldn't do it, it would be weird. And dangerous. And ...

'Okay!' she said.

What?

'They're just eyes. I'll use the time to plan my day tomorrow or something.' She shrugged.

She was clearly trying to make light of it, but her slightly stiff posture told him she would find it challenging, as would he. He'd barely looked anyone in the eye for longer than a brief moment in years. Let alone someone with beautiful almond-shaped brown eyes and long lashes that invited him to look closer. Four minutes, that was all. Four minutes would fly by, for sure.

He moved a little closer to her on the couch and set his phone timer. 'You ready?'

'Are you?'

No response.

'Time starts... now.'

He pressed the start button then took a breath, as he looked up into April's eyes and she looked at his. After a few moments, her eyes diverted for a split second then returned to his gaze. Looking away after an appropriate time was an automatic response, and he had to force his eyes to stay put.

The candlelight gave a warm, shiny glow to her eyes. Though dark brown, tiny swirls of caramel spun within them. He hadn't noticed that before.

She giggled, and her hand covered her mouth, then she tried to resume her composure. Zac smiled a little, but kept his mouth tight. He tried to focus on every little detail to make use of the time. The way her eyelashes lightly kissed the top of her cheeks every time she blinked, and how they curled upwards, opening her eyes to the world. To him. She was wearing eye make-up, a faint glimmer of gold arched across her eyelids, accentuating her olive skin.

Despite looking directly at her eyes, his peripheral vision took in her chest rising and falling, and the curved shadows under her collarbones.

Was she examining every detail of him too? What did she notice?

She appeared to be trying extremely hard not to look away, and not to laugh. How strange it was to look so deeply into someone's eyes and not say anything. And as the seconds ticked by, it felt even stranger not to reach out and at least touch her hand, do something, anything, to detract from the intense vulnerability of the situation.

The air seemed to close in around them, concentrating itself in their personal space. He didn't know what the timer was up to, but perhaps they were halfway. Except something had shifted. She no longer appeared to be on the verge of laughter, and her eyes held a softer, more comfortable look about them. In contrast, he felt his gaze sharpening, intensifying, as though he was no longer simply looking into her eyes, but deeper. The gloss of her eyes increased, like a car windscreen after being wiped with a windscreen wiper. The rims of her eyes became a deeper pink. He could *see* her. Not just the outer her, but the inside. Something that he hadn't seen before... electrifying *and* terrifying. And, he was sure, she saw something new in him, sending a shot of adrenaline through his body.

Something about her drew him in, captivated him. His heart beat faster, his skin warmed, his breath quickened. He wanted to reach out and touch her face, trace around her eyes gently with his fingers. He clenched his hands tight. If that timer didn't go off soon ...

Her face rose slightly as she gulped, and her breathing

quickened. Her chest rose and fell in time with his, like a piece of music about to reach a crescendo. The intensity in her presence was new to him. He didn't know exactly what it was. He was attracted to her, yes, but it was more... an inexplicable, raw, primal connection that simply existed. No reason, no purpose, it just was.

Heat warmed him from deep within. Oh God, he craved her. Right now, right here, he had to touch her. And if he did, an intense kiss would surely follow.

The timer buzzed.

April's gaze dropped, but he couldn't look away. He sucked in a breath, and as his hand reached out to her, some unseen force pulled it back. He stood, ran his hand over his head, and turned away. The bottle on the counter by the knife block caught his eye and instinctively he went to it. He picked up its smooth, curved body with ease. It fit in his hand like a key in a lock, a pillow in a pillowcase, comfortable like an old friend.

He opened the lid. The scent disoriented him for a moment, like he'd opened a bottle of memories and they'd escaped up and out in a rushed haze. He grabbed two glasses and filled the first one, was about to fill the other but his hand holding the stem shook and the glass fell over and rolled. He caught it before it toppled off the counter.

'Nice save,' said April.

He looked at the empty glass and couldn't even wait a second to fill it. He grabbed the full glass and brought it near his mouth, but as his tastebuds tingled with anticipation and his heart pounded, nausea rose in his gut.

He walked to the sink and tipped it down. Then he placed the lid on the bottle and shoved it towards her. 'Please take it. Take it away.'

April took the bottle and stood. 'Zac?'

He doubled over and leaned one hand on the bar stool next

to her bag. He couldn't focus, catch his breath, his head spinning.

'Are you okay?' Her hand touched his back and he straightened up.

He looked in her eyes once again and knew he couldn't keep this bottled up inside. He took a deep breath that would in no way prepare him for what was to follow. 'My name is Zac Masterson, and I'm an alcoholic.'

CHAPTER TWELVE

April stepped back as though the truth had slapped her in the face.

'I mean *recovering* alcoholic,' Zac said. 'At AA they say alcoholic, but I think that reinforces the problem, so I prefer to say recovering. Not recovered, because then that would mean I could have the odd drink and be fine, but I can't, and I'm not. So I'm recovering, and always will be.' He leaned back against the kitchen counter and crossed his arms as he exhaled a long breath. His gaze dropped to the bottle in her hands and she thought for a moment he was going to grab it from her. She went to the door and placed it outside on the porch, then came back in.

She should have recognised the signs, but had been blinded by this man and his unconventional charm.

Recognition. Is that what she had seen in his eyes that had made her feel slightly teary for a moment during the eye-gazing exercise? She hadn't understood why emotion had surged through her, but now she knew.

She had seen her father in his eyes.

The same pain, same need, same hunger... for something no

person could provide. And an emptiness that could only be filled by the liquid poison. But she'd also seen something else. Strength, determination, and... desire? 'How long have you been sober?' she asked.

'Almost eight months,' he replied. 'September first will be the long-awaited twelve-month mark. First day of spring.' He moved behind the counter and filled a glass with water, then sculled it.

Part of her wanted to dash outside and suck in the cool night air in giant gulps, then go home and close the door to the night, and him. But she couldn't. The other part of her wanted to understand. Wanted to know more and more about him. *Needed* to.

'And how long, I mean, were you ...'

'How long was I married to the drink?'

She nodded.

'Around two years or so. Though I don't know exactly when it started. It had just been a few drinks here and there after Johnny's death, and before I knew it, I couldn't get through a day without it.'

April furrowed her brow. 'Your friend died?'

Zac pointed to the mantle. 'My best mate. Like a brother. Watched him die right in front of me.' He moved back to the couch and sat, resting his elbows on his thighs.

April's heart dropped. She sat next to him. 'Oh, Zac.' Her hand tentatively touched his back as it had before.

'One second he was there, the next he wasn't.'

April clamped her eyes closed for a moment. She didn't want to ask what had happened, but assumed it had been an explosion of some kind.

'Our vehicle got hit,' he said. 'I'd hopped out to check something suspicious by the side of the road, and when I turned back ...' He exhaled a long breath. 'All three of them. Gone.'

She placed her hand on his back, cautiously, like he was a bomb about to go off. Heat urged to escape through his shirt. What words were of any value when it came to something like that?

His foot tapped up and down against the floor, his body tensing under her touch. She knew what was happening—he wanted to drink. Her father got impatient twitches when he'd been too long without a fix. Which for him was a matter of hours, not months as it had been for Zac.

'We'd actually been laughing about something just before it happened. Laughing, can you believe it?' He shook his head.

Yes, she could. Just like she'd been singing and smiling right before her crash. The calm, or in this case the fun, before the storm.

'I'm sure he'd be proud of you,' she said.

'Proud? I survived, and what do I go and do? Become a drunk.'

'I mean proud that you stopped. That you had the strength to make that decision. And eight months, that's huge. You should be proud too.'

As his hands formed a triangle while his elbows rested on his knees, she pointed to the tattoo on his wrist. 'Did you get that before or after?'

He glanced at his wrist. 'After. After I stopped drinking actually. I wanted something there so that whenever I picked up a glass or a bottle, I'd see it, be reminded that if I chose to, I could be stronger. I could resist.' He rubbed at the tattoo. 'So far so good.'

April looked at her own wrist. 'I need one to stop me eating chocolate.' Then she covered her mouth. 'Oh God, that's a totally inappropriate thing to say. Sorry.' She tipped her head back and looked at the ceiling.

Zac turned to her. 'It's okay. I like how you say what's on your mind. It's refreshing.'

She caught his gaze. Yes, she did like to voice her thoughts, but new thoughts were creeping into her mind and they weren't ones she could say out loud.

He's an alcoholic.

Like my father.

If only he ...

No. This wasn't the time to allow those thoughts to continue in a domino cascade of increasingly worrisome assumptions. She knew where the cascade would end when the last domino fell, and she wasn't ready to accept that yet. Right now he was in pain, and she wanted to be there for him.

'I have another tattoo here,' he said, pulling up the hem of his jeans. 'For Johnny.'

The letter J was tattooed in medieval-looking font on his inner right ankle.

'That's nice,' she said. 'I guess all you, all we, can do, is remember the good times and hope they meant something.' She looked straight ahead, her gaze falling on the darkened hallway beyond the living room. Zac's room would be beyond there. Here she was, sitting in this man's house, both of them open and vulnerable, baring their souls. She hardly knew him, yet at the same time she knew him so well. She had never met someone who had gotten through to her like this, who had triggered some part of her that wanted to go deeper, wanted to feel things she wasn't sure she could ever feel again.

'Yes,' he said. 'Memories are all we have.'

'Did what happen trigger the agoraphobia?' she asked, then hoped she wasn't overstepping the mark by getting him to discuss his traumatic past.

'When I got back. To the real world, whatever that is,' he said, 'I felt removed from everything, like an alien. And guilty.

How could I go on and enjoy my life when they didn't get to come home?' He linked his hands and ground them into each other. 'I felt guilty if I went out. If I smiled. If I talked to people. Things they'd never get to do anymore. I know it's stupid, and I should have been grateful and made the most of surviving, but that's how I felt back then. And to numb the feeling of separation, I'd go to the pub. Zone out. Becoming even more separated in a sense, but in a way that I couldn't feel the intensity.' He took a cracker but broke it in half, replacing it on the plate. 'Then I started drinking at home instead. And when I finally stopped drinking, I didn't want to go out and have the same thing happen—feel the feelings that triggered the drinking in the first place.'

April nodded as she listened, keeping quiet so he could release whatever was on his mind.

'There was too much temptation. If I was out, I'd end up in a pub or a bottle shop. If I stayed home, I couldn't. Pretty soon it became as simple as that.'

'Hence all the deliveries I've seen arriving at your doorstep.'

He nodded. 'Thank God for internet shopping.'

'Zac, if there's ever anything I can get for you, bring you, please let me know. If I can help, I ...'

'Thanks, April.' He lightly touched her hand, and she knew he wasn't just thanking her for the offer.

'Do you get some kind of government help, I mean financial assistance, for your ...' She didn't want to say disability.

Zac shifted on the couch. 'I have everything covered,' he said quietly. There was silence for a moment and April feared that, as usual, she had overstepped the mark. She may as well have asked him how much money was in his bank account. But then he turned to face her. 'Johnny's adoptive family were well off. He left me so much, *too* much, in his will.' Zac took a deep breath. 'I've given to charity, I've helped out some people, but I feel so bad that I wasted so much of it on the grog.' He leaned back on the couch and crossed one leg over his knee, as though the revelations were draining his energy. 'Apart from charity donation subscriptions, the rest is just sitting there, in my investment accounts. I don't know what to do with it, apart from pay my necessary expenses. I don't want a fancy life, don't need much.' He rubbed his chin then said, 'I should give it all away. I don't deserve it.'

'Zac, he gave it to you. It's yours. Of course you deserve it.'

'Do you want some?' he asked, looking her way. 'Seriously, let me know much and I'll transfer it. You'll make good use of it for your business, I know.'

April's mouth gaped. What she wouldn't give to have a bit more cash. But this was ridiculous. 'That's crazy. I can't and I won't accept money from you,' she said.

'The offer is there.'

Holy crap. He must be loaded.

'I'll never accept it.' She crossed her arms.

'Will you accept another drink? Non-alcoholic of course. Same as before, or something hot—coffee, tea, hot chocolate?'

The thick air in the room seemed to release, like a door had been opened and it all gushed out. 'Thanks, but I better get back home. It's been a long day and I want to get enough sleep for work tomorrow.' She stood.

Zac stood and held out his hand. 'Thanks for the company.'

She shook it awkwardly, then laughed. 'After everything we've told each other tonight, you're shaking my hand like a business associate?' Before she knew what she was doing, she leaned close to him, her arms reaching out.

Zac's taken aback expression morphed into a smile, then he held out his arms and slid them around her waist, as hers wrapped around his broad upper back. 'Thank you for the beautiful dinner,' she whispered, the peppery scent of his warm skin close to her nose. 'And for the conversation. It was the most interesting night I've had in... in... ever.'

'That's the power of Truth Chicken,' he replied, as they pulled back from their hug.

He passed April her bag and *The Prophet*.

'Guess I'll have to alternate between this one and my other one about the farm guy and the jam girl and all the secrets,' she said. 'I'll bring it back when I've finished.'

'Take as long as you like,' he said.

It would probably take her a while. Reading and understanding anything to do with philosophy and self-improvement would take more brainpower than she usually had at night, the only time she had for reading. She would also need time to get used to what she'd learned tonight. But no matter how much time passed, or how deeply she got to know Zac, there was one thing that time would never enable. She could be friends with him, sure, be a good neighbour, yes, but no way could she be more than that with him. Not ever.

Zac went to his room and lay on the bed. He was exhausted; mentally, emotionally, and physically. But not sleepy. His brain was tired but wired. That was the most interaction he'd had in ages, and new yet familiar sensations were scrambling over each other inside, trying to put themselves in order, but tripping and falling over. Should he call his sponsor? He was surprised his sponsor hadn't called *him*, knowing a day like today could reopen some old wounds. But Zac had said he was on track, and would keep his distance from April and stay on course until September first, when he would be in a better position to reassess where he was at and what he was ready for next.

Whether he was ready to start thinking about having someone in his life.

But the desire for companionship was already surfacing, and he didn't want to quell it. Sure, he'd wait till September before starting anything with anyone, but in the meantime, he knew exactly who this anyone was and what he needed to do. He would establish a solid friendship with her, help her get in touch with her inner self and deal with her own past, and, oh, what the heck, he would also flirt like hell. As long as his willpower could take it. Then, when the time came, she would be ready, he would be ready, and they could take things to the next level. He was sure the same attraction that had gripped him had gripped her, when their eyes had focused intently on each other's. But it was more than that. They *got* each other. She already knew a lot about him, and he was surprised by his willingness to open up about his alcoholism, but she'd responded so empathetically. She hadn't expressed any judgement, like she accepted him. And that gave him hope. Hope, that like his blog name, he could win the war within, and hope that he could move forward with his life and live it properly. She was his hope. She was his candle.

Zac rolled over and picked up the pen and notepad he kept by his bed, as poetry sang deep within, its melodic notes wafting up from the depths and out into the night air. Not a complete poem, but words, a phrase, and then another.

This was the beginning of something, he could feel it.

The ballpoint pen rolled an inky trail across the paper as a hopeful smile edged into his cheeks ...

Our fire is burning, I'm stoking the coals
We've already kissed, not our lips, but our souls

CHAPTER THIRTEEN

'Could this be it?' Belinda asked on Friday as she sat behind the counter at April's Glow during a lull in customers. She tilted the computer screen to face April. '*Winning the War Within.*'

April looked at the blog. Zac hadn't told her what his blog was or showed her any of his poems, and when she'd told Belinda that her neighbour was an ex-soldier and poet, she'd set about Googling. She hadn't told her anything else, and wouldn't. And she wouldn't have even told her this much had she not been continually pestering her about Zac after the whole flower on the doorstep thing.

She read the description about how the blog owner was an anonymous ex-soldier who used poetry to help him deal with things he'd been through and things he was going through. Could be him, but he wouldn't be the only soldier who'd taken to the written word to express what they'd experienced.

'Let me have a read,' April said, scanning over one of the poems called 'The Illusion of Time'. Then she read 'Bird in a Cage' and knew. It had to be him. It was about going it alone, and how he should be living 'out there'. It had to be about the agoraphobia and how it was impacting his life. Wow, he was good. No wonder he had so many followers. 'What are you doing?' she asked Belinda as she tilted the screen back to herself and typed into the side of the blog.

'Subscribing you.'

'Hey! Hang on, I don't want him to think I've been stalking him.' She shooed her employee's hands away from the keyboard.

'But don't you want to get notified if he posts another entry?'

'No. Yes. Maybe. I don't know.'

'I'll take that as a yes. Do you have another email address apart from your work one?'

'Oh, give it here.' She tilted the screen and leaned over and typed in her email address, which wouldn't give away her identity. 'There, happy now?'

'Not yet.' Belinda typed in her own too. 'Two new subscribers in one minute. He'll wonder why he's suddenly so much more popular.' Belinda grinned. Then, as April went to refill the oil burner on a back-wall shelf behind the counter, Belinda said, 'Um, you should check this out.'

'Check what?'

'Look.' She pointed to a poem on the screen. 'I could be wrong, but what if he's writing about you?'

UNTOUCHED
We've smiled, we've spoken
Though you don't know that I'm broken
I'm already caught in your net
But we haven't even touched yet

The feel of your skin
My yang to your yin
I want it. But I'm scared
I'm open. I'm bared.

April had to reread it to take it all in. But they *had* touched. Hugged. And she knew he was 'broken', as he'd put it. She checked the date of the entry. Earlier in the month. Before their dinner. After she'd given him the candle.

Something fluttered in her belly. Surely it couldn't be her. Songwriters wrote songs that were just general depictions of love and relationships, but it didn't mean they were about something they were currently experiencing, so it would be the same with poets.

I want it. But I'm scared.

It was like he was reading her mind. But she'd have to get rid of those thoughts and feelings, after discovering his secret. They were no use to her now.

The bell on the door to the store jingled and a young woman walked in.

'Hi,' said April. 'How are you?'

'Good thanks,' she replied. 'Do you have any candles that aren't too feminine, like for a guy? I don't want something too girly.'

April smiled. 'I know just the one.' She led the customer to the cinnamon triple-wicked candle.

By late afternoon, April's right leg was tired. The store had become busier for some reason, and the new winter range was starting to sell, even though it was still a month until winter. She sat behind the counter, but as soon as she did, her phone rang. 'Mum' appeared on the caller ID, so she picked it up. Her mother never called during April's work hours unless she really had to, but sent text messages like 'I know you're busy, call me when you can', or 'when you finish, give me a buzz and let's arrange to catch up'.

'Mum?' she said.

'Sorry to bother you, but your father is asking for us. He's causing a bit of a kerfuffle at the hospital.'

'He's in hospital again?'

'Uh-huh,' Clarissa Vedora replied. 'Nurse says he refuses to take his medication or IV fluids until he can see his wife and daughter. I had to inform her that I'm his ex-wife, but we know he hasn't quite gotten used to the fact.'

Damn. She should have gone to see him earlier when he'd texted her after her birthday. 'So they haven't sedated him?'

'Tried to, but he almost jabbed the nurse with a needle. Flung it across the room, then got up and started yelling and stumbling around, banging into beds and equipment. And ...' her mother's voice shook. 'Then he got aggressive and grabbed one of the nurses by the arms.'

'Oh no.' April stood. 'I'm guessing they can't just give him a drink.' She managed a weak laugh.

'Ah, no. And he's clearly starting to go through withdrawals.'

'I'll get Belinda to close up, should be fine. Will you pick me up from here or my place?'

'I'll see you at the shop in five or ten.'

'Okay.' April ended the call. 'Sorry, hope you're right to close up today?' she asked Belinda.

'Sure, is everything okay?'

'I don't want to burden you with my family dramas, but my dad, he's an alcoholic.' She hated saying it out loud. It blemished the air around her with a stain she couldn't budge. 'He's causing some trouble at the hospital, so I'd better ...' she gestured to the door.

'Oh, I had no idea. Crap. Okay, sure, I can handle things here. You go.' April grabbed her bag and Belinda ushered her towards the door. 'Hope he's okay,' she said.

Instead of waiting out front, April dashed as fast as she

physically could to the bottle shop further up the road, away from the main street. It was crazy, feeding his addiction, but she didn't know what else to do. He needed to calm down before he hurt someone or himself, and barring sedatives if they could get them into him, this was the only way. She picked up a small bottle of whiskey and a hip flask, glad she had her roomy handbag, then dashed back to wait at the store. Glancing around to check no one was watching, she filled the flask with her father's poison. Her mother arrived soon after.

When they arrived at the hospital, it was easy to find his room. They only had to follow his voice, bellowing throughout the ward. 'Ur all a bunch of idiots!'

'Mr Vedora, they'll be here soon. Settle down.'

April and her mother walked in. Her father paced slowly, aimlessly, around the room, his hospital gown hanging limply from his thin frame. 'Dad,' April said.

'My daughter!' His eyes went wide. 'She is here, idiots. She is here. Look.' He came toward her and pointed at her face. 'She's so beautiful.'

One of the nurses managed a smile, and April grasped her father's hands, dry and leathery. 'Dad, hop back in bed. You need to get some fluids and rest.'

'So beautiful,' he said, obeying her command. 'Even with the missing leg.' He looked at the nurse. 'See? She has a fake one.' He pointed again.

April's mother huffed and finally moved closer to her ex-husband, but April rolled her eyes. It didn't bother her.

'Gary, don't talk about April's leg. Just do what the nurses and doctors say.'

April knew her mother didn't want to be there, but she also knew what her father was like and how difficult it could be for medical professionals to deal with him, and her mother would be embarrassed on his behalf.

'And my wife,' her father said, reaching out his hand, but Clarissa didn't let him touch her. 'Still beautiful but getting older, as you can see.' He scrunched up his face. 'We all get old. We all get old and then we die!' he yelled. April's mother backed away and turned her face to the wall.

April talked calmly to him and the nurse took the opportunity to swiftly reinsert the IV line and do other necessary tasks, smiling gratefully at April. April felt compassion for the staff, dealing with difficult patients. She'd seen a lot after her accident and, despite her challenging recovery, some of it was made easier by the caring people who looked after her. Some were just methodical, practical, doing their day's work but a few others had made a big difference, like you could tell it was their passion and they did their best to make things that little bit easier.

'These idiots don't know what they're doing,' he said. 'No one can look after me like you two can. Or used to,' he sighed. Then his weary eyes met hers, hope giving them a hint of gloss.

She knew that look. It was the 'did you bring me anything?' look.

April put a finger to her lips.

When the nurse had finished, Clarissa walked out of the room to talk to her, and April reached into her bag. 'Dad, just a few sips, okay?' she whispered. 'If you behave and let the medicos do their job, I'll bring more tomorrow. And maybe they'll even let you out early. But you have to promise.'

He gulped from the flask without answering. She might as well have said she had one hour to live and he still would have gone for the drink first.

'Okay, Dad? Be good and more tomorrow.'

'My lips are sealed,' he drew a line across his lips with his fingers and April took the flask from his hands, shoving it quickly into her bag. Luckily the curtains around the other beds were drawn. 'Is it bedtime yet? What time is it? Midnight?'

'No, it's early. But you sleep if you need to.'

'Sleep. I need to. Mm, sleep.' His eyes went droopy.

She stayed with him a while as he drifted in and out of sleep, then stood as his breathing changed to a regular rhythm.

Her mother glanced her way. April nodded.

They left the hospital, and before starting the engine Clarissa paused for a moment and took a deep breath. 'Right, off we go!' she said with forced enthusiasm. She had seen it before, her mother trying to counteract the difficult times with overt happiness and excitement. Like once in the past when her dad had sworn at them and told them they were useless... 'Wow is that the time? Let's go out for diner instead, no time to cook!' her mother had said, and they'd gone and pigged out on pizza. Or the time when her dad threw up on the living room floor, and after her mother had cleaned it up, she'd clapped her hands and said... 'Let's go shopping! I need a new sheet set. Oh, and shoes! And we can have lunch.'

April listened on the drive home as her mother blurted random, mildly pleasant but unimportant remarks about anything that popped into her head.

'You're quiet,' her mother said.

'Just thinking.'

'April, I'm your mum. You don't think, you speak. What's got you so silent?'

'My new neighbour. He's an alcoholic. A really sexy one.'

Clarissa made a sound that was a cross between a gasp and a laugh. 'He's told you this? Or have you seen him drinking?'

'He told me. He's eight months sober though.'

'Ah. Well, good for him. But you remember what happened after your dad tried to stay sober, don't you?'

'How could I forget?' The sight of her mother falling from

the top of the staircase had scared the life out of her teenage self. She'd poked her head out of her room when she'd heard the commotion: her father yelling his slurred frustrations, her mother trying to calm him. It was his first day of drinking again after a short break of a few weeks, and Clarissa had hidden the grog from him, trying to get him back on track. But it only made him upset, and without meaning to, he'd flung his arms around and accidentally collided with his wife, who lost her balance and fell backwards. Three broken bones, two ribs and her arm were the result. And the gradual dissolution of their marriage.

'Keep your distance, honey.'

'A bit hard, considering we're neighbours. We've had dinner together. That's when he told me.'

'Dinner? Like a date?'

'Not really, just a friendly thing. He told me about being a soldier. He's been through a lot.'

'Oh. Well, I'm sure he has. But you need someone less complicated in your life, April. What about that nice young man at the bank?'

'That one with the permanent smile on his face?'

'Yes, always so positive.'

'It's weird though, like his smile is fake. I don't buy it. I think he's pretending.' April looked out the window, watching the passing cars. Passing, because her mother always drove ten kilometres under the speed limit. 'Anyway, I'm not attracted to the guy at the bank.'

'Attraction isn't everything,' Clarissa said. 'I was head over heels attracted to your father, look where that got me.'

'Mum.' April sighed.

'Well, attraction will do you no good with this neighbour fellow. A dead end, that one.'

'He's a nice guy. But don't worry. I don't plan on falling for him.'

A twinge of discomfort twisted inside. Had she already fallen for him? She would have to un-fall, because like her mother said, he was a dead end. She couldn't get involved with someone who had a problem with alcohol, simple as that. She would not repeat her mother's mistakes.

CHAPTER FOURTEEN

The next day, April left Belinda in charge briefly and went back to the hospital. She took her father home when they discharged him, and made sure his living environment was clean and safe. She made him eat, then when he was settled on the couch with the television, she left. He would be okay, for now. He would get worse again, but for now, she could leave knowing she'd done what she could. The rest was up to him.

Being a Saturday the store was busy, and by the end of the day she'd almost forgotten about her dad. It was only when things became quiet for a moment that her thoughts would return to him. And then to Zac. She'd already decided not to get involved, but maybe she should try even harder. Maybe she shouldn't even be that friendly with him. Keep things more like they were with Nancy Dillinger next door; occasional brief exchanges, the odd wave and smile, and that was about it. Though Nancy seemed quite comfortable with Sylvia Greene in the next house up, she didn't know why, maybe Sylvia was Nancy's doctor and they knew each other that way. Yes, she would have to keep her distance as her mother had said. It would only make things harder, the more they interacted.

'You look like you're settled in for a long night chained to the computer,' said Belinda, as she grabbed her bag and went to leave work.

April sipped from her takeaway coffee cup as she sat at the counter, going over figures and occasionally jotting down notes and ideas into a word document. 'Just focusing on the business.'

'Not reading a certain person's blog, by any chance?' she eyed her curiously.

'No. No of course not.'

'But you wish you were, right?'

'No. Definitely not. I don't have time.' Her words were short and sharp.

'Worried about your dad?'

April dropped her hands and looked at her employee. 'No. I mean, yes. But he's okay for now. Right now I'm looking for ideas on how to celebrate the first birthday of April's Glow.'

'Oh,' Belinda came over to the computer. 'But isn't that, like, six months away?'

She nodded. 'October. But better to plan early. I want to do something special, like, not only for the store, for the town too. Something to give the store great exposure but also make it a win-win for the community.'

'A candle making competition?' Belinda suggested. 'A colouring-in competition? An everything's-free-for-one-day-only event?'

April chuckled. 'Yeah, not gonna happen.'

'What about having a party somewhere, and everyone gets dressed up as a candle? Ooh! And you could have strippers! They jump out of giant candles and get everyone *glowing*.' She winked.

'Nice try, and as much fun as that would be, I better choose something a bit less... X-rated.'

She stayed at the store until after dark, then remembered

she had clothes hanging on the line at home and should probably get back. She also realised that maybe she didn't really need to start planning the store's birthday celebrations yet and was just trying to avoid an interaction with Zac.

April sprinkled food pellets into Romeo's bowl when she got home, then opened the back door, quickly closing it when she noticed Zac on his deck. His back slightly hunched, he peered at the sky through a telescope. He straightened up and looked her way. She could see him slightly through the door's window, but she moved back into the kitchen and hoped he would finish soon so she could go outside.

What am I doing? She asked herself. *I can't avoid him forever.*

But for now, she had to. Or minimise exposure at least. And after a long day today and night last night, she wasn't in the mood for exchanging banter.

She clattered dishes and pots and pans in the kitchen to sound busy, not that he could probably hear her, and then heated up a dinner she had frozen. When she'd finished, she peered out the back door. No sign of Zac.

She closed Romeo into the laundry to stop him running outside, then carried the basket out to the night air. A cool breeze wafted around her face, her hair tickling her cheeks. She pulled the clothes and underwear off the line (which she'd hidden behind the towels so Zac couldn't see), a few pegs dropping onto the ground in her haste. She bent to pick them up, then her gaze became drawn to Zac's face through his kitchen window. He waved. She picked up her washing basket and flashed a brief, courteous smile, then scurried back inside.

In his eagerness to get to know her, maybe he'd scared her off? Zac frowned as he flopped into bed that night. Juliet leapt onto the bed and curled herself up in a ball on his chest. He stroked her fur while she purred, the vibrating rhythm bringing a certain comfort and calm to his racing heart. An image flashed in his mind, that one day April would be curled up around him in bed, and he'd be stroking her hair as she lay on his chest. He couldn't help it. But as each image intruded into his mind, he allowed himself a brief moment of pleasure at the possibilities. The *future* possibilities. Then he'd replace it with another image, or focus on something around him so that he wouldn't get swept away into the temptation.

His sleep was sporadic, as usual. By the time he woke properly in the morning it was too late to see her, she would be at work. Hopefully they could catch up when she got home. The telescope had been an impulse purchase online, with a free overnight shipping promotion. He couldn't resist. Looking up into the stars reminded him that he was only a small part of this world, and although each person was significant, it reminded him not to get caught up in trivial things or get overwhelmed with his own problems. There was a whole world out there, a whole universe. Even though right now in his life, this house, this street, this town—what little he had seen of it—was his whole world, his whole universe. And he couldn't help but hope that she would become his world, his universe, when the time was right.

As he ate a slow breakfast—mushroom and tomato omelette —he wrote. Questions formed in his mind, and he knew that when you wrote things down, asked the universe, or whatever greater power existed, for help, sometimes the answers came. He just hoped the answers would be 'yes'.

QUESTIONS
> *Will my past mistakes haunt me forever?*
> *Will someone give me a chance, now, or ever?*
> *Will I be able to create something new,*
> *and will you let me create it with you?*

When April arrived home, Zac was sitting on his front porch, sipping from a mug. She tried to look hurried and busy, carrying two bags of shopping. 'Have to get these inside,' she said.

He gave a nod.

When she'd put them away and opened the back door to let Romeo in, she couldn't see him.

Not again!

She tiptoed to the fence and peered into Zac's garden. 'Romeo!' she whispered. 'Stop getting it on with Juliet and come home!'

She spied his tail in the bushes, along with Juliet's as she sat on a tree branch staring at her feline neighbour. Thankfully no hissing this time. But like April, Juliet was keeping her distance.

Romeo scurried to another nearby bush, the bell on his collar jingling. April dashed back inside and got a bowl of food, then brought it back to tempt him. 'Romeo, look! Dinner.' She held the bowl up above the fence. He tentatively approached, his nose twitching.

Zac's screen door squeaked. 'Want a hand?'

She looked his way. 'I thought you liked cats to do their own thing.'

'Yeah, but you seem busy, so I'm guessing you want your cat inside sooner rather than later.'

'I am. And I do, actually.'

As Romeo's nose was hypnotised by the scent of food, Zac scooped him up and over the fence.

'Thanks,' she said, walking with her cat back inside.

A few nights ago they were staring into each other's eyes and now they were avoiding each other's eyes. Well, she was avoiding his.

Had she been too abrupt? At least she'd said thanks. But just because they'd spent a deep and meaningful evening together didn't mean they had to talk at length every time they were in each other's presence.

April looked in the fridge, trying to decide what to eat for dinner. She hadn't defrosted any meat, and was unmotivated to cook. Eggs? She had three left. Damn, she knew she'd forgotten something from the shops.

Her phone beeped, and she glanced at the screen.

I'll have plenty of dinner ready in about an hour if you want to join me. It's in the slow cooker.

Could Zac read her mind? And she *had* read some of the book he lent her. Wasn't she supposed to get dinner for each chapter, or was that only for the whole book? She couldn't remember. But no. She couldn't go over there.

Thanks, but I'm all good here.

She checked her vegetable drawer, her pantry, and then her finger touched the pizza delivery flyer stuck behind a candle magnet on her fridge. No, if a pizza delivery vehicle turned up outside, he'd know she'd blown him off.

Scrambled eggs it would be.

But first, couch and Facebook time for a little while.

She lay on the couch and put her legs up when her phone beeped again.

I thought you hated cooking.

She couldn't get away from this guy. If he wasn't chatting to her over the fence, it was via text.

I don't hate it, I'm just no chef.

She opened the Facebook app on her phone.
A text flashed across the top of the screen:

Can I ask a question?

April swung her legs back down and sat up.

You're asking my permission? And aren't thirty-six of them enough?

There was a longer than expected wait for his reply. The little bubbly dots to show he was typing appeared then disappeared, then appeared again.

I guess you're feeling a bit... exposed? After Wednesday night. Sorry if anything triggered bad memories.

Exposed? She felt... what did she feel? At one end of the spectrum she felt annoyed that she had met an interesting guy, but he was totally unsuitable, and like there was someone behind her pulling her away from him, and at the other end, she felt compelled, like there was an intense and irresistible pull towards him, like she was in a current and couldn't stop being carried closer. But she couldn't say, 'no I feel annoyed that you're amazing apart from the booze and compelled because you're amazing and I'm a woman and you're a man and that's how it works which sucks because I can't be around you without feeling things and I can't feel things because I don't want to end up like my mother'.

She typed back:

> I'm fine.

She waited for him to reply, and ask the question he asked permission to ask, but nothing came. She reread their brief text exchange. Yep, she'd sounded abrupt and a bit rude. *Bugger.* She could never get the tone right in text messages, let alone when words catapulted from her mouth in speech, but at least in those situations she had her hands and face to join in and give context to her words.

She started typing... *sorry if I sounded,* but then there was a knock on her door. Her gaze darted to the white glossy front door, a large silhouette visible beyond.

She got up and went to the door, and didn't need to check out the side window, she already knew it was him. Not by the silhouette, and the fact they had just been texting each other, but she could *feel* it. Somehow, it sounded crazy, she could feel his presence, his energy, his *being-ness.*

'Zac,' she said, opening the door. 'This is a first.' If anything, she thought he'd simply jump the fence and knock on her back door.

He stood there with hands in pockets, and the sunset blazing red and orange behind like he'd brought a fire with him. 'It's good to get out and about sometimes,' he said. 'My question: does knowing about my alcoholism bother you?'

The virtual fire must have grown stronger as its warmth spread inside her skin, tensing her muscles and making her want to run. She gripped the side of the door with one hand and fiddled with her silver necklace with the other.

'It does, doesn't it,' he said.

'Zac—' she was about to bluff.

'Just tell me.' He pinned her with his stare.

'Yes. Okay, yes. It does,' she blurted.

His chest rose sharply. 'So, now you know the ugly truth you don't want to talk to me? At all?'

'No, of course not, it's just ...'

'Well, you're doing a pretty good job of avoiding me and fobbing me off.' His voice was tense and blunt.

So he wasn't Mr I'm-So-Calm all the time. See? She was right. Charming one minute, agitated the next.

Like Dad.

'Okay, yes. Yes, I have been avoiding you and fobbing you off.' She crossed her arms. 'You cook a great meal and I appreciate your hospitality—'

'My hospitality?' he scoffed. 'I think we shared a bit more than my hospitality the other night.'

April took a small step back. 'I know. And you didn't let me finish.' Her father never let her finish things she was saying. He'd ask her something and then in the middle of her answer he'd start talking about something else, usually something insignificant, or some story he'd told her a hundred times but thought he was telling it for the first time. Talking to an alcoholic took a lot of patience. 'And... I appreciate your company, and your empathy about my accident, and I know you've been through a lot and I'm really sorry, but ...' she sighed. 'My dad is an alcoholic. It tore our family apart.'

They fell silent and heat burned the air between them.

Zac dropped his gaze. 'I'm sorry to hear that.'

She shrugged. 'He is who he is.'

Zac looked up. 'And I am who I am. We're all different, even if we share something the same.'

They all said that. But she'd seen other alcoholics her dad had associated with, and the drink united their differences in the same destructive bond. It didn't matter what he said, it only mattered that if he drank again, he'd be different to the man she had dinner with on Wednesday night. He'd be uncharming, un-intriguing, and maybe even worse. Who knew?

'Has your father tried to stop?'

'Yes. Once, but it didn't last long.'

Zac nodded. 'And I take it he's been like this for quite a long time?'

'Most, if not all, of my life.'

Zac nodded again, his face creasing. 'So, what, we can't be friends? Because of this?'

April rubbed her arm, as the cool air finally brushed past the heat and into her house. 'I ...'

'The thing is, April, your dad may not have stopped drinking. But I did. I have. And I have no intention to go back to the way I was.' He hooked his thumbs into the corners of his pockets.

He had a point, but still. 'Intentions are one thing, but they're not foolproof.'

'But the reality is, I'm not drinking. I haven't for eight months. That's all that matters right now. This moment in time.'

Their eyes locked for a moment and she was reminded of their eye-gazing exercise. She'd seen something that reminded her of her father. But she'd also seen other things, and still could. There was a world within his eyes, a universe, and it pulled her in while scaring her out of her mind. She looked away.

'It's just easier to... to keep my distance,' she said quietly.

'What for? It's not like I'm going to come by tomorrow and ask you to marry me or to come over for a passionate night of you-know-what. I'm committed to being dateless and celibate right now.'

Her cheeks burned. 'Oh, you think I can't resist you, is that it?' She planted her hands on her hips. 'Like I could just launch myself at you in any given moment with uncontrolled desire and passion? Huh!'

He was totally right.

'Look, I just mean that you don't have to worry. Right now, I just want to be your friend. Your neighbour. Someone you can chat to here and there, exchange books with, share the odd meal —if that's not too difficult.'

Right now. Why did he keep talking about right now? In the moment. She remembered that he'd said that in September he will have been sober for twelve months. Of course. Alcoholics are advised to avoid getting into new personal relationships until at least twelve months of sobriety have passed.

'It's not difficult, but you revealing this to me, it's brought back a lot of stuff about my dad. And he's just been discharged from hospital. He ends up there a lot. It takes its toll, not only on him, but on my mum and me.'

'Okay, fair enough, I get that.' He relaxed his posture. 'But let's try to be civil, yeah? We've had some good conversations. No need to stop. I understand where you're coming from, I do. But don't forget that I'm not your father.'

That was true, but she also couldn't forget that her father was not her father. Once the drink took hold, it possessed him, as it did with other alcoholics. It was like an evil spirit that lingered and spread itself among all those who allowed it. Zac had allowed it, maybe not now, but once.

She took a deep breath. It wasn't fair to treat him badly because of her father.

'I'm sorry for being rude, I hope you understand. And okay, I'll try to not let my past get in the way of being a courteous neighbour.'

'And friend, perhaps?'

'Sure.' She shrugged. Friends. It sounded simple. But the

thing was, deep down in that forbidden part of her, she didn't know if she could be *just* friends. But she would have to be. And if she ever doubted her resolve, she need only visit her father and be reminded of the reality.

She could not, would not, allow herself to get involved.

CHAPTER FIFTEEN

'Wonder if he ever points that thing at you,' Zoe said, as she peered discreetly out the window near April's back door, spying on Zac as he looked through his telescope. 'I don't know why you won't let me go out there and introduce myself.'

'I'll explain at dinner. Anyway he looks busy, we should leave him to it.'

'Busy?' She chuckled. 'The man's gazing at the stars.'

Well, she did say she'd try to be friendlier. She was surprised he even wanted to be friends, after the way she'd practically accused him of being like her father, who he didn't know, but she hadn't painted him in the best light. 'Okay, but just a quick hello, don't bombard him. He's kind of shy.' She didn't know whether to reveal that he had mild agoraphobia. She told pretty much everything to Zoe, but had Zac told her in confidence? And what about his history, should she even be telling her that? But both secrets had been revealed out of the context of the confidential thirty-six questions, so it was different. She needed to tell her something, to help her manage the whirlwind of emotions swirling up inside. Yes, she'd told her mother, but for her, there would be no discussion on Zac. Once an alcoholic always an alcoholic, she would simply say.

April opened the back door and Zac looked up and across at them. 'Zac, this is Zoe. Zoe, this is Zac.' Even though her friend knew too well who he was.

He smiled. 'Hey.'

'Hey,' Zoe replied.

Romeo dashed through April's legs and out onto the deck, then leapt into the tree near Zac's fence and jumped over into his yard. 'Oh, Romeo!' April called out.

'You called?' Zac asked. Zoe laughed and April shot him an are-you-kidding-me look, and he held up his hands. 'Kidding. I'll get him. Hang on.'

Zac was back. Back to his old tricks.

Zoe and April glanced at each other, and Zoe fanned her face as though she had a hot flush. April nudged her. 'Stop it.'

'Romeo, wherefore art thou,' he said, crouching near the bushes. 'Stop humping Juliet.'

Zoe laughed again. 'Who's Juliet?'

'Zac's cat.'—'My cat.' They both spoke at the same time.

'I might get a cat and call it Shakespeare,' Zoe said.

Zac smiled as he picked up Romeo. 'I think they want to move in together,' he said, handing back her cat. His arm muscles bulged beneath his sleeves and she tried not to look. Zoe looked.

'Thanks again,' she said.

'So Romeo's done this before, huh?' asked Zoe. 'Cheeky thing.'

'Yes,' replied Zac. 'As I said, they're getting serious, I think.'

'Better take him inside,' April said, heading towards the deck.

'When was the last time you looked at stars?'

She turned. 'Stars? Stars. Um, I don't remember.'

'I saw a few stars after my work function last weekend. Spinning ones,' Zoe said.

Okay, she would have to tell her. She couldn't make alcohol jokes around Zac. April was used to the odd one and didn't mind so much when they were light-hearted and not related to her father's condition, but anything that made Zac think of alcohol was probably not a good idea.

'Come look at these,' said Zac. 'It's a beautiful, clear night.' He gestured towards his telescope.

'Oh, we have to get to Café Lagoon, dinnertime,' April said.

'I'd love to!' Zoe moved towards the fence.

April sighed on the inside. She'd probably get used to Zac again, but things were still a little raw and vulnerable, after the recent dealings with her dad, and having opened up to Zac last week. Actually, he had been right. She *was* feeling exposed. She wasn't used to baring her feelings or talking about her past. He was taking her to places inside she wasn't sure she wanted to visit.

'There's a gate around the ...' Zac began, but Zoe had already stepped on the short brick wall surrounding a flower garden near April's side of the fence, and was lifting herself up onto the fence.

'Zoe! What are you, eight years old?' April sounded like Olivia, except Olivia would say to her daughter, 'Mia, what are you, eighteen years old?' when she tried on her mother's clothes and make-up.

Zac was laughing. 'Sure, come on over!'

April took Romeo back inside and locked him in the laundry early for the night. Then she went back outside. Zoe peered through the telescope as Zac explained things to her, something about the big one next to the smaller one.

'Cool,' said Zoe. 'Come take a look, Ape.'

'No thanks, I'll wait for you. Couldn't be bothered walking

around.' Yeah, she'd just used her leg as an excuse. She wasn't about to climb over like Zoe had, and anyway, she was wearing a skirt.

Zoe must have sensed April's discomfort as she moved her face away from the telescope. 'Was that my stomach? Better go eat,' she said. 'Nice to meet you, Zac. Thanks for the astrology lesson.'

'Astronomy,' he corrected.

'Oops!' She slapped her forehead. 'You're a Capricorn, right?'

'How'd you know?' He raised his eyebrows.

'Wild guess.' She went to climb the fence but must have realised there was no brick wall on his side as she stopped and looked around.

'Here, I'll give you a boost.' Zac intertwined his hands and she placed her foot on it. His hands barely moved under her weight.

'Or you could walk around the gate like a normal person,' April joked.

'I'm not normal,' she said, heaving herself up and over, landing back in April's yard.

'Have fun?' April asked.

'Sure did. Thanks, Zac.' She waved, and he waved back.

'Have a good night,' he said.

'Hey, do you want to come too?' Zoe asked.

Oh man! Now she'd really have to tell her everything.

Zac and April's gaze connected and she mouthed 'sorry'.

'Thanks ladies, but it's a quiet night in for me and Juliet.' He smiled and stepped onto his deck, his cat following him.

How did he do that?

'Goodnight,' Zoe said, and April ushered her back inside before she asked him to reveal his life story and declare if he had feelings for her friend.

'Zoe, God, I thought I'd never get you away from him!'

'If you don't want him I'll have him.'

'No. Leave him be.' She grabbed her handbag. 'Let's go.'

'Seriously, why you're not jumping him at every available opportunity I have no idea, girl.'

'He's an alcoholic, alright?' Oops. Blurt number three thousand and forty-seven of her adult life.

Zoe's mouth gaped. 'Are you serious?'

She nodded. 'Sober for eight months.'

'So he's recovered.'

'*Recovering*,' she said. 'He'll never be "recovered", he said that himself.'

'That doesn't mean he'll go back to drinking, just that he can never have a drink without risking it, right?'

'Apparently,' she said weakly.

'You don't sound convinced.'

'I know some go on to stay sober for the rest of their lives, but I also know many don't. And Zac, he's been through a lot. I mean, *a lot*. There's a lot that could trigger him.'

Zoe's brow furrowed and she linked her arm in April's. 'Come on,' she said. 'I think we have a lot to discuss.'

After an hour of dinnertime discussion at Café Lagoon, in which April had talked further about Zac's history as well as the latest on her dad, Zoe had advised she had three options: either stay friends and avoid giving into temptation, forget avoiding him and have a one-night or one-month stand, or move elsewhere and try her luck with internet dating once again. 'What it all boils down to,' Zoe said, 'is living in the moment and going with the flow, or being cautious and avoiding getting hurt, which, although safer, could also involve avoiding what could be an amazing experience that could help you move forward in life.'

'I'm not convinced you're making this any easier,' she said.

Zoe called Jonah over to the table. 'Does the barista have any advice for the candle seller?' Zoe asked.

'Advice on what?' he asked, slipping his hands into his pockets. He'd had a haircut, April noticed. Most shaved off, number three, like Zac. He looked somewhat older now.

'Should April live in the moment and take a few risks, or live with caution and stay safe?'

'You're not talking about climbing Everest or anything are you? Or backpacking around the Australian outback?'

'Um, no, definitely not,' she said.

'In that case, live *cautiously* in the moment.' He grinned. 'No really, live in the moment, otherwise, you're always scared something bad's gonna happen. Who wants to live in fear like that?'

April allowed his words to absorb into her mind. But bad things *did* happen.

'When I was travelling around Europe,' he said, 'some of the best times I had were the unplanned ones. The risky ones, too. I had a plan for some things, but plans often change, and you just have to go with it. Trust life.'

She didn't know if she could do that.

'You're very smart and insightful for a young dude,' Zoe said.

'It's the coffee,' he said. 'It's magic.' He winked, walking back to behind the counter, singing some song she didn't recognise because she hadn't listened to any songs for so long.

Truth Chicken and now Magic Coffee. If the coffee could tell her the future, she'd drink bucket loads of it.

CHAPTER SIXTEEN

It had been two weeks since their heated discussion about alcoholism and her father, and Zac was feeling more positive. She was still a bit reserved in their interactions, in her unreserved 'April' kind of way. Maybe cautious was a better word. But she was making an effort to give him the benefit of the doubt.

As he carried his new outdoor heater, a chiminea, to his back deck, he watched as she filled her backyard birdbath with water.

'Lunchbreak?' he asked. It was a Monday, in the middle of May.

'Even better. Day off,' she said. 'I've hired a new casual employee, Brenda. Which is really confusing because my other one is Belinda, so I keep getting them mixed up and calling one Berinda and the other one Blenda.'

Zac laughed. She was back to her normal self. 'Or you could combine them to save time and call them Blenderinda.'

'Ah, like celebrity couples do.'

'I wouldn't know, I don't keep up with celebrity gossip. Don't even have a television,' he said.

She knew there'd been something missing in his living room when she'd had dinner at his house.

'Well, they combine their names, so Brad and Angelina were called Brangelina, for example.'

He nodded. 'So our cats could be Juleo or Romiet.'

He loved the way her cheeks went glossy and round when she smiled. Like little balloons puffing up inside her cheeks.

He almost added that they could be *Zacril*, but resisted. They weren't a couple, and she certainly didn't want to be one. But he was enjoying getting to know her anyway, and he had figured out that whatever happened or didn't happen between them in the future, he knew that, somehow, they were important for each other. He would persist in building their friendship. He believed in a greater purpose in life, in the journey, and maybe she was here to help him transition back into normal life, whatever that was. And maybe he was here to help her stop deflecting the important things, to stop avoiding the hard stuff just because it hurt, and to understand more about life, the universe, and its wonders. And maybe even help her make amends with her father. And if that was all it would be, then so be it. It would be better than nothing, and better than where he had been before moving to Tarrin's Bay. It was all about progress.

But that didn't change the fact that not a day went by without him thinking of her. Craving her. It was made more difficult by the fact they were next-door neighbours, but even when she was busy and he was occupied and they barely spoke, he still thought of her. Her pretty face was like the sun, greeting him each morning, and the sound of her voice and laugh were his bedtime lullaby. She was the bookends of his days, the support that held him together and kept him going.

She put the hose back on its reel, and a colourful bird came and sat on the birdbath, leaning over to drink from the fresh water. She eyed Zac with a curious expression.

'What is it?' he asked.

'Nothing,' she flicked her hand.

'Bull. I can see the words clambering to get out of your mouth.'

She opened her mouth as her lips stretched into a smile. 'Did you, like, go to rehab or anything? To help you get off the alcohol?' she asked. 'Just wondering, that's all. You don't have to answer.'

'My rehab was in here,' he replied, tapping his head, then his heart. 'And in here.'

Her brow furrowed.

'Mind, heart, and soul,' he said. 'Get those right, and the body will follow.'

'Yeah, I get that you're all new-agey and stuff, but how, like *how*, did you do it?'

This could take a while. In fact, he had thought that maybe he should write about how he had succeeded in making the transition to becoming sober. He hadn't mentioned the alcoholism on his blog. Yet. Didn't know if he ever would. But maybe he should, if it could help others. He sat on the wooden boards of his deck. 'Come here and I'll tell you a bit about it.'

She crossed her arms.

Here we go, defence mode again.

She would say something like, 'Oh, I'm busy, have to go check Facebook', or, 'I should go check on my employees, even though it's my day off'. But she said, 'You come here for once, lazy bum.'

Zac stood. 'You're inviting me over?'

'To my backyard. You can jump over the fence, if you've got the strength. Or take the easy way and go around the side gate.' She eyed him with a challenging stare.

His arms ached from the intense upper body workout he'd done this morning, but he'd be fine. He gripped his hands on the top of the fence, lifted himself up, and swung one leg, and then the other, over it. Romeo stopped chasing some bug on the ground to look up at the intruder. His eyes went wide, as though thinking, 'that's normally what *I* do, you silly human.'

'Water?' April bent down and lifted the end of the hose.

Zac opened his mouth and she laughed. 'I should totally turn this on,' she said.

'You won't. It's too cold. And you'll waste water. They have rules for that, you know.'

'Since when are you interested in rules?'

'In that case...' He walked towards her and took the hose from her, then quickly turned on the tap and sprayed her with water. Her mouth opened wide and she blinked rapidly.

'Hey!' She tried to grab the hose from him. 'It's freezing!'

'Told you.'

She gripped the hose and twisted it to face upwards at him, despite being unable to remove it from his own grip.

Water splashed his face and he laughed. He twisted the hose back to her and she squealed as droplets wet her hair, then reached down and turned off the water flow.

'It's a good thing I don't have to go back to work,' she said. 'I'd have to redo my hair and make-up and that could take a while.' She whacked him on the arm. 'Let's step away from the hose, shall we?'

'Ladies first,' Zac said, holding out his arm but standing close to the hose.

'Um, no,' she said. 'Guests first.'

'Fair enough.' He held up his palms and walked over to her deck and sat on one of the chairs around the table.

'Coffee?' she asked, stepping up onto the deck too.

'Sure.' He didn't have much caffeine, his mind was alert and wired as it was, but it was early in the day.

April brought out two mugs a few minutes later and placed them on the table.

Zac took a sip and the liquid warmed his throat. 'So, how did I do it? Meditation was one of my strategies.'

'Sitting still and chanting?'

'No, sitting still and being calmly aware and present.'

'Wouldn't that make you bored and more likely to want to go and... you know, grab something to deal with boredom?'

'The opposite, actually. Once you get the hang of it. Makes you realise that each breath you take is enough. That in that moment, you don't need anything.'

Her brow creased as she looked into the distance. 'Hmm, I guess that kind of makes sense.'

'Try it,' he said.

'One day.'

'No, right now.' He moved his chair closer to her. 'I'll help.'

'I can't meditate right now, right here in front of you.' She took a long sip of her coffee. 'I'll feel like an idiot.'

'Then I'll do it with you,' he replied. 'Five minutes, how about that? Can't be as challenging as the eye-gazing exercise. We can close our eyes for this one.'

'How do I know you're not going to keep your eyes open and film me with my eyes closed and then put me all over the internet—*Tarrin's Bay candle store owner tries to meditate, it's hilarious, check it out!*'

'Hey, thanks for the idea. I could put it on my blog.'

'Don't you dare.' She eyed him. 'What is your blog address by the way, you haven't told me.'

'And I'm not going to.'

A tiny smile, or was it a smirk, crept onto her lips.

'What?' he asked.

'Nothing,' she said. 'But you should show me some of your poems sometime. Any of them about how annoying your neighbour is?'

'No, but that's the second-best idea you've given me today.' He grinned, and as the late autumn sun's warmth contrasted with the cool air, his inner focus contrasted with his outer desire to simply reach out, touch her hand, her face, anything. Connect with her more. 'Anyway,' he said, 'Close your eyes.'

'You first.'

'Both of us at once,' he said. 'I'll say a few words to help you meditate, then I'll tell you when the time's up.'

'How will you know when the time's up, if you have your eyes closed? Are you going to count to ...' her eyes rolled upwards, 'three hundred seconds?'

'I'll just know,' he said. 'Okay on three, close your eyes.'

She wriggled in her chair to get comfortable and leaned her head back on the wooden slats. He did the same.

'One, two, three.'

She eyed him and waited till his eyes closed.

'Are yours closed?' he asked.

'Yes,' she said. 'Don't you trust me?'

'Do you trust me? I could be watching you and filming you right this second.'

'I guess I'll have to take a chance.'

'Okay, take a big deep breath.'

He took one of his own to guide her, and he could hear her exhalation after a few moments.

'And another,' he added. 'And another. Keep your focus on your breath. In and out.' He breathed slowly along with her, and the air around them fell quiet and calm, apart from the faint hum of the ocean's ebb and flow in the distance, much like their breath. 'If there are any areas of tension in your body, consciously release that tension. When you breathe out, imagine the area melting.' He did the same. 'Since it's your first time, you might find it easier if you think of a calming word and repeat it in your mind each time you exhale. Like calm, or relax, or bliss. If you get distracted, keep coming back to that word.' The word that popped into his own mind was *glow*. April's glow. Not her store, but the glow she had about her. How the room seemed brighter when she entered, how the sky in the backyard seemed to lighten when she was there. 'Keep breathing, and repeating your word. No rush. Be in the moment.'

He meditated with her for a few minutes, then said, 'Okay, if you're ready, slowly open your eyes.' He waited a second or two before opening his, so she wouldn't think he'd been watching her. 'How did that feel?'

Her face was softer, different. 'Weird. Weird, but... interesting. Don't know how relaxed I was, but I did feel more in the moment, so to speak.'

'Good. My work here is done.' He stood. 'Try doing that every day for as long as you can.'

'I'll try to remember.'

'I might have to send you daily reminders,' he said. 'Zac's meditation reminder service.'

'Ah, now there's a business idea,' she said, then tilted her head and looked in his eyes. 'Is that all you did, meditation? And it helped you become sober?'

'That, and learning that addiction is just a habit, not a need. Habits can be broken.'

She didn't respond but nodded slowly as though processing his words.

'It's also a craving for something more. Like... connection. And meaning. And a need to feel something more than you're currently feeling, or the opposite—to stop feeling.'

'Interesting.'

'So I read lots of books, meditated a lot, learned what my body really needed and didn't need, and I'm also stubborn as hell, which helped. Didn't want to quit the quitting.'

April smiled her bow-like smile.

'Plus once I reached the point where I liked the feeling of self-empowerment better than I liked the feeling of being drunk, I knew I had beaten it.'

She eyed him curiously. 'Have you thought about helping others with the same problem?' she asked.

Maybe the meditation had linked her mind with his. 'Yes, I just don't know how yet.'

'Words. You're good with words,' she said, then quickly added, 'so I hear.'

'Yeah. I should just write down everything I know.'

'You totally should.'

'Maybe I will.'

'Good.' April stood and stretched her arms above her head, the arching accentuating her curves, causing warmth to pool in the centre of his body. 'Well, thank you for the impromptu lesson. I shall go and float off inside and get some things knocked off my To Do list.'

'Don't forget to make a To Be list as well,' he said, walking towards the fence.

'Okay, I wish to be able to do all my to dos!'

He laughed, then jumped the fence.

Maybe he did have a greater purpose, to help others. Though he was still in the process of helping himself. For now, at least, he felt there was *another*, more immediate purpose. He went straight to his laptop and clicked 'new post' on his blog, then wrote:

THE PATH TO PURPOSE

Someone else's life I used to wish I could borrow
But as each today merges into tomorrow
I'm realising the reasons I'm here and not there
My daily existence has fruit yet to bear

My aimless wandering through rugged terrain
now has a smooth path that curves into her name
My purpose was only me, up until now,
but now it is her too, some way, somehow

The effects of the spell she has cast can't be cured
Her magic beckons me forward; to her I am lured
Enchanted by her, there is no room for doubt
I will make it my purpose to know her inside and out.

CHAPTER SEVENTEEN

Still meditating?

The text message asked, when April looked at her phone the following week during a quiet moment at the store. She replied:

Ummm…

She'd tried it again a few times. It was okay, but just got boring. Plus she'd been distracted after reading Zac's latest poem, which, as a subscriber, had arrived in her inbox as a new post. She'd thought about going over there and telling him to stop. That she wasn't some conquest. But he didn't know she'd found his blog, and she didn't want to disrupt his creativity if it would help him get through his twelve months of recovery. He wouldn't risk trying it on with her anyway, she knew him well enough now to know he was committed to seeing it through, getting to September first. After that, she had no idea what he'd do, but no point worrying about that now. Besides, his words were like an exotic, undiscovered fragrance, wafting into her awareness in a subtle yet significant way. She'd be lying if she said she didn't want to read more. It was just a fantasy anyway, his poetry. A creative and emotional release for him.

For now, she'd keep the secret unless he wanted to show her his poems.

Zac replied:

> Well, consider this your first of many meditation reminders. Close your eyes right now and breathe.

> What if a customer walks in?

> Then they'll see you with your eyes closed. Big deal.

She liked how matter of fact he was. She closed her eyes and took a few deep breaths. Belinda was on her break, and the store was a quiet haven of soft, slow instrumental music, delicious and inviting scents, and a comforting warmth that enveloped and caressed her. Instead of focusing on a word, she tried to focus on the different aromas in the room, switching her awareness from one to another.

Crisp and cool citrus... orange, lemon, and lime.
Pomegranate, blueberry, raspberry...
Coconut, vanilla, cinnamon...
Za ...

Huh? She opened her eyes. For a moment she thought he was tricking her and had walked in, ready to catch her in the act. He had promised he would walk into her store one day, but she knew he was nowhere near being ready to do that. If he ever would. Which reminded her, she had to read his book. Read the book, and he'd walk in here one day. She better get reading tonight, especially now she had finished the book Olivia gave her, and discovered all its secrets and smiled at the happy ever after.

She texted:

> I did about one minute. That's a start.

> See if you can improve on that tomorrow.
> How's business?

> I need to come up with a way to celebrate my store's birthday in October.

> Something that not only helps you but helps charity?

> Yes, I was thinking that.

> Weather will be nice and warm then, what about something in the park? At night even. You could set up a stall for your candles, and get other businesses to sell some of their stuff too. A percentage of proceeds go to charity. And have a competition. Every purchase goes in the draw.

Excitement bubbled up inside April's mind.

> Shall I employ you as my business coach as well as my meditation mentor?

> Happy to help.

> Thank you, that's actually a really good idea.

> I have a lot of time on my hands to think up such genius ideas.

She chuckled. Then opened her ideas file and jotted down some notes. She could ask some of the local business owners if they'd be interested, see what they thought. Olivia and Mrs

May's would be in on it. Maybe Café Lagoon could set up a portable coffee stand. And some of the crafty people from the monthly markets might also take part. That way it wasn't all about her and her store, it was about the community. Creating a fun event that people would remember. She could also give discount vouchers or special offer vouchers to people who bought her products on the night, to be used in store at a later date and encourage repeat business.

'What's got you looking so excited? Another lovey dovey poem from Zaccy?' Belinda asked as she walked back in, tucking an over-hairsprayed clump of hair from her cheek to behind her ear.

'No, business stuff!'

'Wow, really?'

'Yep. Can you watch things for a little while? I want to go talk to some of the other store owners about an idea.'

April walked around to some of the other terrace shops she thought might be interested. They were. Then she visited Olivia who gave her some more ideas for the night, and said she would help out. Then she went into the ladies boutique in a small arcade behind the brasserie, and almost walked out again. A song was playing, and she didn't know why but it did something to her. As she talked to the store owner, she tried to concentrate on her now perfectly practiced script, but the words from the song kept weaving their way into her consciousness. 'What is this song?' she asked.

'*All of Me*,' the woman said. 'Beautiful, isn't it? My cousin had it at her wedding.'

That was why. It was one of those that-would-be-perfect-at-my-wedding songs. They always made people emotional.

When she walked out of the store, her breaths came faster. Was she having a panic attack or something? Maybe she was dehydrated having walked halfway around town. She should rest. She grabbed a coffee from Café Lagoon and sat at a picnic table in Miracle Park. The same one she'd sat at the day she'd been stood up. She scanned her surroundings and imagined the community event and how it might look. She could use her battery-operated candles on the night to create a glowing atmosphere without causing a safety issue. Maybe she could line the walking and bike track with them, creating a Hansel and Gretel trail towards her store's stall.

The song lyrics suddenly interrupted her thoughts.

Go away, she muttered to herself.

She used to love music, and singing along to songs, and hadn't experienced that sense of connection to a song in a long time. She barely even knew the lyrics to this, but snippets of words crept into her mind. And heart. Something about loving someone for who they were. She would have loved Kyle for who he was, who the accident caused him to be. Somehow. If he'd let her. She missed his smile, his voice, his support. But now *he* needed support, and his parents and carers were providing it instead of her.

A thin film of tears spread across her eyes and she dabbed at the inside corners of her eyes.

No tears.

And no music.

That's all it was. And that's why she didn't listen. Songs only triggered deeply buried emotions and made things more difficult.

Damn memories.

She would just keep focused on her business birthday plans, doing her daily meditation, and reminding herself she was only ever going to be friends with Zac.

By the end of May she had finished reading *The Prophet*. It was a Monday afternoon and she was off work, and had been relaxing on the couch with her legs up.

No time like the present, she thought, getting up and heading towards Zac's house.

She knocked on his front door and waited. She could have called him, but liked to be spontaneous. She had planned to greet him by reciting one of the pieces of wisdom in the book, but the door remained closed.

She peered through the gap in the curtains at the dim interior. Angling her ear towards the window, the faint sound of water trickled, like he was in the shower.

Oh well. She could come back later. Or ...

She dashed back home and got a piece of paper and pen, then came back to his front door. The water sound was still present. She nibbled her bottom lip as she thought, then wrote on the paper:

> The book was great
> It kept me up late
> It made me think a lot
> About the life I've got
> But my words can't express
> I'll have to confess
> It takes talent not luck
> Yep, my poems really suck

She placed it inside the book and on his doormat, then went back home and sent a text:

Surprise on your doorstep. Open it at own risk.

She giggled to herself then flopped on the couch again and scrolled through Facebook. As she ignored a video-gone-viral of some amazing thirteen-year-old singer, the words to that song she'd heard in the clothing store invaded her mind again.

This time it didn't trigger sadness about Kyle. Not as much as before anyway. This time there was something else. Intrigue. Hope. She needed to hear the lyrics, the song, just once, and then maybe she could get it out of her head and move on.

She took a deep breath and searched for *All of Me* by John Legend on iTunes. She only used the account for her store's music. This would be a first.

Her finger tentatively hovered over the preview button, then as she pressed it, she closed her eyes. A sneak peek of the song played and she panicked. She pressed pause.

Okay, okay, it's just one song. I can do this. How can I encourage Zac to get out in the world again if I can't listen to a simple song?

But instead of resuming the preview she clicked 'buy'.

When the song had downloaded, she allowed the music to wash over her, through her, as she closed her eyes and lay on the couch.

As soon as the lyrics started so did the tears. Slowly at first, then in a deluge of overflowing emotion. She leaned over to the drawer under the coffee table and got the box of tissues, dabbing one at her face.

It was too much. She had to press stop.

No, something wouldn't let her. She needed this. Strangely, she needed the pain, the intensity, the cathartic power of the song.

When it had finished, she immediately pressed play again. There was something she couldn't quite grasp the first time, something that made her mind and soul go places that were new. New and intriguing, exhilarating, terrifying, but she wanted it. She wanted it all right now in this moment. The words rang true; some made her think of Kyle, but more so …

It made her think of Zac.

Crazy, weird, amazing, beautiful, damaged Zac.

Oh God, it made her want him. Want to risk it all and accept him the way he was, take a chance. But she had promised herself no. Besides, she'd barely known him long enough to be good friends, let alone more than that. But their conversations had bypassed much of the polite small talk and gone straight to no holds barred, raw, honest interaction.

Why? Why did she have to feel something for someone so wrong?

If the accident hadn't happened, she would be married to Kyle and would never have met Zac. None of this would be happening. But it was. And her life was unrecognisable from the one she'd had and the one she'd planned for.

When the singer sang about crying, she cried even more. The chorus came again and she ached for that unconditional love that she thought would be part of her life by now, that complete acceptance and love for another person that you felt no matter what. Yet here she was, judging someone she hardly knew because he had the same addiction her father had. She didn't know if she could ever love unconditionally again. It was too risky. Too dangerous.

She allowed the tears to flow freely, and played the song a third time. By this time the tears were slowing, but her face was aching and her eyes burning. Halfway through the song there was a knock at the door.

'Oh crap!' She stood, wiping her face fiercely.

She dashed to the bathroom and patted her red face with cold water. Her phone beeped as the song went softer for a second, and when she returned to the living room, she looked at the text:

> I know you're in there. Are you embarrassed by
> your pathetic poem?

If she hadn't been crying so much, she would have laughed.

She glanced at the door, a shadow behind it. His shadow. She could ignore it or say she'd just got out of the shower and was naked. But the song, him, it made her want to try to be honest, open, vulnerable. She needed to let people in, not just on the surface, but deeply. Inside her heart. Even if for a moment.

She opened the door and turned her face away slightly. 'Sorry, I...'

'April, what's wrong?' Zac came in, put something down on the couch, then grasped her arms.

She shook her head and covered her eyes with her hand. 'I didn't want you to see me like this. I'm so embarrassed.'

'Hey, your poem was bad, but not *that* bad.'

She managed a weak chuckle.

His gaze went to the phone on the coffee table, the song still playing. 'You're listening to music?'

She held up her hands in a shrug. 'See? Can't handle it.'

'But you took a step forward. That's good.'

'It's just ...' she wiped her eyes, 'so intense. The feelings, the ...'

'I know, I know.' He slowly slid his arms around her waist, gently pulling her towards his chest. 'Just be with it. Let it flow.'

His voice was smooth and warm beside her ear, like honey; warm, oozing honey that soothed and sweetened the sour, raw intensity of emotion.

He held her like that for the rest of the song, and she tentatively held the sides of his waist. Though his arms were all the way around her, she couldn't quite bring hers to do the

same. But this was enough for now. This was okay. This was...
nice.

'You okay?' He moved his head back slightly to look at her.

'I will be,' she whispered.

'Do you want me to go now? Or should I–'

'Stay,' she blurted, before knowing what she was doing.
'Stay.'

CHAPTER EIGHTEEN

It was late by the time he'd arrived home. They'd ordered pizza and watched mindless TV, which had opened him up to a whole new world he'd forgotten existed. But it was cool in a way, taking a break from the constant awareness and alertness that occupied his mind. He'd also handed her the book he'd brought over, *Ask and it is Given*, by Esther and Jerry Hicks. One of his favourites. She'd said since it was so big it would take her at least till the end of the year to read. To encourage her, he'd promised that for every two chapters she read he'd reward her with some kind of food or beverage. She agreed.

Two and a half months later she was still not finished the book, but was enjoying regular free food courtesy of Zac's Kitchen. And they seemed to have mastered the platonic friendship thing. Tonight's reward was cinnamon cupcakes, made with honey instead of refined sugar, for dessert.

He piped the frosting on top into swirls, pleased with how skilled he'd become in the kitchen. There was one advantage to being home all the time, you had to learn to provide for yourself and get creative. He sprinkled cinnamon on top and smiled at his accomplishment. He placed them on the dining table near the cinnamon candle, which, although burnt down halfway now, still burned bright in the centre of the table.

He glanced at his reflection in the mirror above the mantle.

She'd be here any second.

April knew it had to be done. Zac had suggested it ages ago, but she'd never felt ready. Now she was. Finally.

Before she went to Zac's place for dessert, she needed to put the letter in the envelope and seal it. Sealing the past where it belonged, never to be opened again.

Before she could, though, she had to read it one last time.

Dear Kyle,

This letter has been a long time coming.

I almost didn't write it, and didn't want to bring up the past for you, but the thought of not writing it felt worse, so here goes ...

What I really want to say is: it's okay. It's okay that you didn't want me to stay with you. I'm not angry. I'm not sad. I only want you to have the best life possible with what you've got. You've got a beautiful heart, a strong mind, and amazing parents who I'm sure are doing as much as they can to make your life the best it can be. And your sister, and your brother, too. I'm grateful to them for being there, knowing you have a great support network brings me peace.

I know you think I wouldn't have wanted to stay, but I would have. I want you to know that. Yes, it would have been incredibly hard, the hardest thing both you and I would have ever had to face. But I was committed to you.

I know it hurt you too, to say goodbye. Probably more than me. Definitely more than me. I can't imagine what must have been going through your mind, but now, in hindsight, I think you did what was right for you. And I understand. I'm okay.

I'm doing well, my new leg is making itself at home. So I might not be the best dancer these days, oh well! I have a new business. New friends. A new life. And I want to thank you for that. Because you gave that to me. You let me go, even though I didn't want to leave, so I could have the life you wanted for me. It hurt at first, but now I can see the gift. Thank you.

And thank you for the memories. I'll cherish them. They all matter. You matter. You were an important part of my life, and I'm grateful and honoured to have known you.

I'll say goodbye, once again. But this time with a grateful heart.

And I want you to know that even though our relationship as it was has come to an end, you were, are, and always will be, loved.

April.

She'd thought there'd be tears, but they'd come and gone as she'd written it. Re-reading it was easier, and solidified the resolve within her to finally move on from her history with Kyle and turn the page to a new chapter.

She folded the letter and slid it into the envelope that she'd addressed to his parents' house. She'd post it tomorrow, and didn't mind one way or the other if she got a reply in some shape or form, she only needed to say the words and be done with it.

It was over.

Kyle was her past, and her future lay open and ready for her to grasp and embrace, wherever it may lead.

She slipped her arms into her light cotton cardigan, pushing up the three-quarter sleeves to below her elbows, picked up her phone and keys, and stepped outside. The night was cool but comfortable, a slight warmth teasing and tempting her as the breeze tickled her skin. Spring would be here soon. So would Zac's twelve-month mark. Over the past few months they'd become closer, but more like good friends, and she was happy with that. She could handle that. In fact, she wasn't sure she even felt the same level of attraction as before. Maybe it had only been temporary lust. Either way, things were good. And safe. Because she knew he would not risk his recovery by trying to become more than friends before his anniversary. Even his poems had slowed down, and the ones he did share on the blog were more about his own journey than the elusive next-door neighbour. After September first, however, that was something she had tried her hardest not to think about. *Wait till the time comes,* Zoe had advised.

But tonight: cupcakes.

'What will you do when the book is finished and you are no longer entitled to free food rewards?' Zac asked as soon as he opened the door to her arrival.

'Um,' she said, 'bribe you?'

He smiled and welcomed her inside.

'Oh yum.' She eyed the cupcakes on the table. 'I could get used to this.'

'If you eat more than one you have to help me clean up,' he said.

'Fair enough.' She sat and Zac placed a cupcake on a small plate for her. 'Do you need a fork?'

'Huh?' She glanced at him. 'Oh, a fork. No, cupcakes need to be eaten with the hands, they taste better that way.' She smiled.

Zac grinned. 'What did you think I said?'

'Huh? Nothing. Fork. I don't need one. All good. Let's eat.' She picked up the cupcake and took a bite. 'Mm, very good,' she mumbled.

'Weren't you taught not to talk with your mouth full?' Zac spoke, as he munched on his cupcake.

'Weren't you?'

'Yes, but do I follow the rules?' he replied.

'That was going to be my answer. Answer thief.'

'You started it.'

'How?'

'By talking with your mouth full.'

She tore off a small fragment of her cupcake and tossed it at him. He picked it up from near his plate where it landed and tossed it back at her. She returned the favour; this time, it landed on the floor beside him.

'You mess, you clean,' he said.

She stood, a smug smile on her face, and walked to his side of the table. Kneeling had once been extremely difficult, but she was used to it now, having to bend down to deal with Romeo. She stood right beside Zac, eyeing him off, then slowly bent to the floor and picked up the crumb near his foot. On the way up, her gaze traced the length of his legs, his waist, his torso, and then met his face. 'Five second rule?' she asked, holding the crumb near his mouth.

He took her hand. 'If that's the case, you eat it.'

Maintaining her eye contact with him, she opened her mouth slowly, held the crumb close to her lips.

'You like tasking risks?' he asked.

'Maybe,' she put the crumb down on the edge of his plate and went back to her chair.

Maybe she did.

This was getting dangerous. She was clearly flirting. He could barely keep his eyes off her plump lips when she'd eaten her cupcakes. Two and a half cupcakes, because they'd shared the third one. He had to keep his cool though. Still two weeks until September. And even so, who knew what she'd be like then. She'd made it clear she thought getting involved with a recovering alcoholic would be trouble. She was probably flirting now, testing the waters, safe in the knowledge that he wouldn't give in, his stubbornness and determination standing strong to make the twelve-month mark without any disruptions.

Housework.

That might help.

'Time to clean up,' he said, standing abruptly. He went into the kitchen and filled the sink with soapy water.

'You already licked the bowl?' she asked, sidling up next to him.

'Yep. Sorry.' He shrugged, then picked up the bowl he'd made the frosting in. 'Wash or dry?' he asked.

'I'll wash. You dry.' She grabbed a tea towel and flicked it at him. He grabbed it off her and flung it over his shoulder.

She giggled, then washed the bowl and handed it to him.

'You missed a bit.' He pointed to a microscopic piece of frosting.

She peered closely. 'So I did.' She wiped it off. 'Well, it *is* challenging to concentrate with you looking all masculine and sexy with that tea towel slung over your shoulder.'

He laughed. So much for housework dampening the flirty atmosphere. 'In that case, I'd better take it off.' He caught her gaze then grasped the end of the tea towel and slowly slid it off his shoulder, then flung it around in circles above his head.

'Ha-ha! Are you trying to be a stripper or a cowboy?'

'What do you want me to be?'

'A stripping cowboy?' She eyed him with raised eyebrows then burst out laughing. The sweetest sound filled the room.

He stepped away from the sink and put even more momentum into his tea towel flinging, then attempted to lasso her. The tea towel landed around her neck, and he grabbed both ends, pulling her closer. 'Gotcha,' he whispered.

Her laughter stopped, and she looked into his eyes. Then she gave him a brief, quick, courteous kiss on the cheek.

'What was that for?' he asked.

'To say thanks. For encouraging me to write that letter to Kyle. I did it. Today.'

He released her from the tea towel and she turned to the sink, picking up the cupcake baking tray to wash. 'It helped. Like, really helped. So thanks.' Her body faced the sink, but she turned her head to look at him again.

'My pleasure,' he replied. 'That was unexpected. And... nice,' he said, touching his face where her lips had been. 'I'll never wash my cheek again!'

April pointed the dishwashing brush at him, water dripping to the floor. 'You'd better, or I'm not kissing it again!'

He leaned in closer. 'That's okay, I can kiss yours instead.' He pecked her cheek, warm and soft from laughter.

'But what if I never wash *mine* again?' she asked.

He furrowed his brow and stroked his chin between his thumb and forefinger. 'Then I'll just have to kiss you somewhere else next time.'

She had no idea how to respond to that. Her heart wanted him to kiss her somewhere else, her body wanted it, but her head said, 'are you crazy?' So she scrubbed the cupcake tray like mad. 'These things are hard to clean,' she said.

'Here.' He handed her a different brush with steel wool attached.

'Thanks.'

They washed everything and dried everything and exchanged only necessary information until everything was put away and the kitchen sink and counter cleared.

April's phone beeped with a text from her mum:

> How are things? Long-time no speak. Call me
> for a chat when you can.

> All good, busy atm, call tomorrow.

'Have you listened to any more music, April? Since the last time?'

She turned to face him. 'Music? Why do you ask?'

He shrugged. 'Popped into my head when I saw your phone.'

She leaned her hand against the counter. 'Just the one song,' she said.

'So nothing since?'

'No, I mean, the same song. Over and over.' She brushed her hair behind her shoulder. 'I'm weird.'

'*All of me?*'

'You remember?'

He nodded. 'I've been listening to that one too.'

'It... I...' *It reminds me of you.* 'I just like it.'

'Good,' he said. Then a hint of a smile softened his face and he asked, 'When was the last time you danced, Miss April Vedora?'

'Danced?' she asked. 'Why do you want to know that?'

'I'm curious. I like discovering random facts about people. I like asking weird questions. You know me.'

I know you.

Yes, she did. At what point did he cease to be just her neighbour? She didn't know what they actually were... friends, she guessed, but even that didn't seem to be an appropriate label for their bizarre relationship.

'And I'm guessing if you haven't listened to much music then you haven't danced for a while.'

She glanced down at her leg. 'Not to mention the fact that I probably wouldn't be the most coordinated dancer anymore.'

'That's no excuse.' He folded the tea towel and hung it from the hook on the cupboard door.

She widened her eyes at him. 'Oh, is that right? I'd like to see you try, with this piece of metal.'

'Dancing is done from the heart, not the feet,' he said, patting his chest with his palm.

She crossed her arms. 'I think a lot of professional dancers would disagree.'

He crossed his arms too. 'Oh, I think they *would* agree, that even if someone has expert technical skill, if there's no heart and soul in it, it would miss that something special.'

April uncrossed her arms and put her hands on her hips. 'My wedding day.'

He raised his eyebrows.

'I would have danced at my wedding day. So my last time was at our rehearsal for the dance we were going to do.'

He gave a slow, understanding nod. Then, he moved in front of her, up close, and gently lifted her hand. 'We're going to dance,' he whispered. Before she could spurt forth an objection from her mouth, he pressed his finger to her lips.

You know me too.

Silently, he led her to the centre of the living room, switching off the kitchen light on the way, so that only the light from the cinnamon candle illuminated the room with its warm, orangey glow.

Juliet lay curled up on the couch, but lifted her head sleepily as Zac took his phone from his pocket and placed it on the coffee table.

When the familiar music filled the silence, April's heart beat faster.

No, no. I can't do this.

Not this song. My song. Our *song.*

'Just one dance,' Zac whispered, taking her hand again and holding it up to the side, putting his other hand on her waist. Heat from his skin spread along her arm and up into her body, as the music spread into her awareness, swirling and teasing like a breeze, lifting up stored emotions and flapping them around like leaves on a tree.

Like in a trance, she lifted her other arm up and placed it on his shoulder, her hand barely big enough to fully grasp the roundness of the muscle.

The lyrics began, and it was as though they'd been written for each other. Their connection, her attraction to him, it hadn't dampened through familiarity and comfortable friendship as she'd thought. It was here, in full force. Calling to her.

Whatever this was, it defied logic and reason. It just was. It sent her crazy and completely sane at the same time. It made her light-headed yet grounded all at once.

April moved with Zac as he swayed slowly to one side, then the other side, and back again. Swaying, dancing, though her feet were still. It had been so long, but the emotional rhythm of the music and the heat emanating from his body melted her into submission; a sweet, slow surrender.

When the chorus came, she looked up, and his eyes watched hers, as though the words were being spoken without sound.

Something shifted inside, like she'd trodden on a sandy hill and it had crumpled beneath her foot. There was no stability here, in this moment. Each beat of the song, each sway of her body, led her further and further into unknown territory.

Zac's hand moved from her waist, up, up, until it reached her face. She could feel the tingling warmth before he'd even touched her cheek. And then it was there. The backs of his fingers, trailing gently down her cheek.

And his eyes. On her eyes. Like before when they'd done the experiment, only stronger.

His breath was close, too close. Like he was breathing into her, and she needed it. His oxygen, his power. Him.

His lips were almost on hers. Like his hand, she could feel them without touching them; hot, hungry... heaven.

A small sigh escaped from within her as her lips lightly brushed against his. Not a kiss, but a touch, a hint of things to come.

The song was about love, but this couldn't be love. This wasn't what love had felt like with Kyle. This was different, this was ...

A deep, sharp breath entered her lungs.

This was *stronger*.

And it was that realisation that made her move her face away from his, break free of his hold and dash out the door. It wasn't only about the alcoholism now. If she were to have this and then lose it, for some unexpected reason, it would hurt more than anything else she had experienced. She couldn't deal with that. She couldn't risk it. She had to get out now before it had a chance to take hold of her completely.

CHAPTER NINETEEN

I t was probably for the best that April had given Zac the silent treatment over the past two weeks. Not that she had completely ignored him, she'd sent a message saying she needed some space. She'd even finished reading the book and left it on his doorstep, this time without a poem, just a note saying it had really helped. Zac had just had to live out each day, counting them, waiting for D-day. And now it was here.

He had done it.

He had gone twelve months and reached the milestone he'd promised himself. Promised Johnny. He knew it didn't mean he was magically cured, and that he could forget all the challenges had ever occurred, but it was important to him that he had reached that date without taking one little sip. And without giving in to other temptations.

He rolled over in bed and looked at his strength tattoo. He stroked it with his finger, smiling.

April's face flashed in his mind.

Reaching this date also didn't mean he would magically be ready and able to start something with her, nor did it mean she would suddenly accept his past and the addiction that had once consumed him. But he felt free. Free to start making more progress in all areas of his life.

He stood and stretched, the morning sun streaming through his blinds. No matter what happened or didn't happen between them, this was going to be a good day. He was ready for it.

And, he thought, as a realisation dawned... *I am ready. Ready for her too. I have been all along.*

What he wasn't ready for was the possibility that she may not want anything to do with him. And even if she did, would she ever trust him, trust life, or would she be forever watching him, waiting for the signs, looking for her father in every move he made?

Those questions weren't for now. Today was about him.

He turned on his phone and returned his sponsor's missed call.

Then he looked at his wall calendar and instead of putting another cross on the day like he had on all the others before, he drew a big smiley face on September first.

First thing on the To Be list: satisfied stomach. Time for bacon and eggs.

His stomach grumbled as he prepared breakfast, and when he was indeed satisfied, he jumped in the shower and changed into jeans and a new t-shirt he'd ordered online to wear today. He laughed. He was starting to feel like a woman. But he'd wanted things to be new and different today, to signify the new beginning. And something else that would signify that new beginning was waiting for him outside.

He went out to the back deck and eyed the two small trees he would be planting. One for him, and one to remember Johnny. He put on his gardening gloves and carried each to the area near the fence facing the street. He dug into the soil he'd prepared with mulch the day before, creating a small crater to plant the star magnolias. He removed each from its pot and carefully embedded them into the ground, keeping enough space between them to allow for their rounded shape to grow and develop fully. Juliet scurried around, sniffing the ground and then dashing off like some invisible creature had spooked her. Soon, she'd exhaust herself and find a shady place to laze the day away. He may even do the same.

When both were planted and watered, he stood back with hands on hips and surveyed his new trees; a few small flowers already sprouted. They would bloom into a mass of white star-shaped flowers, reaching up and out. They would remind him to aim high, keep the hope alive, and remember how far he'd come. They would be his daytime stars, while at night he could gaze up at the sky through the telescope and watch the sparkling lights of the universe, shining down on him.

Both small trees were roughly around the same size, though the one on the left was slightly taller. He remembered when he and Johnny had measured themselves and found to be the exact same height at one point. From then on it had become a competition as to who would grow faster and taller. They'd kept measuring themselves, and Johnny would try to stretch his body up as high as possible, but he never reached the same height as Zac again. Zac had had a growth spurt soon after and Johnny was always trying to catch up. 'Yours can be the one on the left,' Zac said out loud. 'Maybe you'll tower over me this time.' He brought his hand swiftly to his forehead and saluted Johnny's tree. 'I'll never forget you, bro.'

Juliet dashed past his feet and up onto the deck, then leapt off the deck and onto the grass again. Zac turned around and watched her playing joyfully, and the slowly moving clouds in the perfect blue sky caught his eye. He gazed up, squinting, at one of the clouds, it had moved and morphed from what it had been a moment ago, but he could have sworn that it had resembled a smiling face. He smiled back, the sun warming his cheeks and the spring breeze washing away the last twelve months and delivering the promise of something new his way.

———

April smiled at Belinda as her employee left the store, excited about some big party she was attending that night. April's plans were a simple dinner with Zoe and Lisa and Olivia, but this time, indoors. Zoe arrived at the store and when April closed up, they went to pick up some takeaway to bring back to April's house.

'You sure we can't invite him over?' Zoe asked, looking between the closed blinds of the kitchen window as she lifted one up.

'Don't spy on him! It's his anniversary today, of going sober. I don't want to disturb him.' She'd ended up telling the others about his alcoholism.

'But haven't you at least congratulated him or anything?' Zoe asked.

'No, should I have? I don't want to get in the way. He's probably planned some ritual or meditation or ceremony to mark the occasion. And what would I do, send a card saying "Congratulations! Hope you have a wild night celebrating your sobriety!"?'

'Just send a text,' said Olivia. 'Something simple.'

'Yeah,' agreed Zoe. 'I'll do it for you. Where's your phone?' She reached for April's pocket.

'Hey! I can text him myself.'

'Well, no dessert for you until you do.' Olivia held up the ice-cream container.

'Pushy lot, you are.' She found him in the text messages and typed:

> Sorry it's late but I wanted to say well done on achieving your 12-month mark. Hope you had a good day.

She showed it to her friends and cousin. 'There, happy?'

Lisa grabbed the phone.

'Lisa!'

She typed something, and April grabbed it back a moment later. Her mouth dropped open on seeing the unsent message:

> Now that it's been 12 months, can we please just get it on?

The others peered at the screen and laughed. Zoe said, 'Yes! Send it!' but April deleted it.

'Seriously, I think you're over-worrying,' said Zoe. 'I get the whole alcoholic situation, but Ape, he's different to your dad. Give him a chance.'

'I promised myself. I promised my mother, that I would never get involved with an alcoholic, or ex-alcoholic, whatever you want to call him,' she huffed. 'Did you know that my mum takes anti-anxiety medication? She's been overloaded with drama in her life with Dad, she doesn't need to be worrying about me too. She's had enough of that the past couple of years, and hey—why not add a man with a history of alcohol abuse into the equation! Daughter of the year, I'd be.'

Olivia placed her hand on April's arm. 'Honey, but what do you want? This is your life, not hers.'

Him. Simple as that. Him. But without the risk and uncertainty, which wasn't possible. 'It doesn't matter.'

'So you like him, but don't want the drama, or the potential for problems down the track,' said Zoe. 'So do what I originally suggested and have a fling—no strings attached. He gets to break his drought, and you get this frustrated attraction out of your system so you can move on. Win-win situation.' She gave a nod and crossed her arms.

Her phone beeped:

Thanks April.

'Is that it?' Zoe asked. 'Is that going to be the extent of your conversation, and if the world ended tonight you'd be happy with that?'

Hell no.

'Interesting perspective,' said Olivia. 'Makes you think, doesn't it? What would we do differently if the world was going to end tonight ...' She nibbled her bottom lip. 'For starters, I'd have to say a teary farewell to you guys and get home to my beautiful daughter.' Olivia took a sudden breath. 'Oh God, why do I allow myself to think such awful things?!'

'Because Zoe put the thoughts in your head,' replied April. 'And the world is not going to end tonight, so we don't need to worry.'

'I'd eat chocolate and binge watch one of my favourite shows,' said Lisa. 'Because I'd hate to die and miss out on finding out what happens next, that would be a disaster.'

April laughed. 'Priorities, huh?'

Her cousin shrugged.

If the world was to end... April would say goodbye to her friends and family, tell her dad she didn't blame him, give Romeo the biggest of cat cuddles, and...

She would go to Zac.

CHAPTER TWENTY

Thankfully the world didn't end the next day, and it was still alive and kicking a week later too. April was staying late at work on a Sunday, busy making plans for her store's birthday celebrations for the next month. The discussions she'd had with the girls last weekend were losing their impact the more she immersed herself into everyday life. But the fact that she was aware of this made her realise how often she'd done that throughout her life—distracted herself with busy-ness, to avoid dealing with the emotional issues, like was she ever going to not feel anything for Zac? Would she ever be able to move on? Or should she, like her friends had suggested, just get the whole thing out of her system? She also realised she must have learnt that distraction coping strategy from her mother; counteract each challenge with other, more 'normal' things.

Maybe Zac was doing the same. She'd been courteous and friendly, but still kept her distance somewhat over the past week. And he hadn't shown any signs of trying to get inside her head again, or win her over, or charm her with his cooking or wit. Maybe he was indeed moving on. Moving forward. Having realised that April was reluctant. And now that the twelve-month mark had passed, that enticing sense of the forbidden was gone. Perhaps that was all it had been between them up till now, something that thrived on temptation and the inability to give in to it.

Before she closed the store, she checked her email. A new post had arrived from Zac's blog, and she clicked the link, expecting another self-reflective insight into his mind or the universe or general life philosophy. But her breath caught in her throat as she read the first line ...

Her smile is a melody I hear with my heart,
    Her eyes a symphony in which I wish to take part.
    The sights, the sounds, all senses consumed,
    By being around her my soul is exhumed.

Temptation offers its hand in a wave,
    Connection, emotion, intensity I crave.
    A synergistic dance of two souls in the night,
    Swaying, merging, ready to take flight.

A single moment ripples the ribbon of time
    Like a drop of my poison, its sweetness sublime.
    But that moment so fleeting, so pure, so raw,
    Leaves a beautiful stain I can no longer ignore.

The chill of July cools my burning heart,
    September's smile promises a fresh new start.
    Like ocean waves my needs ebb and flow,
    But I'll always long for April's Glow.

Her hands shook, her heart raced, her skin became warm and sweaty. Conflicted by the beauty of the prose and the inappropriateness of using her name and her store name, she stood quickly, her balance unsteady. She gripped the counter and tried to calm her breathing.

She had to go see him.

Not to surrender to the power of his words, or get the passion out of her system, but because this had to stop. He had to stop.

Zac had reread a lot of his blog over the past couple of hours, and deduced that there was a decent amount of content to make a start on a book. A book about his journey to recovery, and how self-discovery and poetry had been his saviour. The only thing he needed to work on next was his fear of not being anonymous anymore. He would have to make it known who he was, and be prepared to stand up and announce his experiences, his flaws, his triumphs, to the world. Or at least, anyone who was interested enough to listen. And, he realised, he hadn't even shared his poetry with April yet. And he wondered why she hadn't pestered him about it over the last several months. Maybe if she read some she would see. She might understand more, and see him for who he really was.

He looked up from his deck chair, over his laptop, at her house, the sky darkening behind it. He'd thought he'd heard her front door opening, which meant she'd be coming out back soon to get Romeo inside before he jumped the fence for his evening rendezvous with Juliet. He got up and put his laptop inside, filling a bowl with food for Juliet, then returned to the deck to water his potted plants.

Just as he thought, the back door opened. But she didn't call out for Romeo.

'Zac,' she said, looking his way. That was a first.

'That is me,' he replied.

'I have to confess something.' She walked down the deck steps and over to the fence where he met her. She propped her hands on top of the fence, her pink fingernails curving over onto his side of the fence, shiny and bright.

'Confess? You're not the type to keep secrets, what is it?' Unless, was she about to tell him how she really felt?

'I've read your blog.'

'Oh.' He stepped back a little. 'How did you find it?'

'I didn't. My employee, Belinda did. Sorry. I mentioned ages ago that my new neighbour was a poet and had a blog, and somehow it came out that you were in the army, and somehow, she used her internet powers to find it and she did. *Winning the War Within*, right?'

He nodded. He didn't know whether to be flattered or embarrassed. If he'd known, he may not have posted the poem earlier today. 'So you've seen today's ...'

'Yes.' She took a deep breath. 'Look, you're really good. I mean, *really* good. They're beautiful. But you shouldn't have used my name, or my store's name.'

He slipped his hands into his pockets. 'It was used in a symbolic way. April's Glow, you know, the month, and the glow of autumn colours, that sort of thing.' And her name. And her glow.

'I get that, but anyway, it's not just that. It's the others too. I've read them all. I'm flattered, I think they're lovely, but... please stop, Zac. Please.'

'Why, April?' He removed his hands from his pockets and propped them up on the fence aside hers. 'Why should I stop doing something that brings me joy? Something that helps me express things I'm clearly not allowed to express with you?'

She diverted her gaze, but kept her hands on the fence as though she might fall over. 'Because... because it's uncomfortable for me, knowing you're thinking, feeling, those things, when you live next door.'

'So don't read it then.'

'That doesn't change the fact that—'

'That what, April? That I have feelings for you? Yes, there you have it. Out in the open, laid out in simple terms instead of my fancy rhyming words.'

She caught his eye for a split second then diverted her gaze again.

'It's too hard to be around you,' she said softly.

'We're neighbours. We're going to be around each other occasionally. And I thought we were also friends.'

'I don't want to be friends.' She lowered her face.

It was like he'd been slapped in the face. This was it, she was making a stand, and maybe one of them would have to move house in order to deal with the situation. 'You can't keep going hot and cold like this, April,' he said. 'You need to make a decision so we can both move on with our lives, you need to—'

'I want to be more than friends.'

What?

'But I can't,' she added. 'So we're in a bit of a pickle.'

'Can't or won't?'

She managed a brief look into his eyes. 'You know the answer, Zac. And you know why.'

'So you're judging me based on your past experience again. Assuming I'm like your father, assuming I'm not strong enough to stay sober.'

'It's not just that, it's... I can't... If I ever lost someone again, I don't know if ...' She returned her gaze to meet his.

He moved his hands on top of hers on the fence, holding them in place with assurance. 'Who says you'd lose me?'

He thought something glimmered in her eye, a subtle flicker of possibility, a sign that he was getting through to her. Until she said, 'I can't risk it. I'm sorry.' She removed her hands from beneath his.

'So if we can't be friends, and we can't be more than friends ...' he mused.

She shrugged.

'April, you're thinking too much about the past *and* about the future. And you don't know what the future holds. What about the present? What about living in the now? The moment? You can't live in regret and fear. You can only live right here, right now, take your next best step.' His voice became urgent, impatient.

'Oh yes, live in the moment,' she said, throwing her hands up in the air. 'That's what everyone says. But what about the consequences?'

'And what about the good consequences?' he replied. 'So what if things get messy, or uncertain, or we make mistakes. That's life. That's how we learn. But not embracing something you feel out of fear of what may or may not happen? That's not living.'

She rubbed at her arm.

'You have a life, April. Live it. Do what you want.'

She looked at him, returned to the fence and gripped it. 'And what do *you* want?'

'I want you,' he said. 'Plain and simple.' There was no going back now. 'Whether it's for a night, a week, a month, or years... I want you.'

He was done being patient, if she didn't reciprocate now, he'd leave it alone. Move on.

A loud exhalation escaped her mouth. She was silent, her face tense, her hands white at the knuckles. 'I can't,' she said, then released her grip and walked up to the deck, Romeo following her inside, and the door to her house, and heart, closing with a snap.

CHAPTER TWENTY-ONE

April's body trembled when she got inside. She dropped the cat food all over the floor, then picked up all the pieces one by one, cursing herself. She paced around the living room, then the kitchen. Her body buzzed with unused energy, potential that had failed to be realised, desire that had been building up too long. The constant battle between yes and no and head and heart was waging its own war within, and she didn't know if she could win it.

She should feel better, having made her decision and openly declared what she was unwilling to do, to settle for. But she felt worse. If this was what doing the right thing for herself and her mother was like, then what would risking it all and being proved right feel like? Surely it would be worse. Which meant, she had to stick to her guns. Temporary pain for long-term gain.

She checked her phone and was about to call Zoe when she found herself on Zac's blog again.

She reread the poem about April's Glow ...

Temptation offers its hand in a wave,
Connection, emotion, intensity I crave.

Oh, she craved it too. A relationship was a no-no, but she couldn't deny the fire between them.

Live in the moment.

What if the world ended tonight?

If the world ended, she wouldn't be here at home pacing the house and worrying about things that hadn't happened yet.

She would get out there and live.

'You can't live in regret and fear. You can only live right here, right now, take your next best step.'

She recalled Zac's words.

The house seemed devoid of oxygen. She flung open the front door and sucked in a breath, washing her lungs with the salty night air. In the distance, a couple walked arm in arm towards the town. They were living. Doing something. Together.

She was here. Doing nothing. Alone.

She placed her hand on her waist, at the side, where Zac had placed his when he'd slow danced with her. She tried to recall its firmness and warmth. And the touch of his hands on hers before, on the fence. She could garner a glimpse, a hint, of the sensation, but no more. She strained to remember, to feel, but the sensations were fleeting and just beyond her reach. She needed to feel it again, *him* again. Even if once.

Hell, she needed more than that.

Maybe living in the moment was exactly what was needed. She needn't worry about getting deeply involved, she'd made it clear to Zac where she stood on that. But now, right now, she didn't know how she could go on without expressing this part of herself that was burning inside.

She looked over to his house with its calm facade.

Each step she took towards it lit a trail of flames, desire building momentum and propelling her towards him.

She reached the door and knocked hard and fast.

It opened.

He stood there, shock and surprise on his face.

'I want you too,' she said. 'Right now, I want you too.'

She flung her arms around him and pressed her lips against his in one sudden, urgent, all-consuming kiss. His arms flew around her back, hands moved up into her hair, delving and embracing, pulling her as close as humanly possible.

But it still wasn't close enough.

She kicked the door shut behind her with her good leg, then they moved further inside, lips teasing and tangling, hands everywhere. She pulled up his t-shirt at the back. The heat of his skin, and the curves and firmness of his muscles delighted her hands as they moved up his back. Oh God, this would be the end of her. She couldn't get enough.

She yanked his t-shirt up and moved back a tad to let his arms up as she pulled it over his head, his inked upper body a piece of art right in front of her, urging her to appreciate and explore its beauty. She ran her hands along his chest, looked deep into his eyes; raw, needy, exposed. Mirroring her emotions in this moment.

'You sure?' he whispered.

'I'm sure,' she breathed her reply.

He led her down the hallway and into his room, and as she stood near the entrance, he walked to the corner and turned on a small salt lamp, giving the room a fiery orange glow and an otherworldly ambience. He turned around, the lamp's colour accentuating his tanned, sculpted body. As they slowly moved towards each other across the room, she lifted her slim-fitting black top up and over her head, surprising herself as well as him.

Zac smiled, a delicious, appreciative smile. He brought his hands up to her bare arms, sliding upwards and curving them over her shoulders like he was lathering her with warm oil, then trailed one hand delicately across her chest.

Her skin tingled, every nerve on high alert and hyper-reactive to his touch. When his lips touched her neck, she leaned her head back as the tender warmth softened her, made her crave more. His kisses trailed across her collarbone, to the centre of her chest, to the other collarbone, and up to the other side of her neck. Warm hands travelled from her waist to her back, his fingers lifting and teasing the straps of her bra. He pulled her closer, and as their breaths collided in front of each other in a whirlwind of need, she looked into the endless sea of his eyes. Right here, right now, this was where she was meant to be. As though everything before had been only practice, preparation, leading her to this moment. Nothing else mattered but their primal, inexplicable connection. Their need to be with each other completely.

Holding onto her back, he moved backwards with her until they reached the bed. She touched his chest, moved her hands up and over his shoulders, then leaned close and kissed the tattoo of an eagle that sat between his right shoulder and pec. As though following a sensory treasure hunt, she moved to the side of him, her fingers tracing one tattoo to the next, until she was facing his back. She ran her hand down his spine, following the five symbols inked on his skin. 'What are these?' she whispered, as she leaned in close to his ear.

He turned his head slightly, his hand coming up and over his shoulder to caress her cheek. 'The five elements: earth, air, fire, water, and spirit.'

'They're beautiful,' she said. 'You're beautiful.' She fanned her hands out across his lower back, over the skin poetry she'd seen that night at dinner, then moved to his other side and around to face his front. She sat on the bed, her fingers hooking onto the top of his jeans, as he tousled her hair with exquisite tenderness like he was a sculptor and she was his art.

'There's another tattoo,' he said. 'Right here.' He led her

hand to his right hip, and slid it just under his jeans. She gazed at the muscled V shape that went from his hips to below his jeans, then she unbuttoned and unzipped them. He stepped out of his jeans, and she slowly lowered his underwear to just below his hipbone, revealing four words inscribed at a forty-five-degree angle:

For your eyes only ...

April smiled, leaned forward and pressed four kisses to his skin, one on each word, her fourth kiss lingering. Zac released a delicious, slow, deep sound, like a cross between a moan and a sigh. She glanced up, connecting with his downward gaze, his smile mirroring hers. He bent down and kissed her forehead, then her nose, then her lips, and his hands lowered to the top of her skirt.

She tensed. 'My leg,' she whispered. 'I need to ...' She wriggled out of her skirt, then rolled down the cover of her prosthesis. She pressed the button to release the prosthetic limb and pulled it off, placing it on the floor, then removed her sock and the silicone liner from her stump. 'All done,' she said, looking up at him.

'You're beautiful too,' he said. 'All of you.' He stroked her left thigh and gently squeezed the flesh at the top of her knee. She quivered at his touch, at the sensation of someone touching that part of her that had felt only pain.

Despite the dim light, her eyes were drawn to his left thigh also, where three deep, fragmented scars were embedded into his skin. She caressed the bumpy and fragile textures with her fingers.

'Shrapnel scars,' he said. His hand came down to meet hers at his thigh and she entwined her fingers with his, their eyes and hearts connecting, bonded by their wounds.

Zac leaned down and grasped her face, delivering a soft and luscious kiss to her mouth, and she allowed herself to fall backwards onto the bed as his body moved over hers. He helped her manoeuvre to the centre of the bed then lowered his body completely on top of her. The weight of him against her was like a whole-body kiss. She revelled under his firm reassurance, as their lips shared in the ecstasy of what their souls had been longing to express for so long.

She was transported to another realm, as his lips journeyed down her neck, her chest, and the curves of her cleavage. The subtle release of her bra clasp made her breath quicken, even more so when he delicately caressed and kissed the soft skin of her breast. 'Zac,' she sighed.

There was no self-consciousness in the unfamiliarity of his touch, only pure comfort at being with him in this way, like they'd known each other deeply many times. Yet, at the same time, the moment held an overpowering sense of newness that urged to be explored and discovered.

Zac rolled to the side and opened his bedside drawer. He prepared himself, and as his hands went to her waist, and his fingers lifted underneath the hem of her lace knickers and slid them down, heat filled her centre and she ached for him.

He moved on top of her. She grabbed his hips, hungry for his skin. She breathed out a moan as his body united perfectly with hers, in confirmation of what had already been united deep within.

With ease she matched his rhythm, moving together as one. It felt poetic, like their bodies had their own language… their skin the paper, their warm breaths the words, their rhythm the rhyme, as they formed beautiful prose together.

Time disappeared, the world disappeared, it was only them. Never had she felt so all-consumed, so adored, so exhilarated.

As their connection heightened, he held his hand to her left cheek and his gaze delved deep into hers. Raw, honest beauty looked back at her. Into her. Then his eyes rolled back and a raw, primal sound emerged as the intensity of his release overtook all her senses, each merging together into one glorious mesh of bliss.

They relaxed together into a warm, liquid-like embrace. His skin, her skin, unified. His hands tangled in her hair as he breathed exhausted kisses into the side of her neck, and she cradled his head with her hand, the other rubbing his back slowly and sinuously up and down as though she were trailing her hand back and forth in still water.

They lay together for a long time, until Zac propped his head against his hand as he rested his elbow on the bed beside her. 'How are you, beautiful?'

April smiled softly. 'I'm revelling in sweaty bliss.'

'Sweaty, huh?' he asked. 'You know what you need, right?' He twirled a strand of her hair around his finger.

'A shower and some deodorant?' She giggled.

'I've got a better idea,' he said, climbing over her and off the bed.

She lay with one arm resting above her head on the pillow, her eyes not leaving Zac's body as he walked naked from the room.

Moments later the sound of thick, running water filled the blissful silence, followed by Zac's footsteps as he walked in and out of the hallway, doing whatever he was doing. She smelled a faint hint of rose, and the familiar scent of candle wax melting. She sighed in anticipation, knowing exactly what he was up to.

After a while he returned, and her breath held tight for a moment when he walked into the room. She wasn't used to seeing him that way, but she sure could get used to it. He grinned as he approached the bed, and slid his arms underneath her, lifting her up. She giggled and held on tight.

He carried her into the bathroom, lit only by an array of

small candles, steam rising sensually from the bathtub filled with bubbles.

'I haven't had a bath in years,' she said. Mostly because showering was quicker and easier. 'I think I've forgotten how.'

'Good thing I'm here to guide you,' he said, leaning her closer to the tub and letting her right foot touch the water. 'How's the temperature?'

'Perfect.'

He sat on the edge and carefully slid her into the bath, bubbles sticking to her skin as the warm water enveloped her. The feeling of weightlessness took her by surprise, especially around the stump of her leg as it floated upwards in the water.

Zac stepped in behind her and lowered himself in, one leg either side of her body. She exhaled slowly as she leaned back onto his chest and his hands slid down her arms until they met hers, threading his fingers between hers. She curled her fingers around his hands.

The water lapped lazily around them, making subtle, intimate sounds, highlighting the closeness that tingled between them. The earthy vibration of his chest beneath her head lulled her into a deep state of relaxation as he spoke his poetry to her. His words, his voice, were music to her ears, and she wanted to lay in this watery world of his arms for eternity.

She rolled to her side and placed an arm beside his body to prop herself up slightly, the other reaching up to his face. As she traced the wet smoothness of his jawline, she surveyed the beautiful face of the man she'd tried so hard not to fall for. 'Are you ready for round two?' she asked seductively, then gently teased and nibbled his ear until he pulled her body closer and merged his lips with hers.

CHAPTER TWENTY-TWO

The sound of birds woke him and for a brief moment he'd forgotten about what had taken place the night before. A smile eased onto his lips as delicious memories oozed into his awareness. He rolled over, longing to touch her again, to stroke her skin as he'd done when she'd fallen asleep in his arms and he'd laid there for ages, listening to the gentle ebb and flow of her breath, watching the moonlight dance across her skin as it filtered through the flowering tree outside.

On the other side of his bed lay only crumpled sheets.

He propped himself up onto his elbow. 'April?' he called out with his croaky morning voice. He checked the time. It was still early, he'd hardly slept, and it was Monday—she had a day off today.

Juliet meowed. He got up and dressed his bottom half, walked out of the room. Kitchen—empty. Bathroom—empty. Juliet's food bowl—empty. He fed her and let her outside, then glanced towards April's house. He could see her through her kitchen window. He threw on a t-shirt and walked to her front door.

She opened it and let him in, wearing the same clothes from

the night before. 'Hi, sorry, I didn't want to wake you,' she said. 'I was hungry and thought I should come back here and get my own food.'

'Hey, what's mine is yours. You could have helped yourself to anything.'

Her cheeks went a little pink and she shrugged. 'Had to feed Romeo anyway.' She turned towards the kitchen to put away her breakfast bowl into the dishwasher.

He reached his arms out and slid them around her waist from behind. She tensed, put her hands on his wrists and moved them back. 'Zac.'

'You okay?'

'I'm good. I'm great.' She turned. 'Last night was... incredible.' She locked with his gaze then hers dropped. 'But the night is gone. It's back to reality now.'

'Reality? Last night *was* the reality. *Is* the reality. The start of something even more incredible.'

She furrowed her brow. 'Start? But Zac, I thought we were just living in the moment, as you said. Getting it all out of our system.'

Disappointment hardened in his gut. He'd thought he'd gotten through to her, thought she'd surrendered to the possibility of taking a risk. 'I don't want to get it out of my system,' he replied. 'Never did. I want it *in* my system.'

April sucked in a deep breath. 'Oh God,' she shook her head. 'What have I done?' She leaned back against the kitchen counter onto her hands, then looked up at him. 'I'm sorry. Maybe I should have made my intentions clearer. I thought we were simply going with the flow, finally letting loose. I didn't think you would assume this would be the start of something official.' She rubbed her forehead.

'I didn't assume, but how can it not be, after such an amazing night?'

Her hand twitched, like it wanted to reach out but she wouldn't let it. 'It was amazing. I'll never forget it.'

'Then let's not forget. Why dismiss something that feels so right.'

'It also feels so wrong, Zac.'

He pushed out a breath and turned away from her. 'Not for me.'

'You didn't have my upbringing,' she said.

He turned back. 'And you didn't have mine,' he stated. 'You may not have had the best male role model, the best family dynamics, but you had a family. I would have killed for that.'

She sighed. 'I know, I know. I'm lucky. And my mum has always been there for me. But one night of passion doesn't automatically mean a relationship is going to work. Or that ...'

That I won't go back on the booze. 'That I won't always be the man I am now.'

Her eyes met his and confirmed his statement.

He should leave. He should save his dignity and let her be.

'I'll give you some space,' he said, turning for the door.

'Zac,' she said. 'I mean it, it *was* amazing. I'm not downplaying it, I'm just—'

'It's okay.' He held out his hands. 'No need to explain any further.'

He opened the door and let himself out, while she hung loosely at the door, as though unsaid words had dashed out the door and she was trying to find them.

But he caught them.

He stopped, turned, and looked at her in the doorway, the morning breeze swishing her wavy hair around her face.

Stuff it. He knew what he felt, and he needed to say it.

He went back up to the porch. 'April. Sometimes you have to take a leap of faith. Some things are more important than the fear we attach to them. Feelings like this are rare, they need to be expressed, acted on, explored.'

'Feelings are fleeting,' she rebutted.

'So is life.'

Her silence at his remark only spurred him on. Showed him she was worth fighting for. She knew all too well how true that was, and deep down, he knew that she knew that some things were worth the risk.

'Love is what's most important, April.'

Her eyes widened. 'Love?'

'Yes, love.' He kept his gaze on hers. 'I love you, dammit.'

She gripped the side of the doorframe. 'You... you love me? But we've only known each other, what, six months? And we're opposites. And you know how I feel about alcoholism. So if anything you should hate me, or at least be mildly irritated by me.'

'Opposites attract.'

'So do like-minded people.' She crossed her arms.

'We're also like-minded in some ways. We both like cats. And saying what's on our mind. And cupcakes. And candles.' He attempted a smile but she was clearly not prepared for this conversation, as she found itches to scratch and non-existent bugs to flit away and clothing to adjust. 'Look, I understand your hesitation, and I certainly don't hate you for it. I'm not even mildly irritated. It's a natural response after what you've been through.' He stepped a little closer. 'The only thing that irritates me is how you push aside any real emotions, any real possibility that we could be good together.'

'I'm trying to do the right thing,' she said. 'You should be with someone more stable, more understanding, more spiritual, more supportive. You shouldn't love me, Zac.'

'Can't help it.' He shrugged in resignation, then glanced up at the roof of the porch. 'Love. It's completely illogical and random in the most perfectly imperfect way.'

As he processed his own words she froze, eyes on him, and he noticed a slight softening of her brow. 'You're right.' He thought she was going to grab him and kiss him like she'd done the night before. But she stepped backwards into her house. 'It's illogical. And I can't risk it. Sorry.' She slowly began closing the door, and when he gave a small nod in forced resignation, she let it close completely.

He turned and looked at the horizon in the distance. His legs urged to run there; go wherever they would take him. But they only wanted to walk through that door and talk sense into her. But he'd done enough talking. She could no longer hear the truth in his voice.

But he could write.

And sometimes, the written word was more powerful.

He dashed home and got out a piece of paper and a pen, and let words tumble onto the page. Not as poetry, but as a declaration, a last chance plea, a... something, to let it all out in simple but significant honesty.

I'm ready. I've been waiting, preparing, but I'm ready—now. I just want to feel again. Feel all those crazy overpowering feelings that make no sense and yet fill me with such clarity and purpose that I wonder how I ever lived without them. You've given me a glimpse of that. But I want more. I want a full-on, eyes wide open, heart and soul exposed experience. I want to be immersed in the sensations that being around you triggers; surrender to the intense emotions that will either be my saviour or my downfall. Right now, I don't care which, I just want to feel. Feel life in all its glorious chaos pumping through my body, my heart, my soul. And I want to feel all of it with you.

He folded it up, placed it in an envelope, and taped a small flower to the front. Then he walked out and put it in her letterbox. He felt like knocking on the door and throwing it at her, but that would... *hang on...* he glanced at her house, the door closed to the world and to him. He inched the envelope out of the narrow slit of the letterbox and walked to the front door. He knocked.

It inched opened. 'Zac,' she began, her voice with a downward inflection.

'Here,' he blurted, shoving the envelope through the door's opening and letting it fall to the floor, then walking off the porch once again. He wasn't going to wait for her to read it, or to throw him out again. He was going home to wash his sheets, clean the house, and maybe build some outdoor cat play equipment for Juliet with the timber he had left-over from winter. If she wanted to see him, she knew where he bloody well was.

CHAPTER TWENTY-THREE

April had almost given in. Twice. When he'd so honestly declared his love for her, and then after reading his letter. If you could call it a letter. It was like he'd blurted everything out and hoped it made sense. It did. She'd never known someone so honest and expressive with his emotions. Kyle had told her he loved her, but never like that. Zac was so intense; she could hardly take it. Didn't know if she could take it even if he weren't a recovering alcoholic.

An uncomfortable feeling twisted inside, like there was a knot she couldn't untie and it kept catching every time she took a breath. He'd put his heart and soul on the line, and though she had taken it for a ride, she'd literally closed the door in front of him. It was all too much, she had barely processed their night together even two days later, and couldn't even start to process the possibility of anything more than their brief interlude.

Maybe it was just because of today. September fifth. The third anniversary of her accident. She needed space to get through it, like Zac had needed space to get through his first anniversary. And she needed to get to the first anniversary of her business next month. Show that she had made it on her own, survived the first year. There was too much going on in her mind.

And then there was the email.

It had arrived an hour ago, and she still hadn't clicked on it.

Subject: *Thanks for your letter*

Okay, she had to read it. She'd procrastinated enough.

She clicked open. As Kyle couldn't type, it was obviously from his parents. His mother, in this case, as she read the signature at the bottom.

Dear April,

Thank you so much for your letter. Kyle read it and wanted me to say thank you. He also says he feels a great sense of relief, knowing you are doing well and making the most of your life.

It was the hardest thing he ever did, saying goodbye to you. He knows you understand, and he knows you would have given the relationship your best shot.

In his words: You gave me a gift too: the memories. The possibility. The love. I'll never forget that, or you. Go live your life and make the most of it. Thank you for taking this weight off my heart. Love Kyle.

Now the tears came. Not when she'd read the letter she'd written, nor when she'd sent it, nor when she'd said no to Zac. But now. And not only for his reply, but for the fear that she wasn't honouring him properly. Was she really living her life to the full?

From now on, each anniversary would no longer be filled with sadness, she decided. It would signify a reminder of the gift of life she had. A reminder to live fully as Kyle wasn't able to, and make use of what she had.

She knew this would, at some stage, mean opening her heart up properly again, but right now, she didn't feel ready. Zac was ready, she knew that, but she wasn't. She didn't want to build something only to have it shatter. Maybe Zac had been a practice guy, preparing her for someone more suitable down the track.

Romeo meowed as he approached her, rubbing his head against her right leg.

'It's okay, I'm okay,' she said, sobbing and wiping her face. 'Here.' She picked him up and held him close to her, grateful for the comfort and unconditional love from her pet. 'Will I ever be ready, Romeo?' she asked, to another meow. 'What is wrong with me? Why can't I take away the fear?'

More tears came, and though she felt silly for it, she craved even more. More release, more of the cathartic bliss. If she was going to cry, she might as well do a damn good job.

CHAPTER TWENTY-FOUR

Sometimes the only way to avoid a broken heart was to be the heartbreaker. But that came with its own kind of breaking; a splintering of guilt, an ache of sadness, a painful throb repeatedly saying, 'it's not fair, it's not fair!'

Why is it that the ones who feel so right are so wrong?

The only way April had been able to handle her rejection of Zac was by making herself extremely busy over the past month. Which hadn't been hard. With the store's birthday celebrations all organised to perfection for tomorrow night, she'd barely had time to think about the Zac situation. It was only during quiet moments when her thoughts would return to him, and then before they could take hold she'd find some task she needed to do, or a call she needed to make, or would distract herself on Facebook with stupid quizzes like 'which movie star is your soulmate?'

By the looks of things, Zac was coping in his own way. He was busy too. She'd wake to early morning hammering and chain-sawing, and the sounds of timber banging together. It wasn't like Zac to be up early, but he'd be outside at the crack of dawn building things. Cat things. Like some giant feline cubby house adventure playground. She'd also noticed a wooden stand on the deck housing an array of fresh herbs. If he wasn't a wealthy ex-soldier, poet, and blogger, he could be a carpenter.

She'd thought about going over there and telling him about her event for tomorrow, since it had been his idea, but every time she built up the courage she'd find an excuse not to go. But with one day to go, it was now or never. She couldn't be rude and not at least thank him for the inspiration. And invite him, not that he'd attend. Or maybe he'd surprise her, maybe he'd also been busy working through his phobia and was ready to try taking a risk. He would have been a great ambassador for the event, since the chosen charity would be close to his heart, but she doubted he was ready to announce overcoming his addiction in public, let alone *be* in public.

She took the glossy flyer from her fridge, the butterfly magnet dropping to the floor and breaking in half.

Damn it.

She picked up the pieces and tossed them in the bin.

Bad omen?

No, she didn't believe in that stuff.

She let Romeo inside and fed him, then went out the front door, the sun still blaring despite being evening. With daylight savings starting the week before, she had been able to leave Romeo outside most days while she was at work, which he loved. And despite him jumping into Zac's yard occasionally, it was no longer a problem as Zac would either lift him back over without her having to ask, or she'd ring the new bell she'd bought for him to associate with being fed and patted. Worked a treat.

If only human lives were as simple as those of cats.

She stepped onto the porch, noticing another wooden creation beside the door—a large storage box with a label: deliveries. She shook her head. Zac went to a lot of trouble to make something that was totally unnecessary. Sure, he got a lot of things delivered to his house so he didn't have to step foot inside a busy store, but a box for boxes? He must have really needed something to occupy his mind.

She knocked, and muffled footsteps sounded. She knew he would probably peer through one of the windows so she kept a neutral expression on her face and held the flyer up near her chest, so it looked like she was just dropping something off. Which she was, of course.

The door opened and the scent of Zac's freshly showered skin wafted towards her, her legs becoming unsteady for a split second. A white towel was wrapped low around his waist and tucked in at the right side, the top of one of his tattoos peeking out the top. The tattoo she'd seen that night: *For your eyes only.* She could only see the word 'For', and for some reason imagined another woman in the future seeing the tattoo. A sickening feeling curdled in her stomach and she mentally scolded herself. How ridiculous, jealous of someone that didn't exist yet, or did, but not yet in his life. She'd said no to him, she had no right to feel any attachment to him or entitlement to his damn tattoo.

'Hey,' he said.

'Hey.' April forgot why she was there.

'What's that?' His eyes glanced towards her flyer.

'Oh. This.' She held it up. 'It's for my store's birthday event. Here.' She handed it to him. 'I know you won't come, but I wanted to give it to you anyway, and thank you for the idea.' She avoided looking at his eyes by keeping her focus on the flyer and pointing out things he could clearly read by himself, but she needed to do something with her hands too. 'As you can see, twenty per cent of all proceeds from the night markets will go to charity, the Addiction Prevention Foundation. People who can't make the markets can also donate via a special link on my website. Not that you have to, I'm just saying, if you wanted to it would—'

'I will for sure,' he said.

'Cool. Thanks. Okay, I guess I'll, ah ...' She gestured to her house with her thumb.

An awkward silence filled the gap between them, the gap they had closed before by moving close to each other, the gap that hadn't existed whatsoever that night at his house when they'd lain in bed together as one.

She smiled and stepped off the porch.

'April.'

She turned back and looked at him, standing at the doorway half naked without any self-consciousness. 'Yes?'

'I told myself I wasn't going to chase you. You know where I stand, you know what I feel. But this ...' He raised his hands and let them fall to his side. 'This is just... not us.'

She knew she wouldn't be able to get away without getting caught up in another deep discussion. 'Zac, I think we've said all that needs to be said.'

'No, we haven't. I haven't. And I don't care if I sound annoying, or desperate, or crazy, but we should be together, April. Life doesn't make sense without you.'

Oh God, why did he have to be standing there in that towel, and saying the sorts of things most women would love to have said to them? He was like a perfect disaster waiting to happen.

'And it wouldn't make sense if we *were* together. I'd be forever worried that things would go wrong, that you'd fall back into old ways, that ...'

That I might get knocked down the stairs like Mum.

That I would end up on anti-anxiety medication like Mum.

That I'd lose you like Kyle.

'That... look,' she sighed, 'it just wouldn't work.'

He turned his head away, then back again. 'But life is short and precious, you know that as well as me. We should be making the most of life. Of our lives. Not living in fear.'

'Fear, Zac? Fear?' April put her hands on her hips. 'If we shouldn't be living in fear, then why are you?'

His jaw tightened.

'If life should be made the most of and lived fearlessly, then why aren't you trying to overcome your phobia, huh? I wrote that letter to Kyle to move forward, I read those books you gave me to learn more about myself and the world, I listened to a song for the first time in ages, I took part in those thirty-six questions with you to start opening up more, I ...' She was out of breath. As oxygen rushed into her lungs, she continued, 'I made an effort. But you, you continue to live out your days locked away in your house, building God knows what, and writing God knows what, and avoiding the things that could tip you over the edge. How can I be with someone who can't handle the world? You say you won't go back to your addiction, but how do you know how you'll cope when you're back out there if you won't *get* back out there?' Her wildly gesticulating hands felt like they might fly off and get carried away in the wind. 'God, Zac. You need to just say, "enough!" Take a stand for your life and snap the hell out of it!'

Her exhalation felt rough and gritty, like she'd released some dormant emotions that had festered away for too long. And that wasn't the only thing that was rough and gritty. Zac's face had changed. He no longer held that honest, open expression in his eyes, they only held annoyance. Or was it anger? She hadn't seen it before, even when she'd rejected him after their night together. She'd hit a nerve, and she didn't know whether that was a good thing and what he needed to finally do something about his problem, or whether she had gone too far.

'Sure. I'll do that. No problem. I'll snap out of it,' he said. 'I better get to it, then.' He stepped back inside the house and

April flinched as he closed the door. Not a calm close, but a firm, definite, 'go away' slam.

She dashed back home and closed her own door, and sunk onto the couch as dread and regret weighed down her muscles. She had gone too far. As usual, her big mouth had gotten her into trouble and there was no delete button to undo the damage.

He'd kill for a drink.

A long, slow, indulgent drink that went on forever, gave him that comfortable buzz of happiness and hazy filter over the world and its overstimulation.

He didn't have any. And if he wanted it, he'd have to go out. He couldn't go out. Right now, that was the only thing stopping him. His agoraphobia was saving him, strangely enough. It *had* served a purpose, despite some people seeing it as something that needed to be fixed.

He rushed out back to get some fresh air, even though he'd been standing out front. The air there was marred with her hurtful words. He took a few deep breaths, looked at his strength tattoo, reminded himself of his coping strategies. He should call his sponsor. Before heading back inside, the flowering star magnolia trees caught his attention. Johnny's was still slightly taller than his. He imagined that Johnny was looking down on him, chuckling to himself at his superiority.

No. No sponsor. His twelve months were up. He needed to handle this craving on his own. He needed to step up and make Johnny proud.

And April was right, there was no guarantee he would stay sober. The cravings would come and go. Whether he gave in was another matter. But today, he wouldn't. Couldn't.

Despite being freshly showered, he got to the floor and did

push-up after push-up until his arms could take it no more and sweat formed on his skin. Then he did sit-up after sit-up until he could no longer bend at the waist. Then he sculled a glass of water, took another three breaths, remembered the feeling during meditation of his breath being enough. One breath at a time. He could do this. He could keep it together.

But he needed to write.

Now.

He went to his blog. It was time to come clean.

Today's post is a little different. Actually, a lot different.

No poetry, just some plain honesty.

I've been hiding behind this blog.

My name is Zac. I'm a recovering alcoholic. I've been sober just over thirteen months. Writing this blog, these poems, has helped me, among other things. I'm also an agoraphobic. Haven't always been, though, it started after I came back from Afghanistan. After my best mate died. After I became an alcoholic. Seemed like the only solution. Shut out the world, stay home, stay safe, stay sane, stay sober. And I think it was the best solution at the time. But I know now it can't always be that way. I need to get over it. Somehow. Maybe writing will help me with that too. Maybe now I've gone a year without drinking I can start taking steps to get back into the world. I can only try. I hope you'll continue to read my posts and give the odd bit of encouragement. I may need it. Some people might think it's a stupid condition to have, that you can just 'snap out of it', but you can't. I can't. It's a protective mechanism in response to trauma and fear, and I'm still finding ways of coping with that trauma and fear. It's a process. And I need to live through it.

So no more hiding.

I'm here, exposed. Ready. Sharing my journey with you.

Let's keep moving forward and beat this son of a bitch.

Zac.

Within an hour he'd received a ton of comments. Some offering words of encouragement, others saying they had friends or family that had been to war, and others saying they had phobias of things like spiders and heights. Everyone had their own story to tell. His wasn't the only one. But maybe by sharing his ongoing journey he could help and inspire others. And maybe one day he would have achieved enough to be able to help people more directly who had gone through addiction, and turn his difficult experience into something positive.

As for him and April, it was a lost cause. He'd done all he could do, and in the end, she'd shown that she truly didn't understand him and his challenges, let alone accept them. As much as it hurt to cast aside the greatest, weirdest, most unconventional love he'd ever felt, it was time to move on.

CHAPTER TWENTY-FIVE

Television was no distraction for April, it only intensified the contrast between her life and others.

How can people get so excited about renovating, I mean, seriously!

She switched the channel.

Oh for God's sake, it's a cooking show, not a life-or-death situation!

Switch.

Why are all the female characters in movies young and beautiful and the males are old and grey?

She turned off the TV and headed into her bedroom. It was still relatively early, but late enough that she could try to get an early night and be bright and energetic for her big day tomorrow. Work at the store would be first, then set up for the night markets, then enjoy the night markets and then pack up and go home. She was glad she'd have a busy day to keep her mind off the awful thing she'd said to Zac.

Her eye homed in on the seashell Zac had given her ages ago, sitting on her bedside table next to her candle. She picked it up and felt the ribbed surface, noticing its broken edge and the smudge of discolouration and cinnamon-like freckles.

Just because something is broken and blemished, doesn't mean it's not beautiful and precious.

She didn't know where the words came from as they appeared in the doorway of her mind like unknown visitors turning up at the wrong house. Zac thought of words, April didn't. But there they were, and she felt compelled to write them down.

She tapped them into the notes app on her phone and wrote them on her whiteboard.

Then she pressed her mum's number in 'contacts'.

'Mum?' she asked.

'Yes, darling, is everything okay?'

'Do you regret getting involved with Dad?'

'What? Why are you asking me this now? I'm watching *Rogue Renovators*.'

April could hear the annoying overexcited renovators in the background having happiness attacks at finding the most perfect colour for the feature wall in their living room.

'Do you?' she asked.

The volume went down and her mum replied, 'He wasn't easy, you know that.'

'But would you do things differently, if you'd known?'

There was a brief moment of silence. 'No. Of course not.'

'But why?'

Her mum chuckled. 'Oh, April. Because he gave me *you*. And you were the best thing that ever happened to me. To us.'

The heavy feeling that had filled her muscles lightened as gratitude took its place. Her chin quivered and she sniffed.

'Are you alright, sweetheart?'

'Yes, yes, I'm okay. Thanks, Mum.'

'Are you still having feelings for that man?'

That man.

'Not really. I mean sort of, but I'm not getting involved. And I told him that.'

'Well, good for you. Don't settle for second best,' Clarissa said.

Second best and Zac didn't seem to go together. Why did living without him feel like *that* was second best? She shook her crazy thoughts away. She'd made her decision, and anyway, she'd no doubt hurt him and he would probably never forgive her, and she didn't deserve his forgiveness. She wondered if he had written on his blog, but she'd unsubscribed after their night together so she wouldn't get tempted by his prose.

'So, having me, that made being with Dad worthwhile?'

'Definitely, but even despite the difficulties, there were also the memories. The good ones,' she said. 'He was a real charmer, even sang to me once in public. Embarrassed the heck out of me, but it worked. Charmed his way into my life. I have the memories too, and sometimes that's all we can cling onto.'

She had memories with Zac, even though she'd only known him six months. She could just take them for the gift that they were and move on

'Thanks, Mum. That helped.'

'It did? Oh, good. Well, anything else you want to talk about?'

'No, that's it for now. Thanks.'

'Okay, nighty night.'

'Night.'

She ended the call then called another number.

'Hi, Dad, do you want a visitor?'

She arrived at his stale smelling apartment around nine, her father watching sport on television, a bottle in his hand.

'Hello there!' he said, staggering up to greet her, as she'd let herself in with her key. He kissed her cheek.

'Hi, Dad.'

'Lemme get you a sandwich, hang on...' He stumbled towards the small kitchen.

'No, Dad, it's okay, I'm not hungry,' she replied, 'Are you? Would you like me to make you a sandwich?' He probably needed something to soak up the alcohol.

'Oh, really? Gosh, what a nice thing to do for your old man. Thanks, sweetie.' He made his way back to the couch. 'Salami,' he said.

She got the salami and mayonnaise from the fridge and quickly made a sandwich. She tore a bit off it for herself anyway, not realising till it hit her stomach that she was hungry. She made a half sandwich for herself.

Her dad ate it eagerly, pointing and shouting at the TV occasionally, 'You bloody idiots! Don't know whatcha doin'!'

'Who's winning?' she asked.

'Dunno,' he replied. 'Can't read the bloody scores. Broke me glasses.' He gestured to the smashed glass spectacles on the coffee table, which was more like a booze table.

'Oh, Dad? Why didn't you call? We have to get these fixed.' Damn it, she had a full day tomorrow. She'd have to try and make time at lunch to take them into his optometrist and ask for a replacement. 'I'll take them and sort it out, don't worry.' She popped them into her bag.

'Aye, aye, cap'n,' he said with a salute, then he laughed.

She smiled and pretended he was funny.

'Dad?' she asked, when an ad break came on.

'Yeah?'

'Why do you drink?'

'Tastes good,' he slurred. 'Yum.'

'But why so much?'

He shrugged then lowered his head. 'Nothin' ever feels as good.' He looked at her, his eyes tired and dark bags under them. 'You know I tried to stop once,' he said, and she nodded. 'But didn't work. Nothin' else ever made sense in the world, only my drink.'

'What about Mum?' April asked, knowing what she had sacrificed to look after him for so long.

And what about me?

'I loved chasing your mum,' he said. 'Gave me a thrill it did.' He chuckled. 'Good wife, that woman. But a man needs a hobby, right?' He took a swig. 'This sure beats stamp collecting!' He guffawed and slapped his thigh, then coughed and spluttered.

Boredom. That's all it was. Boredom and lack of purpose in life. That was her dad. Then it had become a habit, and the habit had become an addiction.

Zac wasn't bored. He did things; poetry, building, cooking.

Zac had purpose, or had *had* purpose, serving his country.

And unlike her dad, Zac had found a way to feel good without alcohol. A way to feel *better*. Working on himself, meditating, educating his mind... it had taught him how to get to a state that was more rewarding than the temporary bliss from drinking. If her dad had never experienced that, then of course he would keep going back to the one thing that always brought him comfort.

They were different, Zac and her dad.

They'd shared the same affliction, but for different reasons. And Zac had stopped, her father hadn't.

She'd been wrong. Zac wasn't just like her father, not even close. Yes, he was a risk, and things would never be certain, but she still had feelings for him. Couldn't help it. Maybe like some of his books talked about, this was fate, bringing her to him because she could be the one person who would understand him, understand his past, see what a huge accomplishment it had been for him to recover.

But it was too late. She'd overstepped the mark and made a mistake, said something that should never be said to anyone dealing with any sort of challenge, be it health, mental, or otherwise.

Either way, she had to call him.

Now.

CHAPTER TWENTY-SIX

When she'd made sure her dad was settled and ready for bed (at least he couldn't drink while sleeping), April sat in her car and took a few deep breaths. She hardly drove, with everything being within walking distance of her house, but as she glanced down at her prosthetic leg, she felt a flicker of gratitude that it had been her left leg and not right that had been lost, making driving much easier. She had a lot to be grateful for; her right leg, her prosthesis, her life, her business, her friends, her house, her mum, even her dad despite his challenges. If this phone call didn't go well, she'd be okay. She'd survive, as she'd always done.

The sound of his phone ringing gave her heart palpitations.

She prepared herself to speak.

It went to voicemail. *Damn.*

Maybe he was in the shower. No, he'd just had one when I got there.

She called again. Voicemail.

Text message? No, she was a voice person. She called again and this time left a message:

'Hi, Zac, it's me. Obviously, you would have seen my name on the caller ID. Anyway, I just want to say how sorry I am for what I said. God, I feel like an idiot. I'm so sorry. Sorry. Okay, I'd better... sorry.' She ended the call. So much for being a voice person.

She drove home and listened to the radio for the first time in ages. Two songs came on that she didn't know, along with a couple of others she had heard in the past. Then she was home.

That wasn't too bad. While driving too. I deserve some chocolate.

She got herself ready for bed but by the time she was about to snuggle up and wind down with some chocolate, she didn't feel like it anymore. Sleep was calling, and unlike Zac, she answered.

***

There was no response to her voice message when she'd woken, though he could have been asleep, but by lunchtime on Saturday there was still no response.

'Call the guy again,' Belinda said, stuffing some of the items for tonight into a box.

'That'll make me look silly. And desperate, and grovelling.'

'You are silly and desperate and grovelling.'

'Hey,' she said, pointing her pen at Belinda. She ticked a couple of items off the store birthday To Do list. But there was something else she had to do. 'Oh!' She held the pen to her lips. 'Crap. Can you mind the store a bit longer for lunch? I need to go get new glasses for my dad. I could leave it till Monday, I guess, but I don't want him to trip over a step or something.' She stood.

'Of course, chicky babe. I mean, boss. Go.' She flicked her

hand to the door. 'And maybe on the way back you could stop by Zac's house and see if he got your message.'

'Yeah, yeah,' April muttered. 'Might not have time.'

'Make time.'

April left and went home first to get her car, then drove to the optometrist in the next town. She organised a replacement to be made and paid the bill, then gave her dad a quick call. Then she drove back into her street, but when she neared her house, there was another car there. At Zac's house. His Ute was there too. Had he bought a brand new, fancy, black Audi? Talk about going over the top, the guy hardly went anywhere.

Someone got out of the car. A woman. She looked vaguely familiar, and as the smartly dressed woman walked up to Zac's porch, April drove into her driveway and noticed the logo on the car.

Oh no.

Desperation and apprehension gripped her inside. It *was* too late. And she *had* made an irrevocable mistake with Zac. And now he was going to sell his house and leave this street and her life forever, and some old guy would move in and he wouldn't have a cat like Juliet, he would have a dog that barked late at night and woke her up, and he would be one of those annoying people who whistled all the time and sang old tunes that you couldn't get out of your head and he would come over at random times and ask for sugar and anything else he needed, and chat to her for hours like she had all the time in the world, and then he might collapse and have a heart attack and she'd have to give him mouth to mouth and call an ambulance, and ...

She jolted herself out of her worst-case scenario fantasyland and noticed Zac had opened his front door, and both he and the real estate agent were looking her way, as she stared at his house and sat idle in her car. She put her foot on the pedal and the car jumped forward suddenly towards her carport.

When she got out, the estate agent had gone inside. April began her walk back to work, walking as briskly as she could.

No, no, no, no, was all she could think.

And when she arrived back at the store, a customer was wanting a refund for a candle that hadn't lasted as long as the label said, and she knew this for certain, because she had kept a timer and noted down the burning duration each time she had lit it.

April forced a 'customer is always right' smile and hoped bad things didn't come in threes.

———

When they had dealt with the candle disaster, April told Belinda about what she'd seen at Zac's house.

'You need to take drastic action, girlfriend.'

'Like what? Stand out the front with pieces of white cardboard with things written on them to apologise and make him forgive me?'

'Hey, cool idea!'

'That stuff only works in movies.'

'They should totally put that in a movie,' said Belinda.

April's mouth gaped. 'You're not serious?'

'Yeah, why? It'd be awesome.'

'Have you not seen *Love, Actually*?'

'No, actually.' She chuckled. 'Is this one of those moments where you're too old and I'm too young? Cool!'

April shook her head. 'Anyway, he's obviously made up his mind. I should just leave him be.'

'Uh-uh,' Belinda said. 'You've only just called him, right, like last night? Guys need time to think about stuff, process stuff. Anyway, maybe you should try communicating with him at his level, like in writing.'

'A letter?'

'Maybe? Or a poem. Or a text; put it down in writing and then he'll be able to think about it properly.' She stood on the stepladder to rearrange a display on a high shelf. 'And that way, you'll get it all off your chest, and you'll be able to focus on enjoying tonight's event, knowing you did as much as you could to make it up to him.'

She had a point. Though she didn't know if she'd be able to do it justice, putting it all in a text, but then again, she'd written that letter to Kyle and that had turned out well. Maybe that had been practice for this, in a way.

'Here,' said Belinda, handing her a candle. 'Burn that baby and just do it.'

April took hold of the candle-in-a-jar with the word 'courage' on the label.

What the hell.

She went to the storeroom and sat on the fold-up chair, put the candle on top of the filing cabinet, and lit the wick.

Courage, come my way. Words, come my way. Forgiveness, come my way.

She texted:

Zac,

You're better with words than me, but I'll do my best.

Once again, I'm sorry. Really sorry. I shouldn't have said those things, I regret them. Your life has been hard and you're fighting a battle I know nothing about. Of course you can't just snap out of it. I can't believe I said that. I wish I could press delete on my voice sometimes. If I could, I would delete delete delete. And I would say this instead:

You're the strongest person I know. You're inspiring. You're talented.

That's all that matters. You can do anything you set your mind to, I know you can. I'm still learning that, learning to get rid of doubts and fears when it comes to relationships.

I saw my dad last night, and he told me why he drinks. I don't think I've ever asked him that before. His reason was simple, yours wasn't. I know now that you're not like him. Just like I'm not the same as other amputees. Having something in common doesn't make people act the same. I'm sorry I didn't see this before.

You are you, Zac. One of a kind.

If we never see each other again I wanted you to know that I'm sorry, and that I understand you. I accept you. You are enough just as you are. You have changed my world, woken me up to greater things, all through your words, your presence, and your love that I feel undeserving of.

I hope you will forgive me, and I hope that one day we will share a meal of Truth Chicken again, as friends if you still want to be one, or as neighbours while you're still around. Or just as two people with a past that has tested us, challenged us, and made us better people for living and surviving through it.

April.

Her hand was shaking by the end of it, from the sheer effort of typing a long text into her phone, or the enormity of what she'd written, she wasn't sure.

But Belinda was right. When she'd pressed send, it was like an autoreply of relief had been delivered back to her. Whatever happened from here on in was his choice, and she'd be okay.

She walked out of the storeroom.

'Done?' asked Belinda.

'Done,' she replied. 'Now, only a few hours till the markets begin, let's get this show on the road!'

'There you go, that'll get you glowing.' Jonah handed April her coffee over the portable coffee stand in Miracle Park, where a crowd was beginning to form.

'Nice pun,' she replied. 'So do you ever get days off?'

Maybe she should try her luck with a younger man, and one whose only vice (that she knew of) was coffee.

'Days off? What are they?' He furrowed his brow.

'I know the feeling. Though Mondays are working out well for me now.'

'And let me guess, you spend them doing other business work?'

She shrugged. 'Maybe a little.'

'The joys of running a business, eh?' he said. 'My parents do most of the work so I'm lucky, though I help out a bit. But one day they're going to retire so I'll have to decide if I want to take over the business completely.'

'You're young, though, do you want that kind of commitment?'

Or any commitment? What was she doing?

'Maybe. Maybe not. I'll see where life takes me. Might head back overseas sometime too.'

Yeah... too young. Needed to go live his life and be free to do as he pleased.

'Hi there,' April said to a customer who approached her candle stand. The middle-aged woman eyed the colourful display and April tried not to hover and watch, knowing that customers often liked to take their time and see what they were drawn to.

'How much do I have to spend to go in the competition draw?' she asked.

'One entry for every twenty dollars you spend at any of the stalls here tonight,' said April. 'The winner will be drawn at 8:30 pm.'

'Is that café any good?' she asked. 'I'm new in town.'

April gestured at Jonah. 'Absolutely, Jonah here works at Café Lagoon, and he'll most likely serve the winner's free dinner for two.' She smiled.

'Oh, sorry,' said the lady. 'I didn't see!' She picked up a candle pack that was forty dollars and paid for it, and filled out two entry slips.

'Tell you what,' said Jonah. 'I'll give you an extra entry to welcome you to Tarrin's Bay.' He winked at her.

'Oh gosh, what a lucky woman I am!' She blushed, then filled out another slip and thanked April and Jonah.

The sound of guitar strings humming turned April's attention to the middle of the park, beside the walking track. Local musician Barry Reynolds had set up and was about to begin.

'Shame Drew's not able to make it too,' said Jonah. 'Would have got a bigger crowd.'

'Drew Williams?'' April said, even though she knew who he meant. Australia's favourite singer-songwriter, Tarrin's Bay born. Though she knew he was in and out of town, she hadn't yet seen him or met him.

Barry began playing a lively number and a few people gathered around him, while others smiled appreciatively as they walked past and eyed the stalls. Battery-operated candle lanterns hung from the tree near the Wishing Fountain, its branches swaying slowly, the candles emitting a subtle white light. A warm feeling embraced April as she looked around at what she had created. The town was here, local businesses were getting some exposure and new customers, and she was celebrating her store's birthday, Tarrin's Bay style. If only Zac could come and enjoy the atmosphere, then he might see that it wasn't so scary. He would be welcomed, supported, and part of the community. But she knew he wouldn't just turn up and say, 'Surprise! I don't have agoraphobia anymore, I snapped out of it!' And she already knew he had made a sizeable donation, as she'd received a notification via email from the payment system linked from her website to the charity. It was listed as 'anonymous', but she knew it would have been him. The donation had come in a couple of hours after her long text, so maybe her message had had a positive effect? Or maybe he had simply made the donation as he'd promised and nothing else had changed. Anyway, she wouldn't think of him tonight, she would focus on enjoying the evening as planned.

Belinda arrived and helped to serve customers, and the crowds increased. April, busy with customers, waved to Zoe and Olivia as they walked past and gave her a thumbs up, and her mother waved from one of the bakery stalls. Children ran and played around the park, the playground equipment getting an evening workout.

As Barry's music played, April was relieved that it didn't feel uncomfortable. She could now enjoy listening to songs and not think back to that awful day. If anything, now they simply gave her hope for the future.

She noticed her neighbour, Nancy, chatting nearby to the local doctor who lived on the other side of Nancy's house, Sylvia Greene. Nancy caught April's gaze and wandered over with Sylvia. 'Good evening,' she said. 'Nice event you've got going here.'

'Thanks,' said April.

'Yes, well done,' said Dr Greene. 'And it's great that you're raising money for the addiction charity.'

'Every little bit helps,' April replied. She had considered a charity for those affected by paralysis, to help Kyle, and then one for amputees, but with all that had gone on this year, supporting addiction seemed the most appropriate option. And each year, she'd decided, she would support a different charity to make at least some difference with the life and business she'd built up.

'And prevention is often better than cure,' said Sylvia. 'Although I've got a few patients who have successfully overcome addictions and stayed clean or sober. It's good to see.'

'Oh really?' April's heart twinged with reassurance. 'That *is* good to see. Thanks for telling me.' April smiled.

Nancy leaned over the stall table towards April. 'The charity is something close to home, isn't it. I can tell,' she whispered.

April fiddled with her hair and said, 'Umm ...' Then she thought, why not. Why should she hold any shame for who her father was. He may have a problem, but he loved her and in the end that was really all that mattered. 'Yes. It is,' she said. 'My father is an alcoholic and will never change. If there's a way to help stop other families from being affected by the condition, then I'd love to be able to help. Though it's too late in my dad's case, maybe the charity can help someone who may be heading down that road to not cross that line into addiction.'

Nancy patted April's hand. 'I understand,' she said.

Sylvia nodded with an expression of understanding concern too.

'You should join me for a cuppa and chat sometime, dear,' said Nancy. 'I make lovely scones.'

April smiled and nodded. 'That would be great, thank you. I would never say no to scones.'

'And you can tell me all about that young chap who lives next door to you. I've been trying to figure him out whenever I walk past but he doesn't seem sociable.'

April was uncomfortable discussing Zac with someone she didn't know well. 'I think he's moving away, actually,' she said. 'He's um ...' *the most interesting person I've ever met... The best lover on the entire planet... The most beautiful kind-hearted man... My soulmate... wait, what?*

April's cheeks flushed warm, and she sipped more of her coffee.

'He's um... a nice guy. But he's been through a lot and likes to keep to himself,' she said.

'Have I seen you two conversing over the backyard fence on occasion?' Nancy narrowed her eyes a little.

'Yes. Yes, you have.' *Let's hope that was all she could see through her windows.*

'Oh well, maybe he might like to join us for a cuppa sometime too. Before he moves, that is.'

'Maybe,' she replied, brushing hair off her face as the breeze flapped it around. Sylvia caught April's eye and the doctor gave her a knowing glance, like she intuitively knew that perhaps there was something beneath the surface that April didn't want to discuss. Damn, those doctors were used to assessing people.

'Anyway, Nancy, weren't you saying that you wanted to get

some candles?' Sylvia pointed to the display. 'Those are nice,' she said, looking at the Jasmine range.

Nancy picked one up to smell it. 'Oh, that reminds me of my youth,' she said. 'I'll take three.' She paid and entered the competition. 'Youth... seems just like yesterday. Time is slipping away, isn't it?' she mused. 'If I could go back, I would...'

'Would what?' asked April.

'Oh nothing, you don't want to listen to an old lady such as myself waffle on while you've got customers to serve.' She waved her hand.

'Yes, I do.' April locked her gaze with Nancy's.

'I wouldn't waste time worrying and trying to plan everything, I would enjoy life for what it is and make the most of every moment,' she said.

'Like you're doing now,' said Sylvia, and Nancy nodded, then blushed.

'Definitely,' Nancy said. 'And that includes getting to know a lovely chap on Facebook I've been conversing with. I think I'm ready to meet him and invite him out or something. He could be a righteous wanker, but he could also be the second love of my life, who knows?' She held up her hands and both April and Sylvia laughed.

April pondered Nancy's advice... Stop worrying, enjoy life, make the most of every moment. She glanced around at the vibrant community gathered in the park, as twilight teased into the horizon slowly and effortlessly. Each day would pass, time would pass, and before she knew it, she would be Nancy's age and thinking back on her own past and wondering what she would do differently. She didn't want to have regrets. She didn't want to have only half lived.

Yes, she was relieved to have sent that message to Zac, and knew that in reality, her life would turn out perfectly fine without him. But what if she needed to give it that extra boost?

What if life was waiting for her to take more of a stand and declare what she really wanted?

What did she really want? Did she just want to go with the flow and let whatever happened happen? Partly, yes, but mostly, no. She didn't want pain, or hurt, or disappointment. But she did want love. Love and connection. And sometimes you had to take a risk in order to get them. Which meant living life with trust, and without worry.

No more fear or assumptions, she said to herself.

Love, only love.

If there was a chance, she had to take it.

She wanted love, and she wanted Zac.

April got out her phone and turned away from the customers at the stall as Belinda served them. 'Give me a sec,' she said, opening up a text message window. She typed:

> Me again. Sorry for long text before, but I forgot to add something: I still understand if we go our separate ways, and I thought I was okay with that, and I would be okay, but that doesn't mean I want it. I know I've been a bit of an idiot, okay, a LOT of an idiot, but Zac— please don't go. Don't leave. Don't move. I'm ready now too. I want you. All of you. Scars and all. Let's be wounded and weird together. Let's just jump in and go for it.

> If you don't want to, fair enough, I had my chance and may have blown it. But at least by doing this I'll know that I gave it a shot. And I've put my heart on the line, like you did, which was so brave and I can't believe you did that for me. I can't believe someone as amazing as you wants, or wanted, me.

So there. I've fallen for you. It might even be love, as you said. I'm not used to this, but all I know is that I'm a goner. You've swept me up in your world and I don't want to live anywhere else.

If you still want me, I'm here. Ready and waiting.

April.

When she hit send it was like she was spinning, spinning with the exhilaration of taking a risk, of baring her feelings without knowing how he would respond.

For the rest of the evening she chatted and served customers, caught up with her mum, feeling on such a high she didn't know how she would get back down. No matter what happened, she was living. *Now*, she was living.

And when Jonah took to the mic at Barry's music set-up and asked for everyone's attention, she smiled a huge smile when he announced the winner of the dinner for two was Nancy Dillinger, her next-door neighbour and reason she had just sent that message to Zac.

Nancy clapped her hands together in delight as she accepted the prize, and then grabbed hold of the microphone. 'Now, I know you'll probably all be lining up to have dinner with me, but I already know who I'm taking to dinner, so I'm sorry to disappoint.' She grinned, and a few people feigned overt disappointment and rejection with frowns and slumped shoulders. Then she caught April's gaze as she walked away from the microphone and over to April's stand. Nancy gave her a suggestive wink and smiled, then whispered with a giggle in her ear. 'Maybe I'll even get lucky.'

<h1 style="text-align:center">CHAPTER TWENTY-EIGHT</h1>

Luck. Maybe a lot of life did come down to luck. But it also came down to creating your own luck, or at least, doing your damn best to give it a shove in the right direction. It had been late by the time April had arrived home after the very successful night markets, and Zac's lights were off. She hadn't heard back from him after either of her messages, but maybe he needed to process them and think things through. She wouldn't rush him or be annoying and ask 'did you get my message?'

And having to be back at work early on Sunday morning left no time for crossing paths with him, so she focused on keeping busy in the store by planning her Christmas stock and display ideas.

'Don't forget Halloween,' Belinda said. 'We should push that as much as possible before letting the Christmas stuff take up space.'

'You want to take over the store one day, don't you, Bee?' April asked. She'd never called her Bee before and didn't know why she did just then, but it had popped out and felt right.

'Already planning my strategy to climb my way to the top.'

She laughed a fake witches cackle and rubbed her hands together.

'Crazy woman,' April chuckled.

'I have a good mentor,' she replied.

'Hey, so the newspaper emailed and said it'll be a two-page spread on Wednesday, showcasing the photos from the event and talking about the charity and encouraging more donations.' April jiggled on the spot.

'You did well, boss,' she said.

'*We* did well.'

They high-fived each other, and April went out back to the storeroom to unpack more of the Halloween stock.

The bell on the store's door jingled, and she heard Belinda say, 'Howdy, what can I do for you?'

'I'm here to see April,' said the voice, and April's heart stopped.

No way, it couldn't be. Not *here*.

She returned to the store and her mouth fell open. 'Zac?'

Belinda's eyes went wide and she pretended to be busy in the corner.

Zac's presence bombarded her with a collision of disbelief and surprise. He wore jeans, as usual, darker ones, his hands in their pockets, and a thin, short-sleeved grey shirt with buttons down the front, of which the first three at the top were undone, exposing parts of his tattoos. He also wore an accomplished smile, his eyes bright and alert, gaze alternating between her and the store's surroundings, like he was stepping into her world for the first time.

'Zac, what are you doing here?' She took a tentative step closer, but stayed next to the counter until she knew of his intentions. He could be here to tell her he was leaving. Today. And this would be the last time they'd see each other. Her hand shook as it leant on the side of the counter.

'I made a promise, remember? To walk into your store one day.' He removed his hands from his pockets and surveyed the displays to his right, then looked back at her. 'You said it could be in a million years but I figured I might not be looking too great by then and you wouldn't recognise me, so thought I better do it now.'

A quick smiled flashed on April's face, sending warm shots of excitement to her cheeks. She took another step closer. 'Wow. I can't believe you did it. I wasn't expecting, I ...' Thoughts came and went, but none made sense. 'I'm glad you came,' she said, then her body softened and she walked closer, and they stood with only a small display table separating them. 'Zac, I'm sorry. Again. I hope my message made sense. I know you can't just snap out of it and I wouldn't expect you to. I hope you forgive me.'

'I do,' he said. 'It's okay, don't beat yourself up. I know you were frustrated. But you were right in a way, I do need to start taking action to overcome it. So today, I thought why the hell not, I'll take a little walk down to my favourite candle store.' He lifted his palms up in the air. 'Even though I almost changed my mind and turned back at least forty-seven times.'

She chuckled. 'How do you know it's your favourite candle store if you've never been before?'

He rubbed his chin. 'Something about the name, reminds me of someone.'

She found herself twirling a loosely curled strand of her hair.

Zac's face became serious. 'The thing I've realised is, I've always found it hard to ask for help. I've always been the helper. Call me proud, I don't know, but now, I know I need to get some of that help stuff. And if there's anyone I'd want to help me with the help stuff, it's you.' He moved towards her and grasped her elbows gently. 'Will you?'

She looked deep into his eyes and saw the part of him she'd seen that night during the eye-gazing exercise. The part she'd connected with, desired, wanted. She gulped. 'I can't imagine any other alternative.'

He smiled softly. 'So we just jump right in, hey? As you said?' He rubbed his thumbs back and forth across her arms. 'Take a risk and give things a shot, otherwise ...'

'Otherwise we just stay friends and have occasional really hot sex,' she blurted with a shrug.

A laugh burst from Belinda's mouth, as it did from Zac's. 'Sorry. I'll just ah... I have to go check something ...' Her employee scurried off to the storeroom.

'The things that come out of your mouth, April.' Zac shook his head with a smile. 'I love them.' He leaned in closer and whispered, 'I've got a better idea. We take a risk and give things a shot, *and* we have occasional really hot sex.' He winked.

She moved her hands to around his neck. 'Replace the word occasional with frequent and you've got yourself a deal.'

'Deal,' he said.

He leaned closer and she tilted her face up and received his eager kiss. His lips were like sinking into a soft, supportive, welcoming bed at the end of a hard day. She wanted to stay there, immersed in him, for as long as she could. His hands held her cheeks firmly but tenderly, and then moved around her back, pulling her in close.

She nestled her head in his neck and whispered in his ear. 'I'm with you, Zac. One hundred percent.'

'Oh man this is *so* going on Facebook!' Belinda appeared with her phone camera. 'And hi, I'm Belinda,' she said, holding out her hand for Zac.

He shook it and laughed.

And as the vibration of his laugh reverberated through his

chest as she rested against it, she knew she had found her true home.

CHAPTER TWENTY-NINE

'You sure we're not leaving Belinda in the lurch?' Zac asked as he stepped out of April's Glow, April's beautiful soft hand in his.

'She's used to it,' April said. 'And besides, she's a fan, so she'd do anything for you.'

'Ah, what?'

'Of your blog. She found it. Remember, I mentioned it a while ago when I told you I'd read your blog?'

'Oh yeah. Huh. I've never met any of my *fans* before,' he said, chuckling at the word. Then again, he'd never met anyone who'd read his blog, fan or otherwise.

'You've met me.' She swung his arm in hers.

'You're a fan? Really?' He spoke with fake enthusiasm.

'Your biggest.'

'And what does my biggest fan wish to do this afternoon?'

April stopped and looked around. 'Hmm, do you think you could handle a stroll down the main street? I could take you on a little tour?' Her eyes held hope but caution.

Zac's insides felt unsteady. 'Um, I think visiting your store was enough adventure for one day,' he said. 'One step at a time?'

'Of course, one step at a time. Or two steps for me, because your steps are much bigger than mine.' She walked two to his one as they went up the hill towards her street.

'I'll go slower.'

She gripped his hand tighter and spoke softly, 'No more slow. We've done enough slow.'

He knew what she meant. They'd spent six months getting to know each other, going back and forth, hot and cold, fast and slow, mostly slow, except for that one night, and it was time to amp things up. Life was short and went by fast, there was no point waiting, or wasting time.

'Hey, I could take you on a proper tour of my house. You haven't seen it all yet,' she said.

'Good idea.' He smiled.

'And there's one room in particular I think you might like,' she spoke with a teasing tone.

'Kitchen?' he asked.

She shook her head.

'Bathroom?'

'Nope.'

'Laundry?'

'Uh-uh.'

'Um, geez, I dunno. Help me out here, candle woman.'

'I'll take you straight there,' she replied.

Their walking speed had picked up after her mentioning the house tour, but there was only one room she wanted to be in with him right now. April led him through the living room and down the small hallway, and into her bedroom. The blinds were drawn, and only tiny thin slits of light slid through making faint stripes on her bed.

'I present to you the master bedroom,' she said with a flourish of her hand. 'Built in the last quarter of the twentieth century,' she added in a posh tour guide voice, 'it was created by some unknown builder who realised that the occupant or *occupants* would require a place to rest one's head at night. As you can see by the presence of the queen-sized bed, it fits the purpose for which it was intended.' She led him around the side of the bed, next to her bedside table, and trailed her fingers up and down his arms. 'And also, the room was built with the assumption that it may provide a useful space in which to... how does one say this... *get it on*, in the comfort of said queen-sized bed.'

The expression of amusement on Zac's face was utterly adorable. He was both masculine and cute at the same time, and also sexy, and despite knowing him well, still held an air of irresistible mystery.

She pushed gently against his chest so that he sat on the bed in front of her.

'How could we not use the room for the purposes in which it was intended? It would be a waste,' he said.

'Indeed,' she replied, unbuttoning his shirt from the top to the bottom, then spreading it open and exposing his well-defined chest.

He kicked off his shoes, as she removed his shirt. She held it up in the air and swung it around in circles.

He grinned. 'Doing the stripping cowboy? I thought that was my move.' He raised his eyebrows.

She hooked the shirt behind his neck and pulled him close to her, pressing his lips with hers. 'Cowgirl, perhaps?' she said, teasing kisses across his cheek, neck and under his ear.

'Sounds good to me.' He took the shirt from her hands and flung it behind her onto the floor. 'Nice shell,' he said, eyeing her bedside table.

'Some guy gave it to me.'

'Yeah?'

'Zander, Zeb, Zee... I can't quite remember his name.' She furrowed her brow.

'Will this jog your memory?' Zac pulled her towards him into an urgent kiss and she fell onto him as he leaned back on the bed.

'It's coming back to me,' she whispered. 'Oh wait,' she said, getting back up. 'I should light my candle.' She grabbed her gas lighter and held it towards the hope candle on the bedside table. Flame emerged on the well-worn wick, then flickered out. 'Bugger.' She tried again. 'Nope, it's out.' She laughed.

'What so funny?'

'Not funny, just... interesting.' She lifted up the candle and breathed in its remaining, sweet candy scent. 'This candle has lasted so long. It was given to me by my cousin to lift my spirits and give me hope. It gave me the idea for the candle store.'

Zac took a whiff of it too. 'The smell reminds me of you.' He tangled his fingers in her hair.

She smiled. 'It's like I don't need it anymore. The hope I needed, I got. It served its purpose.' She placed the jar back down. 'So unless you want me to disrupt the flow of our romantic mood by rummaging through my cupboards for a suitable replacement to light our... *rendezvous*, we'll have to go glow-less for this one.'

He let out a cute, mischievous chuckle, and she nestled her thighs between his as she stood between his legs against the bed. 'Oh, don't worry, I'll just give you a glow of your own.' He gathered the hem of her lacy chiffon top and lifted it upwards and off, then gathered her body in his arms and pulled her onto the bed by his side.

'I think I'm already glowing,' she replied, with an eager smile of what was to come.

It was exactly like he'd imagined. In bed, her laying on his chest stroking his skin as he played with her hair. No words, just silence. Comfortable, perfect silence. The sun was lower now, shining more of a warm orange, as it filtered through the cracks in the venetian blinds and cast light and dark shadows across their relaxed bodies. Looking down at her, he watched as her eyelashes fluttered gently up and down as she blinked every now and again. Such a simple, automatic response, yet so beautiful. Her fingers moved with a flow and rhythm that calmed him, and as his chest rose slowly up and down, so too did she as she rested on him.

With each breath, he fell more and more in love with her.

April. His neighbour, his friend, his lover. And now, his partner, his ...

He gulped as he realised.

She was his soulmate.

The one he had wanted. The one he had asked for long ago. The one he had waited for.

'Don't tell me you're getting ready to go at it again?' she asked with a giggle, turning to look up at him as his breathing became faster.

'No. Well, yes. Maybe, but... hang on.' He rolled her gently to the side and sat up. 'Just remembered something. I have to show it to you.' He got up quickly. 'It's at home, I'll duck over and be right back!' He grabbed his keys and went for the door.

'Ah, Zac?' April propped herself onto her elbow, the sheet embracing her body. 'I'm more than happy to watch you wander around naked, but the lovely Nancy from next door might see you and freak out.'

He stopped and eyed his clothes on the floor. 'Oh yeah. I should at least wear something I guess.' He stepped into his trunks. 'That'll do. I'm so used to not being seen that I forget sometimes.'

'Forget. Please forget,' April laughed. 'But maybe not right now, you exhibitionist.' She flung a pillow at him, and he gently whacked her back with it.

'I'll forget again when I get back.' He grinned, then walked out the bedroom door and let himself out the back door to her deck.

Romeo meowed hello and looked up with wide eyes.

'Hey buddy, not right now,' said Zac. 'Important human stuff going on here.'

He stepped onto the low brick wall around the garden and heaved himself up and over the fence and into his yard. He let himself into the house and went to his hall cupboard where he had stored a few small boxes of mementos.

He couldn't believe he had forgotten about it until now.

He looked in one but it wasn't there, then opened the smaller box that held a few photos he'd yet to put up, and a tattered soft teddy bear he'd found in Afghanistan. He was going to give it to the next kid he saw, but then the explosion had happened and changed everything. So he'd kept it, for some reason. Maybe it was symbolic way of bringing Johnny home when he couldn't for real.

But that wasn't what he was looking for.

Underneath the bear was a folded piece of paper. He lifted it out and opened it up.

This is it.

He didn't even read it before dashing back out of the house. Though he couldn't remember all the details, he knew the gist of what was written on it, and wanted to experience it alongside April anyway.

He jumped back over the fence, in his undies, waving to

Nancy in her house across April's yard as she peered out the window with a big grin on her face.

'Sorry, Romes,' he said, as he passed the cat and went back inside, making his way to the bedroom.

'That was quick,' April said. 'Not that I have any idea what you're doing and how long it might take.' She was still laying on the bed, half propped up, her eyes curious and sparkling. 'Oh, and aren't you forgetting something?'

'Huh?' he said. 'Oh yeah, I'm forgetting to forget.' He smiled and took off his trunks then slid back into bed next to her.

'Much better,' she said. 'Now, what is it you have there, Mister?'

He never knew if this day would come. But it was here, and he was as happy as he was when he was a young boy and had discovered girls weren't so bad after all. But this was much better.

'When I first went sober, I wrote this.' He held it out in front so they could both read it. 'It's a letter, except at the time, I didn't know who I was writing it to.' He slid his free arm around her and held her close. 'But now I know.'

Dear Soulmate,

I already love you. Even though we're not yet together, and I don't know who you are, or whether we've met or are yet to meet, I already feel a deep love and connection with you. I woke this morning with a strong urge to write to you, my mystery woman, my future best friend, lover, soulmate.

If you walked into my life right now, I would want you, but I wouldn't be ready. I will be, one day, but not yet. There are things I need to take care of, things I need to resolve. I need to get my life back on track and be the man you would want to have in your life. That is keeping me going, knowing that you are out there somewhere in this vast universe, and it is up to me to be the best man I can be. Not only for you, but for me.

Maybe you're on a journey too, finding your way in the world, or overcoming personal trauma or challenges. If you are, I know you'll come out on top. I can already tell that you're a strong, inspiring woman. Somehow, I have this sense of you, like we're already bonded by our future, though it hasn't happened yet. I feel a kind of promise, a knowing, that you are on your way to me and I am on my way to you. It could be in a year, it could be in five years, who knows? But I trust that perfect timing will be on our side.

I love knowing that as my heart beats, so too does yours. As my lungs breathe oxygen, so do yours. Right this minute. I exist. You exist. And one day we will exist together. I will place my hand on your heart and feel your heart beating, I will be close to you, breathe the same air you are breathing, feel your breath on my skin. You will no longer be a thought, a hope, a dream, but my reality.

If I am brave enough to show you this letter, it means I've looked into your eyes and realised that you're the woman I've written this letter to. It will be the most magical moment of my life, knowing that you're her. And I'll never take you, or us, for granted. You're so important to me. Even now, not knowing what you look like, what your favourite food is, or how you sound when you laugh, you're important. All I know now is your essence, the core of who you are. I can feel that deep in my heart, beating along with my own.

My beautiful partner, always remember this:

I love you.

I loved you before I loved you.

I loved you before we were us.

Thank you for coming into my life, for taking a chance on me, for accepting me. Let's make every moment count.

Love, Zac.

He finished reading before she did, and so he waited, his

heart racing, his hand shaking as it held the letter. And then she turned her head and looked at him, tears brimming at her eyelids and a quivering smile on her lips. 'To think I almost let you go,' she whispered, her voice trembling. 'My beautiful, beautiful man.' She brought her hand to his face and caressed his cheek, tenderly, urgently, her eyes scanning his face as though taking in every detail. 'I feel like I'm in a dream.' She nestled closer into his side.

'I'm dreaming with you,' he said, then turned to face her and placed his hand on her chest, over her heart. 'I can feel it,' he said. 'Your heart. Finally here, with me.' His eyes became warm and the strong emotion welled up inside his own heart, filling him with a love that was even stronger than he'd imagined.

She put her hand over his and held it tight to her chest. Her eyes overflowed with tears and they spilled onto her cheeks. 'That is most beautiful, magical thing I have ever read.' She shook her head in awe. 'You are amazing, Zac Masterson.'

He smiled and kissed her forehead.

'It's like the advice in that book you gave me, to ask for what you want in life and let it manifest. It's like you wrote this letter, and the universe answered, and led you here,' she said.

'Exactly,' he replied. 'Amazing. I'm so grateful I moved in next door.'

'I'm so grateful my cat went into your yard that day.'

He chuckled. 'I'm so grateful you're a bad cook and needed to keep coming over for dinner!'

'Hey!' She flapped the letter onto his face. Then she looked at it again. Her mouth opened wider. 'Oh my God,' she said.

'What is it?'

'The date! Look.' She pointed to the date written at the top, September fifth, one year ago. 'That was the date of my accident, except it was three years ago now.' She shook her head.

'You wrote this on a date that holds such significance to me. What are the chances?'

'Wow,' Zac eyed his blue ink handwriting scrawled across the page. 'It's not chance, April,' he said, taking the letter and folding it, placing it under his hand and over her heart. 'It's fate. It was always meant to be you.'

And as he wrapped her firmly in his arms while tears flowed down her cheeks, he finally, *finally*, felt like he had truly found peace and won the war within.

'I hope you're not really a serial killer,' April said as Zac blindfolded her and helped her into the front seat of his Ute.

'Serial *kisser* maybe.' He smooched her with those lips she had grown so familiar with and yet still felt so enticing and new.

'Happy to be your victim.' She laughed, when he started the engine. 'Oh wait! Babe, can you take a picture of us? It's my birthday tradition, I usually do a wacky photo with Zoe and the girls, but I think we should do it too. Me—blindfolded, perfect. Except I won't know how it looks till after this surprise, whatever it is, so I'll just have to trust you.'

'What an awesome idea. Should I pull a silly face or something?'

'You wouldn't have to try very hard.'

He nudged her in the side. 'Enough, smart mouth. Okay, hang on, let me prepare.'

She felt him lean over and open the glove box, then heard a shuffling of some papers and unknown things.

'What are you doing, getting your own blindfold or something?'

'Nope.' After a few moments he said, 'Okay I'm ready. Here we go, selfie time.'

She had no idea what Zac was doing but she poked her tongue out and pointed to the blindfold with both hands. *Click!* 'All done!'

He put something back in the glove box and then drove out and down the street, and then onto the highway. April could tell, based on the speed he was going and the sounds of the other cars.

'Just one hint? C'mon!' She was itching to know what he had in store for her birthday.

'Nope.'

'Have you secretly finished writing your memoir and you're taking me to the book launch?' She jiggled up and down in her seat.

'Nope,' he repeated with the same smug tone. 'Remember I've enrolled in that memoir writing course, starting in town in May? So nope, no book launch.'

'Couples sexy photo shoot?'

'Nope, but there's an idea for my birthday.'

'Mm,' she whispered. 'Okay, I give up. I'll wait. Because I'm so patient.'

'Oh yes, Patient April who wants to know everything yesterday.'

'Life's short.'

'So is my patience when it comes to your impatience.'

'Now you're just getting all fancy and wordy.'

'It's what I do best.'

April covered his hand on the gearstick and whispered, 'Actually, it's not the main thing you do best.'

She could feel his gaze on her for a moment.

'Mm. Anyway, don't distract me, birthday girl, I'm trying to drive!'

'Okay, okay.'

After around twenty minutes the car came to a stop. 'Now, no peeking. I'll help you out.'

The door opened and Zac's hands held hers as she stepped out of the car.

'Are there people around? I'm going to look like an idiot. Am I on television, some reality birthday show? Is my mum here?'

April had explained her feelings about Zac to her mum after they'd committed to their relationship. At first her mother had been worried and cautioned her, but when she'd told her about the soulmate letter her mum had practically cried. She'd gripped April's hands and said, 'Sweetheart, hold onto him. I can't promise that it'll be easy or perfect, or that things may not change down the track, but that kind of love needs to be grabbed with both hands.'

As for her dad, he had moved into an assisted living facility and had easy access to help when he needed it, while still having the freedom to live life on his terms; in other words, to keep drinking.

'Patience, patience,' said Zac. 'Almost there.'

April felt unsteady, but Zac's supportive arms helped her. 'You must look like a real meanie, you know, blindfolding your amputee girlfriend. It's hard enough to walk normally, let alone when I can't see!'

'Oh stop it, you. You can walk perfectly fine. And look, here we are. Oh wait, you can't.' He laughed, and she nudged him with her elbow.

The temperature cooled when she stepped inside a building of some kind. Or was it a room? There was faint chatter but it stopped when Zac led her to a chair.

'Okay, you ready?' Zac asked.

'Yes! Now can I take this thing off?'

Zac kissed her cheek. 'Here we go.'

She squinted as light rushed into her eyes. Then as she blinked and took in her surroundings, she covered her mouth with a gasp. There was art on the walls, and chairs, and a table, and equipment. Tattoo equipment. 'Oh my God!' she cried, looking around.

'Welcome to Inkling!' a heavily inked man said, a smiling woman with a single rose tattoo on her arm beside him.

'You're getting me a tattoo?' she asked Zac. 'I'm getting a tattoo?' She didn't know whether to be scared or excited. She knew what it felt like, but was she ready for another?

'I thought today was as good a day as any,' said Zac. 'You've been saying for a while how you want to get a new one.'

'Yes. Yes, I have! And I do!' Her head was spinning. 'But I haven't decided what to get yet, um, oh gosh, what should I get?'

'I took the liberty of coming up with some options,' Zac said, showing her some pictures. 'Or, you can choose something completely different. Whatever you like.'

April's mind ran through the possibilities. She didn't want another one like the one she'd lost on her leg. It had to be something different. Something to acknowledge this new life she was living; show how she'd grown and matured and met the love of her life. She clasped her hands together. 'I want skin poetry!' she said.

Zac grinned. 'Really? You sure?'

'Yes. I'm sure. Poetry, or a saying, or words of some kind.' It would be a great tribute to him and the words that made him who he was. 'On my back!' She pointed behind with her thumb.

'Rightio then,' said the man. 'When you're ready, let me know what words you want and I'll show you some fonts.'

April tapped her chin. She thought about how her life had taken such an unexpected turn. Twice. When she'd lost her leg and Kyle, and then when she'd gained Zac. Life was unpredictable, but somehow, it always led her in the right direction. She wanted to honour that beautiful unpredictability, by doing something completely crazy. 'I want you to choose,' she said to Zac. 'You choose my tattoo.'

His eyes widened and his mouth opened. 'You want *me* to choose something for you?'

'Yes,' she said, taking hold of his hand. 'I trust you,' she whispered. 'You're the word expert, pick something meaningful for me.'

He asked if she was absolutely sure about a hundred times and then raised his hands with a smile and said, 'okay then'.

Zac disappeared behind a curtain to chat with the tattoo artist, while April covered her ears and sang 'la-la-la'.

He emerged with a big grin. 'One surprise tattoo coming right up!'

April took off her top and kept her bra and cami on, then got comfortable on a forward-facing chair so the tattoo artist could prepare her upper back. Zac sat next to her and held her hand.

The sound of the needle brought back memories of her first tattoo, and then, the scratching and slightly burning sensation.

'Doing okay?' Zac asked.

'It's nothing,' she said, then faked a huge grimace.

Zac laughed and got out his phone. He took a few photos as the artist worked.

They chatted about random things, and before she knew it, the guy said he was all done.

'It looks so good,' said Zac.

'Show me, show me!' April said, trying to turn her head over her shoulder.

'One sec.' He snapped a couple of photos, one up close, and sat next to April again. 'You ready?'

She bit her lip and nodded. 'If it says "Zac is the best

boyfriend in the whole world", I'm so getting you back on your birthday.'

He laughed. 'Actually, it says Zac is the best lover in the whole world.'

She shot him a glare. 'Just show me,' she said.

Zac held the phone in front of her, and a soft gasp escaped her lips. Then a smile. A big, satisfied smile.

Words that she'd seen before had been inked onto her back. Words that had also been inked onto Zac's back:

As my heart beats, so too does yours.

'I'm speechless.' She clamped her lips together. 'It looks so nice, I love the script font,' her finger hovered over the screen. 'And the words... it's perfect,' she said, looking up at Zac.

She'd loved it when she'd first seen Zac's tattoo, but now it held even more meaning for her, after reading those same words in the soulmate letter. He'd not only meant the quote to signify that all people were the same on the inside, but that somewhere out there, his soulmate's heart was beating. Hers.

She flicked to the wider shot of her back, then when she flicked through the other photos, she found the selfie he'd taken in the car with her blindfold on. Her tongue was protruding, and he had a big goofy, hopeful grin on his face, his eyes wide open, and something in his hand.

'Oh my God,' April said. 'Oh my God.'

For the second time that day she covered her mouth with a gasp.

In the photo, Zac was holding up piece of paper with the words:

Marry me, dammit!

She turned to face him, and he had the same goofy, hopeful grin on his face.

'For real?' she asked.

'For real,' he said, taking her hands in his, her heart melting at his touch and his request.

'Yes, dammit!' she said, laughing and crying in equal measure. 'Abso-bloody-lutely!'

He held her face close to his, they gazed into each other's eyes, and he kissed her mouth with the promise of another new beginning yet to come. 'I was going to wait until after the tattoo to ask you, but when you suggested the selfie it seemed like the perfect opportunity! And I didn't get a ring, because I thought you might want to choose your own.'

She smiled. 'I don't want a ring,' she said, glancing around. 'I have a better idea.' She matched his goofy, hopeful expression. 'Will you agree to it? Do you trust me?'

'You want me to agree to something before I know what it is?'

'Uh-huh,' she nodded. 'You like taking risks?'

'Hmm, I just so happen to like them quite a bit,' he said. 'What's the deal?'

'Oooh!' she said, rubbing her hands together. 'Let's get tattoo rings. Both of us, the same design, on our ring fingers. Instead of gold and diamonds.'

'Cheaper too.' He shrugged and nodded. 'Nice thinking, fiancée!'

He held out his hand and she high-fived him.

The tattoo guy came over and shook both their hands. 'Congrats to the lucky couple. So, tattoo rings you say?'

And the next photo Zac took on his phone not long after, was of his left hand and April's side by side, a simple, thin, relaxed line tattooed around their ring fingers, curving around into a figure-eight infinity symbol.

Bonded by ink, and bonded by love, they walked hand in hand together down the urban street in the small city of

Welston, Zac breathing normally for the first time as crowds of people walked past.

'I'm so proud of you,' she said. 'Step by step, you did it. Faced your fears.'

'I had some help from a certain woman,' he replied. 'And I still like hanging at home, as you know. But this,' he glanced around the busy street, 'this feels okay... I can manage it. It's all good.' He smiled and slid on his sunglasses.

'So,' said April, excitement bubbling in her belly. 'It appears we have a wedding to plan.' The idea of choosing the perfect candles to decorate the reception may have made her slightly more excited than the fact that she was getting married. Just for one brief moment.

'It appears we do,' he said. 'So, I'm thinking... backyard wedding, yours, mine, or both.' They had not moved in together, but stayed at each other's houses as the mood arose. 'Maybe the celebrant could stand in my yard with me, and you stand in yours, and when he or she pronounces us husband and wife I have to leap over the fence—'

'In your undies!'

'In my undies, yes, and then kiss my bride.'

April laughed, then recalled their first dance when she'd felt the strength of their attraction and they'd almost kissed. 'And I know the perfect song for our wedding.'

Zac looked at her, and they both said it at the same time with a knowing smile:

'"All of Me".'

They walked closely together in blissful silence, and April heard the meaningful lyrics in her mind as memories surfaced.

She thought about the first time they'd met. 'And what about Romeo and Juliet? Perhaps a double wedding?'

'Not a bad idea. I think they're already going steady.'

'Oh!' April blurted. 'And the celebrant can say to them, "you may now hiss at the bride"!'

Zac chuckled, then said, 'Don't give up your day job for stand-up comedy.'

'Not a chance,' she replied. 'I love my day job too much.' She removed her hand from his and slid her arm around his waist. 'And I love you.'

'I love you too.' He slid his arm around her back.

'Ouch! My tattoo!'

'Oops!' Zac lowered his arm to her waist, then leaned in and kissed her temple.

They walked along the street, and Zac stopped when they came to a pub.

'You okay?' she asked.

He stayed silent for a moment, looking through the window of the establishment. 'You know, I just don't feel any desire to go in. None at all. It feels foreign to me now, it's weird.'

'Good weird,' she said.

'Very good weird.'

After a moment, they continued walking, and April knew that she would continue loving him, supporting him, and standing by him no matter what.

And though nothing in life was one hundred per cent certain, she had a feeling, an *inkling*, that Zac would be able to stay sober for good.

Some things were stronger than addiction, and he had found that strength within himself. Not only that, he had found love, and helped her find love. And April knew that love, *their* love, was stronger than anything.

THE END

<u>Also in The Tarrin's Bay Series</u>

The January Wish

February or Forever

Miracle in March

Memories of May

Home for June

ACKNOWLEDGEMENTS

Thanks once again to my editor Belinda Holmes for helping me polish up these books before publication, and of course to my publisher, Bloodhound Books.

To fellow author, Lea Darragh, thanks for reading this manuscript so quickly and giving helpful feedback and encouragement! You are a gem. Thanks also to Ruth Donald for reading this manuscript and helping me with the army related details and characterisation for Zac, not to mention your moral support and encouragement.

Thanks to my mum for helping me with flower and plant information for Zac's garden, because I have no idea about that stuff! And thanks also for reading the draft and giving me a boost in confidence by saying it was good!

A special mention and thanks to Dr Arthur Aron and the team involved in the research paper *The Experimental Generation of Interpersonal Closeness,* for permission to mention within my book your thirty-six questions that involve self-disclosure between participants to build a closer relationship and connection, and to utilise some of these questions in a scene for my characters.

I'd also like to acknowledge the song *All of Me* by John Legend, which inspired part of my story and is mentioned by the characters in the book, as well as two books that the characters read and that have inspired me: *The Prophet* by Kahlil Gibran and *Ask and It Is Given* by Esther and Jerry Hicks (The Teachings of Abraham). And thanks to the Australian candle store, Dusk, for inspiring my character April's candle store and for keeping my home well stocked with delicious-smelling candles!

Thanks also to my writing buddies and friends who I couldn't imagine this writing journey without, and to my readers who keep reading my books and the reviewers who help support them.

ABOUT THE AUTHOR

Juliet Madison is a bestselling and award-nominated author of books with humour, heart, and serendipity. Writing both fiction and self-help, she is also an artist and colouring book illustrator, and an intuitive life coach who loves creating online courses for writers and those wanting to live an empowered life.

With her background as a naturopath and a dancer, Juliet is passionate about living a healthy and positive life. She likes to combine her love of words, art, and self-empowerment to create books that entertain and inspire readers to find the magic in everyday life.

Juliet lives on the picturesque south coast of NSW, Australia, where she spends as much time as possible dreaming up new stories, following her passions, being with her family, and as little time as possible doing housework.

You can find out more about Juliet, her books, and her courses at: http://www.julietmadison.com and connect with her on social media at Facebook http://www.facebook.com/julietmadisonauthor and Instagram http://www.instagram.com/julietmadisonauthorartist